Invitation to Murder

Also available by Carol Floriani

Writing as Carol Robertson

A Summer to Remember

Writing as Carolyn Ross

Dancing in the Dark

Invitation to Murder

A MYSTERY

Carol Floriani

NEW YORK

Published in the United States by Crooked Lane Books, an imprint of
The Quick Brown Fox & Company LLC.

Crooked Lane Books and its logo are trademarks of The Quick Brown Fox & Company LLC.

Library of Congress Catalog-in-Publication data available upon request.

ISBN (hardcover): 979-8-89242-537-7
ISBN (paperback): 979-8-89242-538-4
ISBN (ebook): 979-8-89242-538-4

Cover design by Lulu Dubreuil

Printed in the United States.

www.crookedlanebooks.com

Crooked Lane Books
34 West 27th St., 10th Floor
New York, NY 10001

First Edition: May 2026

The authorized representative in the EU for product safety and compliance is eucomply OÜPärnu mnt 139b-14, 11317 Tallinn, Estonia,
hello@eucompliancepartner.com, +33757690241

10 9 8 7 6 5 4 3 2 1

For Morgan

"Give it all you've got, no matter what."

—Isabel Carrera Langdon, Lacey's mom's mantra

Chapter One

Last spring, when life had suddenly thrown me a wicked curveball, I knew I had two options: swing away and try to hit it out of the park, or duck and run for cover. Faced with a truly impossible situation, I chose the former, and I wish I could say I had never regretted that decision. But, as it turned out, at the end of April, I was suddenly catapulted from the energy of New York City back to my sleepy hometown of Willow Bluffs, New Jersey, the pride of the Palisades.

And, on this bright, crisp September afternoon, I found myself standing, or I should say pacing, on the front porch of the storied Eduard Vander Horn House, nervously awaiting the arrival of the grand dame of the stage and small screen, Miss Tessa Langdon Vander Horn, who, in fact, happened to be my great-aunt on my father's side and my only living relative. Relieved when I finally spotted her beloved, vintage 1995 black Lincoln Continental turning into the estate's long, winding driveway, I bolted down the front steps to meet her. The driver rolled to a stop under the ivy-covered carport, and I eagerly opened the rear passenger door.

"Aunt Tessa, just in time. I was beginning to worry." I reached for her gloved hand as I helped her from the back seat.

"Lacey, dear, you know I never miss a cue."

And that was true. Onstage or off.

"You're looking better every time I see you, dear. Fabulous, I'd say, considering the year you've had."

Yes, not bad for me, I told myself, but I knew I'd never have the Langdons' striking good looks and innate poise. "Let's join the others," I said, taking my aunt's arm. "The ceremony's about to start."

She glanced back at the familiar, nineteenth-century Italianate manor she had called home for so many years. With its newly painted, white clapboard exterior and dark green shutters, it sat high on a rocky cliff above the western bank of the Hudson River, proudly commanding the Palisades.

"Second thoughts?" I asked.

"No, not for a moment," she insisted.

I hoped she meant it. After all, there was no turning back.

Although today's groundbreaking ceremony for the construction of Vander Horn Estates and Community Park was not the typical production to which Aunt Tessa was accustomed, it would prove to be a fitting finale to the drama she had set in motion many months before when she decided to dispose of the Eduard Vander Horn House and almost all of the grand twenty-six-acre estate that had been her late husband's family home for generations. The offer made by Cliffside Custom Builders had been too good to pass up, and as much as she hated to admit it, the money was welcome—a relief, in fact, and precisely the boost her finances needed after several less-than-prudent investments.

The town council had initially opposed the subdivision, but once Aunt Tessa announced that she would grant ten acres to Willow Bluffs for municipal use, Mayor Ariana Nikolas, up for reelection, suddenly began tripping over herself to expedite the deal. The manor house would be tastefully renovated and sold, and as many new homes as the builders could squeeze in would be built on the property. The closing papers had finally been signed in the morning, with one of Aunt Tessa's financial advisers representing her with full power of attorney.

"Uncle Jonathan is undoubtedly spinning in his grave," Aunt Tessa said with a sigh. "But what's done is done. Isn't it, my dear?"

She and her late husband, my great-uncle, manufacturing mogul Jonathan Vander Horn, had lived in the Italianate manor for years when they weren't at their penthouse on Manhattan's Upper East Side, just a few miles away but a world apart. She vowed she would never give up her haven in the city, but she couldn't completely sever her ties to Willow Bluffs either.

As an irrevocable term of the sale, she insisted on retaining the spacious carriage house on the property, Riverview Cottage, and when she offered me the first floor as my living quarters, that sealed my decision once and for all to move back to my hometown from New York during a time that was probably the saddest and most vulnerable of my life. She also kept a portion of the expansive backyard, the East Lawn, which extended to the rocky Palisades, just right for my yellow lab, Dylan, to explore.

"I'll need someone to look after things, Lacey," she had said. But I knew she understood that I needed to be close to my roots.

Now, ironically, she had returned to her home as the guest of honor in a ceremony marking its sale.

"Are you staying over, Aunt T?" I asked.

She had converted the upper floor of Riverview Cottage into a suite for herself, decorated to the nines with overstuffed floral chintz furniture and an ocean of pastel silk throw pillows.

"Yes, I believe I will stay tonight. I'd like to enjoy the cottage as much as I can before the construction starts. You know what a mess those people make of things."

All eyes were on Aunt Tessa as we crossed the South Lawn to the excavation site. No one knew exactly how old she was, not even me, but I assumed she was a very well preserved seventy-something. Tall, fair, and slender, she wore a timeless navy-blue Chanel linen suit with a pale yellow pin-tucked chiffon blouse, accessorized with taupe suede pumps, a queen-worthy matching handbag and, the piece de resistance, a navy and yellow feathered fascinator hat that veiled her platinum blonde bob and emerald green eyes with a wisp of netting.

I wished I had inherited a fraction of Aunt Tessa's style and charm. I played it safe in a hunter green jersey sheath with a matching fitted jacket that cleverly hid the six and a half pounds I'd gained after moving back to Willow Bluffs. I pulled back my long, dark, chestnut brown hair into a tight ponytail, neat and out of the way. And although my hazel eyes would never be as green as Aunt Tessa's, they sometimes appeared to change color if the light was right.

The guests buzzed with excitement, anxious for the event to begin. I noticed the owners of Cliffside Custom Builders, Jim Barclay and Ron Valenti, studying the blow-up of the site plan I'd displayed on an easel on the grandstand stage with Mayor Ariana Nikolas, a five foot two, raven-haired dynamo. Aunt Tessa was hard to miss. The mayor immediately approached us.

"Mayor Nikolas, I believe you've already met my aunt, Miss Tessa Vander Horn."

Aunt Tessa smiled, always delighting in the title "Miss" whether on a marquee or in conversation.

"Of course. Truly a pleasure to see you again, Miss Vander Horn. I'm sure I speak for everyone here when I say I'm a huge fan," she gushed. "We're overwhelmed with your most generous land grant and absolutely thrilled to have you here. I can't thank you enough for taking the time to join us today."

"The pleasure is all mine, Madame Mayor, I assure you."

"Please, call me Ari." Smiling, she leaned in and added with a hushed voice, "Maybe later you will give us the scoop on *Edge of Darkness*."

Aunt Tessa had starred in the wildly popular soap opera since it premiered in the late 1960s, and she had never leaked a single thing about the compelling story lines, not even to me when my curiosity was piqued. "They don't tell me anything until I get my daily script, dear," she replied with a sly grin. "You'll just have to watch."

"Oh, no. Not sure I can wait. But my DVR is set," Ari said. She then turned toward me and placed her hand on my shoulder. "Lacey, wonderful job on the arrangements. You were born to do this, you know. Your mother would have been proud."

I certainly hoped so, but I knew I'd never be my mother. "Trust me, Ari, it wasn't without drama."

I noticed our youngest town councilman making his way through the bottleneck of guests surrounding Aunt Tessa. Young and slightly disheveled with longish, sandy blond hair and tortoise shell horn-rimmed glasses, he always looked exactly like I'd remembered him from Willow Bluffs High.

I politely made the introduction. "Councilman Derek Conover, my aunt."

"Delighted to meet the star of the event, Miss Vander Horn," he said, oozing with charm.

"On the contrary, Mr. Conover," Aunt Tessa replied with feigned reproach. "I believe today's leading lady is this old, rambling estate."

"Ah, well said."

"Derek, if you'll escort Miss Vander Horn to her seat on the grandstand, we'll get started," Ari said. "By the way, where's Glenn?"

"Oh, sorry, I meant to tell you," Derek said. "I spoke to him last night. He said he'd definitely be here, but he might be a little late. He was due in court on a zoning matter this morning."

"Zoning matter? Hopefully not a cease and desist order," Ari said.

I hoped she was joking.

"Too late for that." Derek pointed out. "They closed the deal on the estate this morning."

Glenn Hartman, a longtime town councilman, had been one of the chief roadblocks to the Vander Horn sale, and I never knew exactly why. Actually, no one did, or at least they never spoke about it publicly. Willow Bluffs had its secrets, but this one seemed to be especially well-guarded.

"I hate to go ahead without him, but I suppose we'll have to," Ari said. "Lacey, is everything set?"

I nodded. I had triple checked every detail. "Photographers and reporters from the *Willow Bluffs Gazette*, the *County Record*, the *Paterson Herald*, and *Palisades Life Magazine* are here and ready." I smiled and added, "Not to mention *Soap Opera Weekly*. Just follow my cues after your remarks."

Ari looked pleased.

I glanced at my watch and saw that we were already running a few minutes late. I made my way to the grandstand next to the construction site. An eight-foot black banner with bold, gold letters promoting Vander Horn Estates and Community Park hung from the framework that had been constructed above. I had propped up five gold ceremonial shovels on a wooden stand that the VIPs would use to ceremoniously break ground. The first structure on the Vander Horn project to be built would be the foundation of the state-of-the-art, two-story field house that would anchor Willow Bluffs' new park, a coup for our mayor in her reelection year.

Mayor Nikolas stepped up to the podium on the grandstand, stretching to reach the microphone. "Good morning, everyone. Welcome!"

My mind drifted as Ari paused and waited for the crowd to settle into their seats adjacent to the construction site. I thought about how I had fallen backward into the role of event planner. As I got into it, I found that it was, of course, terribly different from my previous position as a book publicist with Corcoran Publishing, but just as challenging. Even though I thought I was ready for change, this was a whole new ball game.

Tragically, barely eight months before, I had lost both of my parents in a horrific car accident during a heavy winter storm on the Hudson Parkway in Manhattan. Day after day, I was slowly coming to terms with my grief. Very slowly, in fact. At times I thought I'd never recover, but moving back to Willow Bluffs helped immensely. Both my parents had been beloved in the community, and I felt that every day. My father, Joseph Langdon, had been an attorney in town, and my mother, Isabel Carrera Langdon, owned a well-established business, Letter Perfect, known for producing exquisite printed materials and beautifully innovative invitations. It was only natural that over the years she had also become a sought-after event planner. Of course, no one missed my parents more than I did.

After much consolation from Aunt Tessa in the weeks after I'd lost them, I finally accepted her generous offer to move into Riverview Cottage, an exclusive residence. Living there completely rent-free was something I could only have dreamed about if the cottage hadn't remained in the family. I knew in my heart that moving out of Manhattan was the only way to start a new life. At the time, I'd felt that the best way to confront my grief was to dive right in and pick up where my mom had left off by taking the reins at Letter Perfect, hopefully without falling off the horse.

The plans for the ceremony proved to be more challenging than I anticipated, anything but "letter perfect." In fact, it was a perfect storm of Murphy's Law mishaps. The invitations had to be redone twice because of typos, United Shipping temporarily lost the gold-toned shovels I'd ordered, and early in the morning, the caterer had initially sent royal blue instead of pine green table linens. But, with the help of my fabulous assistant Jeremy, I managed to correct the glitches in time.

The mayor sounded like she was winding up her remarks. A born politician, Ari glowed in the spotlight. She concluded with a few introductions and thank yous, turning slightly to acknowledge the VIPs seated behind her. "Today marks a true milestone in Willow Bluffs after a year of teamwork, late-night meetings, determination, and of course, compromise. We owe everything to the woman of the hour, Miss Tessa Langdon Vander Horn, who has personally made our Community Park a reality with her most generous ten-acre land grant."

Aunt Tessa nodded graciously as the guests applauded. She knew that her grant had been more of a necessity than a charitable donation. She would have been the first to tell you that she wasn't the shrewdest businesswoman in the world, yet she knew how to use her celebrity. She pulled out all the stops to forge ahead with the sale of her property. Who could have said no? Even those who didn't want to see houses shoehorned into the magnificent Vander Horn property had been intrigued by the proposition of a new park.

"Also joining us in today's ceremony are Mr. Derek Conover, representing our town council, and Mr. James Barclay and Mr. Ronald Valenti, the principal partners in Cliffside Builders."

Ari beamed with excitement. "Without further ado, please join me as we break ground for the first stage of our project—the Vander Horn Field House, the gateway to our new community park."

I signaled the photographers to come forward first and then the dignitaries.

Taking Aunt Tessa's arm, Derek Conover helped her down the few steps to the construction site. Ari and the builders followed, each taking a shovel.

"This is the moment we've all been waiting for—a huge moment in Willow Bluffs History. Let's dig in," Ari said.

The VIPs lined up on the edge of the grass posing as if to plunge their gleaming, golden shovels into the dirt. The photographers snapped away. Some of the guests stood up to get a better look, many capturing the moment on their cell phones.

And that was that. The *County Record* would run photos and a story in the evening paper, the *Gazette* would feature the event in the morning edition, and *Palisades Life* would undoubtedly feature a pictorial essay in the next issue. I couldn't wait to see how *Soap Opera Weekly* would spin it.

While Ari and the others held court with the photographers and reporters, I headed for the grandstand microphone. "Refreshments are now being served under the tent on the East Lawn," I announced. "Please, join us."

The guests ambled across the lawn. Sensing the light and festive mood, I could finally exhale. The most difficult part of the event had gone off without a hitch. Now, if we could manage to serve lunch, lemonade, and miniature pastries, we'd be home free.

Decked out for the occasion, the East Lawn looked as I imagined it would, warm and welcoming, with a sweeping view of the Bronx and Upper Manhattan across the Hudson River. I relished the compliments so many guests tossed my way as I surveyed the festive yellow and white striped tent with baskets of deep purple mums hanging from the canopy. Bright sunflower centerpieces surrounded by tea lights accented the hunter-green covered tables. "Lovely party, Lacey," I heard someone say. "Beautiful day." "You obviously take after your mother, Lacey."

Clad in khaki pants and crisp, white, button-down shirts, the young wait staff, mostly local college students the caterer had hired, circulated enthusiastically with trays of elaborate hors d'oeuvres and fancy tea sandwiches.

I spotted Derek Conover gallantly strolling arm in arm with Aunt Tessa. She was in her glory, and being seen in her company certainly wasn't hurting his image. He cordially excused himself when I joined them. "Miss Vander Horn, I regret I'll have to share you with our other distinguished guests," he said as he slipped into the crowd.

"That young councilman is a lovely gentleman, dear."

"Derek?" I shrugged. "I suppose. He was in my class at Willow Bluffs High."

"Was he now," she said, in a tone suggesting her approval.

"I hardly knew him, Aunt T," I told her. "I hung out with my softball teammates, and he was more the student government type." I fidgeted with my ponytail.

"I see," she replied with eyebrows raised.

"We haven't had much contact since twelfth grade. He went on to law school, started his practice, and ran for town council. I was in the city. We've both been busy."

"Pity, Lacey." After a dramatic pause, she added, "You're not getting any younger, you know."

"Aunt T, I'm twenty-eight!"

"Exactly, my dear."

Something told me the subject of Derek Conover wasn't closed, but thankfully, I could see that it had been temporarily deflected. I noticed an exuberant, fortyish woman barreling toward us from across the tent.

"Who's this?" my aunt muttered under her breath.

"No idea," I said, smiling. I knew we were about to be cornered.

"Miss Vander Horn, such a thrill to be here," the woman gushed. "You're my favorite soap star, and let me tell you, I watch them all! I can't believe I'm standing here with Caroline Manchester at Manchester Manor. I mean, the Eduard Vander Horn House. I mean, wow! Totally overwhelming. And the estate! It looks exactly like it does on TV. You know, in that amazing opening sequence of *Edge of Darkness*."

Aunt Tessa was intrigued. The woman had all the earmarks of a super fan, I thought, and she seemed pleasant enough.

"Yes, isn't it marvelous," Aunt Tessa said. "Those opening sequence shots were filmed many, many years ago when my husband and I had just moved in. How funny that this was exactly the exterior the producers were looking for. I'm told they searched for weeks for the quintessential Manchester Manor, and there it was, looming right here over the Palisades. My very own residence."

"They'll still be using the same opening shots, I hope. I mean, with the sale of the estate and all."

"Oh yes, my dear. I'm quite certain they will," my aunt assured her.

The woman smiled nervously, trying to collect herself. "Thank goodness. The *Edge* just wouldn't be the same without it, you know. And that haunting music, of course." Still flustered, the woman continued, "Pardon me. I haven't even introduced myself. I'm Natalie Summers. I'm so excited to be here. Star struck, I suppose. I just started writing for *Soap Opera Weekly*. I couldn't believe it when I got this assignment. I'm hoping to spend a few minutes with you later, Miss Vander Horn. I'd love a couple of quotes for my story."

"Yes, of course. Get some lunch, dear. We'll talk later."

Aunt Tessa had been the queen of the small screen for more than sixty years, playing the inimitable leading lady, Caroline Manchester, in the soap opera *Edge of Darkness*. Dominating the ratings since it first aired, the serial had won countless daytime awards, largely due to Aunt Tessa's formidable presence on the show. Tens of thousands of dedicated viewers who worshipped her formed a national fan club and demanded her presence at soap opera conventions across the country. She always graciously obliged. The sponsors loved her as well, and the producers knew that as long as Miss Tessa Langdon Vander Horn headlined the cast, the show would never be in danger of cancellation.

With the reception in full swing, I snagged a salmon canapé as one of the waitresses breezed by. She nodded and then motioned for me to step aside. "I thought you should know, Ms. Langdon, a couple of police cars just pulled up in front. I saw them from the kitchen. The cops are standing in the carport talking."

"Thank you. I'll check it out immediately." I turned to my aunt. "Excuse me a moment."

I rushed across the South Lawn toward the front of the house to see for myself. Sure enough, two police cruisers were parked behind Aunt Tessa's car in the carport. Police Chief Paul Hennessey and two officers were absorbed in an animated conversation. Something seemed very, very wrong. I hurried toward them.

"Chief Hennessey, I'm Lacey Langdon. I'm directing today's event. Is there something I can assist you with?"

"Yes, ma'am, I'm afraid there is," the chief replied.

"What can I do?"

"I have an announcement to make to your guests," the chief said, looking somber.

"Of course," I said, anticipating bad news.

"I'd like to address the group all at once, if you don't mind," he stated.

"Please, follow me." My heart raced as I led them around across the lawn to the tent behind the house. The two-minute walk lasted an eternity. We stopped just inside the canopy.

"May I have your attention?" I managed. My voice cracked. No one seemed to hear me over the din of the reception.

Chief Hennessey stepped forward and abruptly took the lead. “Quiet, please, ladies and gentlemen,” he announced in an imposing baritone. The guests quickly took notice, many looking as startled as I felt. “Come forward as far as you can,” he commanded, leaving no doubt that he meant business.

At that moment, everything seemed to stop, including my heart, as the guests gathered around. Chief Hennessey paused a moment until everyone was within earshot.

“Ladies and gentlemen, I apologize for the interruption at this most inopportune time. Unfortunately, we’ve had a serious incident here in town. I regret to inform you that earlier today a jogger encountered a dead body on the bank of the Hudson River directly below the estate.”

Chapter Two

Nothing sucks the life out of a party like an uninvited corpse.

Festive turned to somber in a nanosecond. As shaken as I was, I knew I had to come through, sweaty palms and all. Even my mother would have been thrown off her game if a disaster had been tossed into the mix at one of her events, but I knew in my heart that she would have quickly recovered and ultimately triumphed. *Give it all you've got, no matter what*, she would have said. The path was clear—that is, if I could manage to keep my head together.

So much for sleepy, comfortable, boring Willow Bluffs, the small town where nothing ever happened. The guests, now gathered in a close group under the tent, seemed as stunned as I was. Some were frozen and expressionless. Others were agitated and visibly horrified. Several bombarded Chief Hennessey with questions over the audible gasps and speculative murmurs.

"Chief, can you tell us what happened?"

"Suicide?"

"A man or a woman?"

The chief quickly took charge, flanked by rookie Officer Jane Kowalski, looking uneasy, even slightly pallid, and veteran Sergeant John Martinelli, already carefully scanning the crowd, undoubtedly searching for reactions. The local reporters, who had come to cover a fluff story, hovered close by, ready to break the Willow Bluffs scoop of the century.

"Settle down, folks," the chief said. "We've just begun the preliminary investigation. I have no further comment at this time."

With palpable tension in the air, the commotion continued.

"Have you identified the body?" someone shouted.

"Was the victim from here in town?"

"Quiet, please," the chief insisted, visibly annoyed. "Let me repeat. I have no further comment at this time. There is nothing more I can tell you now except that we are looking into every possible angle."

"Chief, when *will* you be able to tell us something?" someone called out.

"Can't say," he barked. "Furthermore, I need all of you to remain on the premises until we've taken statements from everyone. We want to hear about anything unusual you may have seen this morning. Anything at all. Now, if you'll all take a seat, we'll try to get through this as quickly as possible."

The buzz of curiosity among the guests quickly gave way to a wave of grumbling.

Turning to me, he added, "Miss Langdon, do you have a copy of the guest list?"

"Certainly, right here on my phone."

He handed me his business card. "Forward it to my email address right away."

A couple of clicks and done. *Off to a good start*, I thought. I sent him the list of invitees and attendees. Who knew what that would tell him? I realized then and there that as the event coordinator, I was going to be involved in the investigation whether I liked it or not. If the body had, in fact, been discovered just below the estate, maybe someone had seen something. I couldn't imagine what, but I had to admit I was intrigued.

As the bewildered guests found their seats at their tables, the VIPs—Aunt Tessa, Mayor Ariana Nikolas, Councilman Derek Conover, along with Cliffside Custom Builders partners Jim Barclay and Ron Valenti—joined me at the table closest to the house.

Ari spoke up immediately. "Chief, if there is anything I or anyone on the council can do, we are available to you twenty-four seven."

"Appreciate it, Mayor. We're stalled waiting for a positive ID from the next of kin."

"Well then, you must have some idea," she observed, expecting an explanation.

"Sorry."

"I assume you're working with other agencies," Derek said.

"Yes, of course. The county medical examiner and the sheriff's department are still on the scene."

"The M.E. will be doing an autopsy?"

"Yes. We may not know anything for a couple of days."

If Derek had been trying to pump the chief for information, he hadn't gotten very far, but I knew he wouldn't give up easily. Besides making a name for himself as an up-and-coming local attorney and town councilman, I'd recently read in the *Gazette* that Derek had also begun teaching Law and Justice in America 101 two evenings a week at Oakdale College, a small school in nearby Westerville. Even back at Willow Bluffs High he'd been a go-getter, a member of the Student Council every year until he was ultimately elected president, and a reporter for the school newspaper, *On the Bluffs*.

"The sheriff's team will be joining us shortly. We'll conduct a thorough investigation of the property along with them."

"Mind if I tag along?" Derek asked.

The chief shrugged. "I have no objection if the sheriff doesn't mind."

I was relieved. Derek was more than welcome to pinch hit. I certainly didn't want to be around for that. The bluff behind the house that jutted out over the river was treacherous, probably three hundred feet above the water with a clear drop. It had always been fenced off from the rest of the property, but if someone had really wanted to go back there to explore, it was accessible. It had never been my thing. For as long as I could remember, I wasn't particularly fond of heights. I never ever ventured out to the cliff. In fact, when I lived on East Seventy-Second Street in the city, even the view down to the street from my fifth-floor apartment made me woozy. I never looked straight down. In fact, I hardly ever opened a window.

"Ms. Langdon—" the chief began.

"Call me Lacey, please."

"Lacey, for the sake of privacy, we'd like to conduct the interviews inside the house. Anywhere suitable?"

"Perhaps my aunt could help with that."

"I'll defer to Mr. Barclay and Mr. Valenti," Aunt Tessa said. "They own the house now."

"Whatever you need," Jim Barclay said. "We intend to fully cooperate. You know the interior better than we do, Miss Vander Horn."

Aunt Tessa nodded. "Yes, I suppose I do. I suspect it's a bit stuffy inside," she noted, "and some of the furniture has probably been covered up, but there is plenty of space you could use on the first floor. I'd say the parlor, the library, and the morning room would do rather nicely."

"Good. We'll get started right away."

"Lacey, why don't you show them the way?" Aunt Tessa suggested.

Chief Hennessey, Sergeant Martinelli, and Officer Kowalski followed me across the lawn, through the French doors at the rear of the house, and down the creaky back hallway that led to the library. Stopping at the library doorway, the chief motioned for Officer Kowalski to go inside. The rooms in the back of the house were always dark, and the mahogany wainscoting and floor-to-ceiling shelves crammed with dusty old books made it look even drearier than it was.

I opened the ivy green velvet curtains. "There, that's a bit better," I said, pulling off the drop cloth from a couple of worn leather chairs. "Use whatever you like."

Officer Kowalski glanced around the room, grimacing. She looked even sicklier than before. I imagined a dead body on a riverbank, probably grotesquely waterlogged, would do that to a rookie cop, despite her best efforts to hide it. I was incredibly relieved that I hadn't seen the body myself, or even worse, that I hadn't been the one to discover it. I often took my dog, Dylan, on the winding path just north of the estate along Hudson Road that led down to the river. We would walk along the very path where the jogger had made the gruesome discovery. In fact, I had considered taking Dylan for that walk early in the morning but, thankfully, I was far too busy with last-minute plans for the groundbreaking.

After my assistant, Jeremy, had rectified the near fiasco with the table linen, he brought Dylan with him to Letter Perfect. A part time student at Oakdale, he always managed to pitch in when I needed him.

I knew the shop was in good hands while I was tied up with the groundbreaking.

"The house isn't haunted, Jane. It's just old," the chief said.

"I'll be fine," she said. "Fine."

She didn't look fine to me. Ever since she'd arrived, she looked like she'd seen a ghost.

Sergeant Martinelli headed down the hall to the parlor, an airy sitting room facing the front of the house. Aunt Tessa had done her best to keep it true to its history, full of antiques that had been passed down through several generations of Vander Horns. The sergeant removed the covering from the royal blue damask sofa and matching club chair.

"Are you sure it's okay to sit on this stuff?"

"No problem. They've been there forever, and my aunt has had them refurbished many times over."

"That's what I mean."

If the Willow Bluffs Historical Society had its way, nothing would have been touched, but that was another issue altogether. I reassured them that the furniture was indestructible. When I was a kid I used the sofa as a trampoline—when no one was looking, of course. And I would take the cushion off the seat of the club chair to practice tumbling. Aunt Tessa and my mother would have been appalled. My father would have laughed.

I directed the chief further down the hallway. "The morning room is just off the conservatory. You can't miss it."

"Send in the guests—say one table at a time," he said.

"Easy enough. Just one thing. The staff was just about to serve lunch."

"Go right ahead. We don't want to intrude."

Don't want to intrude? That ship had already sailed. An unidentified body. Police presence. The medical examiner on the way. No real answers. Speculation everywhere. What else could possibly have intruded on a lovely groundbreaking ceremony for a new town park and condo complex? The guests had all but forgotten why they had come. I headed back outside to the tent and sent the first group of guests into the house for their interviews before I took a seat at my table.

"Everything okay?" Ari asked.

"Yes, I suppose so."

"Ari, why don't you say a few words to get this thing back on track?" Derek suggested.

I nodded in agreement. If anyone could hit a couple of foul balls and deflect everyone's attention back where it belonged, Ari could.

I continued funneling the guests into the house until all were accounted for. When Chief Hennessey, Sergeant Martinelli, and Officer Kowalski finally exited, it was difficult to tell whether they were satisfied. Then, after the chief took brief statements from me, my aunt, the builders, Ari, and Derek, he wrapped up the interviews.

"Ladies and gentlemen, thank you for your cooperation. At this time, you're all free to go," Chief Hennessey announced.

Obvious that no more information would be forthcoming, the guests began to slowly depart.

"The *Gazette* will have the story," Derek said. "Eventually."

Ari was as impatient as the rest of us. "My office will be in constant touch with Chief Hennessey. We should know more tonight. At least, I hope so. All we can do is wait."

"My, my. This certainly is a cliffhanger," Aunt Tessa remarked. "Pun intended. I'd say it's worthy of *Edge of Darkness*."

No one laughed.

We immediately spotted two investigators from the sheriff's office distinctively dressed in crisp, black trousers and white shirts. They crossed the East Lawn and quickly approached Chief Hennessey. One carried a digital camera. After a short huddle, they appeared to be ready to go to work, but not before heading straight for our table.

"Miss Vander Horn," the chief asked, "is the gate that leads out to the bluff locked?"

Aunt Tessa shook her head. "I doubt it. I have to say, no one was ever crazy enough to venture out there."

Ron Valenti and Jim Barclay glanced at each other. "We haven't changed anything," Jim said. "Never even thought about locking it."

"Let's take a look, Paul," one of the investigators said to the chief.

The officers headed for the bluff with Derek trailing behind.

"Wait a sec, Derek," Ari called. "Have you heard from Glenn?"

"Not yet. He said he'd text me when he was finished at court, but he's before Judge Clemons. Could drag on into the afternoon."

"Let me know."

Aunt Tessa gracefully rose from the table, politely saying her good-byes. "A pleasure, Mayor. Mr. Valenti. Mr. Barclay. Do keep me in the loop."

"Certainly, Miss Vander Horn. I'll be in touch."

"Until later, Lacey," Aunt Tessa said. "I'll be at the cottage."

"Get some rest, Aunt T. I'll bring dinner from Grimaldi's."

"And a nice bottle of cabernet, dear." She paused, leaning in close to me. "Or two," she whispered.

Amen to that.

I walked over to the entrance to the South Lawn to say good-bye to the remaining guests as they left. Many seemed to have enjoyed the event despite the interruption. I noticed a few, however, who seemed miffed.

Mrs. Edna Quartermain, president of the Willow Bluffs Historical Society, stopped to let me know exactly how she felt.

"Ms. Vander Horn, I've most certainly never been questioned by the police before," she snapped.

"They were only following procedure, ma'am."

"One would think I was a suspect."

"I'm sure they don't think that at all, Mrs. Quartermain."

She exited in a huff.

The president of Republic Investments, Thomas Pierce, who had handled Aunt Tessa's investments for years, also expressed his displeasure.

"If I had known I was going to be part of a police investigation, I wouldn't have come," he grumbled. "Unthinkable that I would be involved. My family has lived in this town for more than fifty years."

"I know, Mr. Pierce. It was just a formality, I assure you."

"Oh, Tom, really," his wife scolded. "I thought it was all rather exciting." She put her hand on my shoulder. "Don't give it a second thought, Lacey. We had a lovely time."

"Thank you, Mrs. Pierce,"

I hoped the rest of the guests agreed with her.

Before long, most of the guests were gone, the caterers were packing up, the tent was being disassembled, and the carpenters were tearing down the temporary stage at the excavation site. I headed back to my Volkswagen Beetle, more than ready to join Jeremy and Dylan at Letter Perfect, hoping to spend the rest of the day with some semblance of normalcy.

As I left the estate, I turned left onto Willow Street, Willow Bluffs' quiet but picturesque main street, and followed it about a half mile to the business district. Since the early 1950s, the zoning board had had the foresight to consistently resist the construction of strip malls. The freestanding businesses, mostly Cape Cod–style cottages or bungalows, had been converted into stores or restaurants. The winding, red brick paver sidewalk connecting the shops gave the center of town a quaint look that attracted people from all over the county.

I parked in my usual spot on the side of the charming little white house with yellow shutters that my mother had transformed into our town's popular stationery store more than twenty-five years ago. I couldn't wait to get inside, away from the craziness of the day. The afternoon sun was intense for mid-September but welcome and comforting as it kissed my skin. The moment I entered Letter Perfect, Dylan jumped off his perch on the cushy, chintz-upholstered seat in the bay window and greeted me with his usual exuberant jumping and tail wagging. I was just as glad to see him. I kneeled, scratched him behind his ears, and kissed him on his nose. I didn't care about the yellow lab hairs all over my dark green dress. The day had been unsettling, and it seemed that Dylan was my one true friend. I imagined that by now the entire town was buzzing with speculation about what had happened. One thing was for sure—an unidentified body that had turned up along the riverbank wouldn't stay quiet for long in a place like Willow Bluffs.

Jeremy, engrossed in a weighty textbook, looked up from his seat behind the cash register. "Hey, Lace. It's been quiet here. You didn't miss anything."

"Well, *you* sure did," I replied.

"Yeah, so I heard."

With Dylan at my heels, I collapsed onto the window seat. "What exactly did you hear?"

"Not all that much. A couple of people came in before lunch and said a body had turned up. Pretty weird stuff."

The front screen door breezed open and slammed shut in a flash. Jess, the manager of the coffee shop next door, burst in like a whirlwind. "I saw your car. Thought you could use this."

It was hard to be anonymous when you drove a sunflower yellow VW, but I didn't mind a friendly face.

She handed me a piping hot latte. "You read my mind, Jess."

"And, Jeremy, your Americano," she offered, sliding the coffee across the counter.

"Wow, thanks. Just what I need."

With short, blonde, curly hair and an athletic build, perky Jessica Santoro had been manager of Willow Bluffs' coffee shop, Bean Around, for years. We'd played varsity softball together at Willow Bluffs High School, and although she was two grades ahead of me, as teammates we had become close friends. She was another Willow Buffs lifer. People tended to stay—or people like me, who'd flown the coop, tended to come back. Her coffee shop next door to Letter Perfect had become the town's bona fide gossip center, and Jessica, in perpetual motion, was everyone's personal barista, psychologist, and best friend.

"You're amazing, Jess," I said, sipping my frothy latte.

"And you sure know how to throw a party," she commented.

"Tell me about it."

"Yeah. Talk about a bummer," Jeremy said.

"What's the deal?" Jessica asked.

"I wish I knew."

"People are talking. Like big time," she said.

"No surprise there. Who came in today?"

"The usual crowd, except a couple of outsiders who were at your event. Natalie something. From one of the soap rags. Totally wired. The last thing she needed was a double espresso."

I laughed. "I know. I met her."

"Funny thing. She said she was doing research into the Vander Horn family. Because of your aunt, I guess."

"She didn't seem all that interested in the, um, unfortunate occurrence."

"Who knows?" Jessica responded.

"Interesting. I wonder what she's after. Except for Aunt Tessa, I've always thought we Vander Horns were rather ordinary."

"I have to say, most of my customers have been buzzing about the story of the day. Story of the decade, actually."

"The police are being extremely tight lipped," I told her. "They took statements from everyone."

"Why? Do they think someone actually saw something?"

"I guess. You never know."

"Probably just procedure," Jeremy chimed in. "Or maybe they were more interested in who *wasn't* there."

"Hmmmm. Kind of makes you wonder." Jess sighed. "How was your event, otherwise?"

"Seriously? You mean the groundbreaking ceremony before all hell broke loose? It was fine, Jess. Just fine."

"Hey, I'm sure you did your best," Jess assured me.

"Unfortunately, the whole takeaway after all of my planning will be the corpse on the jogging path."

"Uh, just out of pure curiosity," Jeremy said wryly. "Did the body float in or drop down?"

"I believe they are assuming it fell," I told him. "Hit the riverbank."

"Oh, man." He gestured with a diving motion. "Kerrr-splattt."

I shot him a disapproving look. "The investigators checked out the cliff behind the house."

"Wow. This is epic. I mean, when was the last time we had a jumper?" he quipped.

"You know, not since I can remember," Jess said.

I was thinking out loud. "Could have been an accident, I suppose. My knees wobble just thinking about those cliffs. Maybe whoever it was simply slipped."

"A hiker?" Jess wondered.

Jeremy shook his head. "I don't know. I've hiked those paths along the Palisades a lot in the past couple of years, and I've always thought they were pretty safe. Some of the overlooks even have railings."

"Don't worry, the *Gazette* will have the gory details," Jess said.

"For sure. All of them," I said.

"I'd better get back before the four-thirty coffee stampede. Listen, promise you'll let me know if you hear anything more."

"Will do. You, too."

"You know I will, sweetie."

That I could count on.

"I have to take off, too, Lace. Five o'clock class at Oakdale."

"Thanks, Jer. I couldn't manage without you."

"Got that right!"

I was relieved to finally be alone. The situation occurred so quickly I hadn't had much chance to gather my thoughts and process what had happened. I'd planned to stay at the shop till our regular closing time, five-thirty, then grab some takeout from Grimaldi's across the street. I was craving some classic comfort food like veal parmesan and linguine with marinara sauce that Aunt T and I could share, and of course, her personal request, a bottle or two of cabernet.

With Dylan curled up at my feet, I sat alone at the conference table usually reserved for eager party givers or nervous brides-to-be. I finally began to decompress in the comfort of the shop. Shelves of binders containing samples of every type of invitation imaginable lined the soft, pale gray walls. Meticulously arranged tables, all covered with floral cloths displaying gifts and party favors, were strategically placed throughout the store. I could feel my mother's presence. I hoped she would somehow guide me. A stack of her business cards remained at the center of the conference table. *Isabel Langdon, Letter Perfect Events, Perfection to a T.* A tough act to follow, for sure. I couldn't imagine when I'd have the self-confidence to replace my name for hers.

My phone vibrated, interrupting my musing. A message from Ari Nikolas lit up the screen. A text from her was most unusual. My heart suddenly sank. She must have had news, and I doubted it was good.

i was going to call but can't even speak

I typed as quickly as I could.

what's up
hennessey just released the name of the deceased—it was glenn.
glenn hartman? From the council? are they sure? can't be—i thought derek said glenn was in court
nope positive ID by his wife
angela? i thought they were divorced
no—they had separated but got back together—they're calling it an apparent suicide

I hesitated a moment, frozen in shock. *suicide?*

jumped from the cliff behind the estate
OMG but why
no idea—in utter disbelief
oh lord me too

Chapter Three

I woke up the next morning with a dull headache, a lingering reminder that sharing the second bottle of cabernet with Aunt Tessa until midnight hadn't been a great idea. I quickly showered, dressed in no-fuss khakis and a black crew-neck sweater, and headed to the kitchen for a caffeine fix. Thankfully, Aunt Tessa, due on the set of *Edge of Darkness* at ten, had already made coffee and was studying her script, obviously unimpaired by our evening. Her face scrubbed and her blonde bob covered by a chic Hermès scarf, she was dressed simply but elegantly in a black gabardine pencil skirt and pale blue silk blouse. She would be transformed into the glamorous soap matriarch Caroline Manchester by the show's magical hair and makeup staff when she arrived at the studio.

"Have a cup, Lacey," my aunt said, pouring me a large mug. She shot me a disapproving glance. "Lord knows, you look like you could use one, dear."

I sat down next to her at the kitchen counter and took a big gulp.

"Julien's picking me up at nine. We're taping this morning. Three episodes."

Julien LaFontaine had been Aunt Tessa's devoted talent agent for as long as I could remember, booking her appearances, negotiating her contracts, and running interference for her whenever necessary. And he made sure she never missed a beat, socially or professionally, not that she would have. In short, she never made a move without him. Sometimes I felt he was too devoted. But then again, he'd known her and Uncle Jonathan since childhood.

I hadn't rebounded as quickly as Aunt Tessa did after yesterday's debacle. I didn't have hair and makeup people to transform me or an agent to guide me through my day. A cup or two of coffee would help. I simply wanted to spend a normal day at Letter Perfect. Normal—back to the sleepy Willow Bluffs where nothing ever happened.

"Are you staying in the city tonight?" I asked.

"No, I think I'll come back to the cottage. I could use another quiet night. Let's get takeout again. I love Grimaldi's."

The coffee had diminished my headache somewhat, but I vowed I would stay away from the second—and third—glass of cabernet if I spent another evening with Aunt Tessa.

I noticed Dylan sitting patiently by the cottage's front door. I let him out and grabbed the morning paper. I anxiously unfolded it on the kitchen counter. The headline glared at us. COUNCILMAN DIES BY SUICIDE.

"Those people at the *Gazette* certainly got the story fast," Aunt Tessa said. "Like vultures."

We quickly scanned the article, which reported significant details, including that the police determined that Glenn had jumped from the cliff behind the estate.

"I hope we don't get a parade of gawking trespassers," I said.

"The builders own the property now. Let them worry about it." Suddenly, Aunt Tessa looked pensive. "The whole thing's a pity, though. Tragic. And, I must say the timing's a bit uncanny."

"I don't know what you mean."

"I dreamed about poor Cousin Sophie last night."

"Cousin Sophie? I'm not following you, Aunt T."

"The sad, sad story of Sophie and Sebastian. I was reminded of it when I was cleaning out the library in the big house a couple of weeks ago. My mother-in-law had recounted it in one of her diaries. She had researched family records and went into great detail."

"Aunt T, I must say I've never heard of a cousin named Sophie."

"That's most likely by design, my dear. Goes way back to around 1840, I believe. She would have been a cousin several times removed, by marriage on your Uncle Jonathan's side." Aunt Tessa pointed out. "So, not a blood relative, of course. And, as it was, the story was buried for generations. Yes, buried. A black mark on the family."

"Please, go on."

"Sophie lived with a broken heart for years. It ultimately killed her, as these things do, you know."

"I can't even imagine." My curiosity was piqued. I poured myself another cup of coffee and buttered a blueberry muffin.

Aunt Tessa fixed her eyes on mine. "Let me start at the beginning. The patriarch of my husband's family, Eduard Vander Horn, my great-uncle by marriage, lived on this estate in the nineteenth century. In fact, he had it custom built once he had established the very successful The E. and F. Vander Horn Silk Company with his younger brother Frits, Sophie's father. The brothers were very close. In fact, Frits, his wife, and

Sophie lived right here on the estate with Eduard's family. Eduard and Frits also had a much younger brother, Emil, your Uncle Jonathan's grandfather, but Sophie's story is the most fascinating. And, as you know, the business they built is still operating today as a textile company in Paterson."

"Yes, I know. I never realized its roots went back that far."

"Cousin Sophie was truly lovely—tall, lithe, the belle of the county. I just found a beautiful painting of her in the attic. Which reminds me, I have so many things to send into storage, but I digress." She gathered her thoughts and continued, "Sophie fell in love with a dashing young Frenchman, Sebastian DesChamps. His family had come from Avignon at the beginning of the nineteenth century. The DesChamps, also in silk manufacturing, became bitter business rivals of the Vander Horns over the years."

"Ah, so Sophie and Sebastian were star-crossed lovers?"

"Exactly. From what I could glean from my mother-in-law's account, the DesChamps were, shall we say, rather unscrupulous at times, spying on the Vander Horns's production line, stealing buyers from Eduard and Frits. Unsavory things like that. Just the fact that Sebastian was of French descent was most distasteful to the Vander Horns."

"Not good."

"No, not at all. Sebastian, a young clerk in his family's company, became quite taken with Sophie, and she with him. Despite his family's reputation, Sebastian was an upstanding young man. But Eduard and Frits had personally selected another suitor for Sophie from a Dutch family, like the Vander Horns. The Dutch were awfully clannish back then, and the Vander Horns were no exception. Eduard and Frits insisted Sophie should be courted by the young Dutchman Lucas Van

Dyk, who lived right here in Willow Bluffs. Lucas was a promising young clerk who worked for the Vander Horn Silk Company. Perfect for Sophie, or so they had decided."

Aunt Tessa rose to her feet, her expression becoming intense. "But Sebastian was steadfast. As the tale goes, he came to the estate, barged into the house, and confronted Sophie's uncle Eduard in the library. They had a huge row. Eduard was the head of the family, and his demands ruled. In fact, he absolutely forbade Sebastian to see Sophie again. And then, by a cruel twist of fate, Lucas Van Dyk happened to arrive at the estate with some contracts for Eduard to sign."

"What timing!"

"Indeed. Lucas blasted his rival Sebastian with an awful tirade and professed his love for Sophie. Eduard insisted the wedding date should be set as soon as possible. Devastated, Sebastian stormed out of the house."

"Oh, no. I can only guess."

"Yes. Unable to imagine his life without Sophie, Sebastian ran to the cliff and, well, jumped. Later that morning, his body was found below on the riverbank."

"Oh my God. I can't believe no one ever told me this."

"For years, the cliff was known among the locals as Sebastian's Point. But then interest faded. The story was swept under the rug for generations."

"What happened to Sophie?"

"Oh. Very sad. She was the true victim."

"Absolutely."

"Poor Sophie became a shadow of herself." Aunt Tessa's voice softened, and its intensity quickly turned to sadness. "As the story goes, she would go to the cliff and stare out over the river. All alone. Day after day. Constantly mourning Sebastian.

She was forced to marry Lucas. It was a completely loveless marriage, of course. She suffered with a broken heart her whole life. It ultimately killed her, as these things do, you know."

"What a story! I assume they had no children?"

"I believe they did have a daughter, Annabella Van Dyk. But even she couldn't save Sophie from her broken heart."

"Family secrets."

"They say Sophie was committed to an institution a few times."

"No doubt. Is all of this documented anywhere besides in the diary you found?"

"I honestly don't know. There must be records of Sophie and Lucas's marriage. And the birth of Annabella. Perhaps the town records here in Willow Bluffs or in the county seat would have the marriage and birth certificates."

May be worth pursuing, I thought. "I wonder if anyone ever researched our family tree."

"I haven't come across anything like that. Well, at least not yet."

"What a story, Aunt T."

"As good as anything the writers on *Edge* have come up with. I told Julien about it and maybe a few other people along the way. I'm sure I've told you Julien's been developing a Broadway show based on *Edge*. He thinks this old tale would make quite a storyline."

"Could work."

"I don't know. I'm all for pathos, particularly when it comes to *Edge*. But some things are better put to rest, aren't they, dear?"

"Yes, I suppose so."

"I left my script and bag upstairs. Excuse me a moment."

I heard Dylan barking in the distance and suddenly remembered he was still outside. When I opened the door to call him in, I noticed Julien's car parked in the carport. He was crossing the lawn and heading toward the cottage.

"Dylan! Come, boy," I called.

Julien arrived before Dylan. "I come when called," he joked.

"Good morning, Julien."

"I saw the dog way over by the gate," he said as he walked in.

"He usually doesn't stay out this long." I walked outside onto the lawn. "Dylan! Dylan! Come on in."

He bolted inside looking like he'd been rolling in leaves. "You've been on serious squirrel patrol this morning, Dyllie," I said, brushing the leaves from his golden coat. I gave him a treat, and he settled down.

"Have you had breakfast, Julien?"

"Yes, I'm fine. I missed the excitement yesterday. I was held up in the city the entire day in production meetings."

"All I can say is it wasn't the day I had hoped for. But Aunt Tessa was marvelous at the ceremony. She'll be down in a minute."

There was only one way to describe Julien LaFontaine: impossibly handsome, even in his seventies. I couldn't think of any other man I knew who looked as good as he did. He was six foot two, with perfectly groomed silver hair, high cheekbones, a classic square jaw, and piercing green eyes. And he was always impeccably dressed, as if he'd just stepped out of the pages of *GQ*. Yet he was the first to describe himself as a "failed actor extraordinaire," and that became a blessing in disguise. His ambition turned from the stage to actors' management. After a couple of apprenticeships with well-known talent agencies, he formed what had become the highly sought-after LaFontaine Creative Arts Agency, employing a staff of powerhouse reps who managed top Broadway and screen personalities. He knew how to turn on the charm when it counted, but from what I had seen there were times when he could be as cold as ice. Julien always handled Aunt Tessa's affairs personally. No one else in the agency dared to interfere. He looked out for her with a vengeance.

"*Edge* is taping three episodes today. Wrapping a story line," he explained. "They can't do anything without Tessa, of course."

Aunt Tessa made her grand entrance, sweeping into the kitchen. "Well, of course not, Julien," she said. "Caroline Manchester wouldn't hear of it."

"Good morning, my dear," he replied with a smile. "You're looking ravishing, as always. I'm anxious to get on the road. The George Washington bridge can be a nightmare."

"See you tonight, Aunt T."

"Lacey, would you bring home something from Grimaldi's again? Oh, and that same cabernet. It was wonderful, wasn't it?"

"It certainly was! I'll pick up another bottle and maybe some bronzino."

"Perfect."

My head was still a little foggy. I had learned my lesson. Maybe half a glass, tops, for me tonight.

I decided to get to Letter Perfect to open up early. There was nothing for me to do in the cottage except replay the events of the day before, and that served no purpose. Moreover, I was curious about what Jess would have to say about the story in the *Gazette*. She would surely have her finger on the pulse of the reaction in town. I checked the kitchen clock. Ten after nine. There was just enough time to stop at Bean Around—when I heard a knock on the front door. My first thought was that Aunt Tessa might have forgotten her script. I took a quick look, thinking I'd grab it, but I didn't see it on the kitchen counter.

Standing on my tiptoes, I peeked out the small window at the top of the door. I was surprised to see Derek Conover, looking, as usual, like he'd just rolled out of bed. He probably had.

"Hey, just thought I'd stop by on the way to my office," he said, stepping inside.

"Oh. Okay. Coffee?"

"No, thanks. I just came from Jess's. Quite a buzz in town. Everything okay here?"

"Yes. Considering."

"I thought you might be rattled after yesterday."

Puzzled, all I could manage was, "I appreciate your concern."

He paused and looked around nervously. "Hey, this is a great place. Listen, Lacey. I want to ask you a favor."

So that was it. I figured there was more to his visit than concern for my well-being. "Sure. What's up?"

"Truth is, I didn't get to see much of the cliff yesterday. As a matter of fact, I didn't see any of it. Chief Hennessey was okay with me tagging along, sort of, but the county investigators didn't exactly agree. I had to stay in the background. Like way in the background. Behind the fence."

"Why are you so interested in the cliff?"

"The course I teach at Oakdale. Law and Justice. Thought I might find something useful for my class about police procedure. Besides the usual textbook stuff, that is."

"Makes sense." It really didn't, but I played along.

"They must have removed the crime scene tape by now, so I doubt anyone would mind if I went over there."

"I certainly don't mind. But it's not my family's property anymore."

"Yeah, I know. But you do have access."

"Yes, I suppose I do. Just be careful out there."

"Why don't you come along?"

"I'm not a fan of heights, you know."

"Oh, come on. You don't have to get close. Bring this guy," he said, patting Dylan on the head.

"Why not?" I shrugged and grabbed Dylan's leash and my jacket from the hook next to the door. I was more than a little curious about why Derek was so curious. "Come on, Dyl. You get to go out again."

The vivid colors of the changing leaves from the day before now seemed muted under the gray autumn sky. The weather had turned much cooler and breezy, not even a hint of sun peeking out from the clouds. I shivered. My light corduroy jacket clearly wasn't warm enough.

"Eerie, isn't it?" Derek said, trying his best at small talk.

"What?"

"The thick haze hovering over the river."

"We see that a lot in the morning. I guess I'm used to it."

"Listen, I want to ask you something. Is it just me, or does Glenn's suicide seem a little, you know, drastic?"

"Yeah, maybe. A bit," I admitted.

"I know his wife wanted a divorce, but even so. People get divorced every day, and they tend to get over it."

"I heard that they had reconciled, but you never know what's going on in someone's head."

"Yes. Or behind closed doors, I suppose. But even so . . ."

"You're the lawyer and college prof."

"Adjunct instructor," he said, correcting me. "And just one course."

"Don't overthink this whole thing, Derek."

"I tend to do that. However, I have heard Glenn's wife is a real shrew."

"Angela?"

"Maybe she just put him over the edge, so to speak," he quipped.

"Not funny."

Dylan suddenly sprinted ahead of us, pulling his leash from my hand. He dashed straight across the East Lawn, through the open gate, barking in a high-pitched tone that signaled something was wrong. We ran to catch up with him, past the rocky side of the cliff and about twenty feet into the woods. Sniffing wildly, Dylan turned, kicking backward with his hind legs until he had brushed away a small pile of branches and leaves.

"Dylan, what's up?'

Finally, it seemed that Dylan had found what he was digging for, still sniffing and alarm barking, until his bark turned into a howl. He had exposed a rock about six inches in diameter. He sniffed and circled.

Derek approached slowly. "Look at this," he said. "The rock is covered with a thick red substance on one side."

I stepped closer, very gingerly. My proximity to the cliff made me woozy.

"Be careful not to touch anything," he warned.

"Do you think it's blood?"

"I do." Derek took a couple of steps backward, assessing the scene. "Dylan obviously sensed it."

"Must have come from an animal. We see deer, foxes, coyotes, lots of wildlife."

"I wonder. The county team obviously missed it," he noted.

"It was hidden out here under the brush. Practically buried. The police must have focused on the cliff," I offered.

"Seems that way. Or maybe they didn't look hard enough. Yesterday the investigators had basically resigned themselves to the idea that this was a suicide."

"Wait, you don't think it was suicide?"

"I'm just saying I think it looks suspicious," he said matter-of-factly.

"So, what's next?"

"I'm calling Hennessey."

We heard the chief's squad car arrive within two or three minutes. He quickly spotted us in the woods and joined us.

"What were you two doing back here, anyway?" the chief asked.

"My dog broke free and ran through the gate. He headed straight for this spot."

"Not far from the cliff, as you can see," Derek added.

"Thank you," the chief said sarcastically. Turning to me, he asked, "The dog led you directly here?"

"Yes. We had to retrieve him," I replied.

Chief Hennessey spent several minutes studying the rock, and then he pulled out his cell phone and called his dispatcher. "Get Kowalski and Martinelli over to the Vander Horn place pronto. And call the county team and get them back here, right away. With the M.E."

"What time did your crews start setting up yesterday, Lacey?"

"Seven a.m. sharp," I replied.

"Interesting. We'll take another look at the early morning security tape. Wasn't much good yesterday, but the lab is enhancing it as we speak."

Officer Jane Kowalski and Sergeant John Martinelli arrived together minutes later.

"New information?" Sergeant Martinelli asked.

"Take a look for yourself," the chief said, pointing to the area Dylan had uncovered. "Kowalski," he added, "see that this entire area gets taped off."

Sergeant Martinelli circled the rock and then kneeled down beside it, taking a closer look. "Quite an accumulation of dried blood. Matted strands of hair," he observed. "Possibly human."

"That's what I thought," the chief said. "If the M.E. finds that they match Glenn's, we'll have a full out murder investigation on our hands."

Chapter Four

That bloody rock had made me late. Once I'd settled Dylan down and coaxed him into the cottage with a few treats and a fresh bowl of water, Derek walked me across the lawn to my yellow Beetle, parked under the carport in front of his Prius.

"Listen, as far as I'm concerned, there's only one way the M.E. could possibly go on this," he said, getting into his car. "Talk to you later."

I knew he was right. I braced myself for what was to come.

He pulled out of the driveway just ahead of me as one of the county investigators pulled in. I headed to Letter Perfect, and Derek to his law office, about a quarter mile further down Willow Street. When I arrived at 9:40, Jeremy had already opened up the shop.

"Hey, Lace, where've you been? The phone's been ringing off the hook."

"No surprise there." I had a feeling customers were looking for excuses to pump me for information. Anything unusual that happened on the Vander Horn estate immediately became town gossip, and the "suicide" of Glenn Hartman was bigger than anything I could remember that had happened in Willow Bluffs.

Thankfully, I knew Jeremy would be able to handle whatever came our way. Sometimes, I felt guilty for saddling him with so much responsibility, but I certainly couldn't have managed without him. His boyish good looks, long brown hair, and casual demeanor were deceiving. Barely twenty-one years old, he possessed a steady work ethic. He put in several hours every day at the shop, took night courses year-round at Oakdale College, and occasionally filled in as a bartender for Classic Caterers. He had already accumulated almost half the credits he needed to graduate.

"Anything urgent?" I asked.

"Mrs. Reed needs a rush on those baby shower invitations."

"I'll take care of it," I replied. "I've had a most unusual morning."

"Yeah, you look a little pale."

With his elbows on the counter and his head in his hands, Jeremy's dark brown eyes were fixed upon mine as he listened intently to the whole saga.

"Wow, who would want to off a Willow Bluffs town councilman?" he quipped.

Good question, I thought. And I knew I wasn't going to rest until it had been answered.

I sighed. "Nothing's official yet, Jeremy. They'll probably be doing the autopsy this afternoon. Listen, keep this between you and me. At least for now."

"It's in the vault."

Leaving Jeremy to deal with the walk-in customers, I sat down at my desk in the small office in the rear of the shop. Perhaps I shouldn't have blabbed all the details about the morning's discovery to him, but I'd been bursting at the seams, dying to get it off my chest. Who wouldn't have been thrown off their game? I felt like it was the bottom of the ninth inning, the score was tied, and my team was down to its last out, destined to lose. There would be no winners in this game—a tragic loss for the Hartman family, and a black mark on both the town and the Vander Horn estate and, by association, on our family name.

I wasn't sure I could focus on work with one hundred percent concentration until the medical examiner had finally determined the cause of Glenn Hartman's death. Somehow, bridal showers, birthday parties, and wedding invitations didn't seem like my highest priority at the moment, but they had to be. I could feel my mother looking over my shoulder. Once again, I heard her mantra. *Give it all you've got, no matter what.* Weeding through phone messages and emails, I dug in and did what I could to catch up. After a couple of hours, I was ready for a break.

"Jeremy, I'm going for coffee. Do you want anything?"

"Thanks. An Americano would be amazing right about now."

"Something for lunch?"

"I brought leftover pizza."

"That's lunch?"

"Yeah. Usually breakfast, actually. A delicacy."

"If you say so. I'll be right back."

I took a shortcut across the grass to Bean Around. The weather, still hazy, dreary, and gray, fit my somber mood. Jess had a way of cheering me up, although under the circumstances that would be a tall order. The coffee shop itself was welcoming—warm and rustic, with walls lined with barn siding and tables and chairs made out of old, distressed, reclaimed wood. But even the rich, familiar aroma of exotic coffee blends wasn't enough to raise my spirits. I walked straight up to the counter to order.

"I've never seen the folks around here so worked up," Jess said.

"Yeah, well, with good reason."

"Your usual?" she asked.

"Please. And Jeremy's. But make mine a grande. And I'd love a ham and cheese on a croissant with honey mustard."

"You've got it."

I recognized most of the chatty customers sitting at the tables, but I tried my best to avoid eye contact with anyone. I noticed the owners of Cliffside Builders in the back corner. So did Officer Jane Kowalski as soon as she came in. She approached them immediately.

"Mr. Valenti and Mr. Barclay?" she asked.

I strained to listen over the whir of the espresso machine.

"I've been trying to reach you all morning," she continued. "I left word with your secretary, but as long as you're both here, Chief Hennessey would like you two to stop by headquarters as soon as possible."

"Is something wrong, Officer?" Ron Valenti asked.

I'll say, I thought to myself.

"No, no. Just a couple of new developments in the Hartman case he'd like to discuss."

"We'll be right over," Jim Barclay replied.

Officer Kowalski ordered a corn muffin and promptly left.

"What was that?" Jess said under her breath.

"I have a feeling we should all stay tuned."

"Do you know something?" she asked, looking intrigued, but I decided to keep my mouth shut for once.

"Just that they are probably doing the autopsy today," I replied.

I made my exit before she could question me further.

When I got back to Letter Perfect, Jeremy seemed much more relaxed. "Any more emergencies?" I asked.

"Get this. Angela Hartman called. She'll be stopping in soon. She wanted to make sure you'd be here."

"Why?"

"She didn't say."

I had just finished my incredible croissant sandwich when Glenn's widow walked into the shop appropriately dressed for mourning in a black pantsuit, white blouse, flats, and no jewelry except a gold watch. She neglected to remove her oversized sunglasses. I wasn't sure if they were meant to hide the fact that she had—or hadn't—been crying.

"Mrs. Hartman, I'm so sorry," I offered.

"Thank you. Call me Angela, please."

"Your husband's passing was such a shock to everyone."

"I am beyond devastated."

I struggled to think of something kind to say. "His years of service to the town were admirable. He will be greatly missed in Willow Bluffs."

"Thank you."

"Is there something I can do for you?"

"I was hoping you'd be able to print a program for Glenn's memorial service. Something special. Something more than the funeral home would do."

"A celebration of his life."

"Precisely. I suppose we'll need it rather quickly."

"Of course."

She reached into her purse. "I've jotted down a few things."

She handed me a sketch of the layout for the program along with a short bio of Glenn, the hymns that would be sung, and the charity they would support. It seemed rather well thought out and detailed, considering her husband had been dead just over twenty-four hours.

I showed her two or three tasteful programs that we had previously designed. Nothing overwhelming.

"We'll need about two hundred copies. I'm sure we'll have a good turnout."

"Yes, of course. I'll print extra, just in case."

"I imagine the service will be in a couple of days. I just spoke with the funeral director. He expects the county to release Glenn's body later this afternoon."

I thought she sounded rather glib, or perhaps she was in denial, but then again, everyone mourns differently. "I can have the programs ready in a day."

"I appreciate it. I'm inundated with details at the moment. This will be one less thing to worry about."

She sounded like she was simply checking off chores on a to-do list.

"Call me if you have any questions, Lacey. I left my number with your young man."

She left without having shed a tear. I opened my laptop and started working on the program layout immediately. It was simple enough, and she had basically done the job for me. I chose a heavy, white stock paper with a charcoal grey double border. To save time, it could be printed right here in the shop.

My phone suddenly buzzed with a text from Derek.

cant talk now but ck the WB police site
ok will do
meet me at the bean after work

I put my phone aside, saved my design work on the memorial service, and nervously searched my laptop for "Willow Bluffs Police." I then opened the website, immediately clicking on "recent press releases." I easily found the release dated today.

For Immediate Release:
After the discovery of new evidence today, the suicide of Glenn Hartman, reported yesterday by the WBPD, is now being investigated as a homicide. Anyone with information may call our confidential, anonymous tip line, 800-555-6666.
WBPD

And there it was, in black and white. Homicide. Murder. No room for speculation now. Soon the news would be all over town. The next couple of hours dragged. Even though I was interrupted many times with print orders and event issues by phone and email, I managed to complete the layout for the Hartman memorial programs. I'd give the template a final check in the morning. And I remembered to call Grimaldi's to order Caesar salad, veal marsala, and eggplant parmigiana for pickup later. As Aunt Tessa requested, I'd get the cabernet at the wine shop next door.

Jeremy called to me excitedly, "Hey, Lacey, you won't believe this!"

I could tell the urgency in his voice that he'd just read the press release on the WBPD website. Ready to leave, I joined him in the front room. "I know. I saw it," I replied. "Let's call it a day. I'm meeting Derek Conover at the Bean."

"Not without me you're not," Jeremy insisted. He grabbed his books for his evening class, stuffed them in his backpack, and followed me out the door.

Derek was already there when we walked into Bean Around. Jeremy and I stopped to place our orders and then joined him at his table in the back.

"Hey, Mr. Conover," Jeremy said.

Derek gave him that "I know you, but I can't place you" look.

"I'm in your night class at Oakdale College," Jeremy reminded him. "Law and Justice."

"Of course," Derek recalled. "Front row on the right."

"Best class ever. Never miss it."

Jessica's part time baristas were taking care of the coffee orders. She left them to handle the stream of five o'clock customers and took a seat next to Jeremy.

"I suppose you've heard," I said to her.

"Are you kidding? The homicide investigation is all people are talking about," Jess replied. "It's been crazy around here the entire afternoon," she said.

Jeremy quickly chimed in. "A murder right here in Willow Bluffs is great stuff for class, isn't it, Mr. Conover?"

"That's one way of looking at it," Derek admitted. "We'll be able to focus on police procedure. The autopsy today must have been conclusive."

Jess had no idea that we already knew what she knew. "They supposedly found the suspected murder weapon. A rock that was thrown into the woods. Sounds rather amateurish, don't you think?"

Derek, Jeremy, and I looked at each other, surprised that she had already heard. But bad news traveled fast in Willow Bluffs, even news that was supposedly confidential.

"Yeah, you'd think the murderer would have thrown the rock over the cliff," Jeremy said.

Jess offered her theory. "Maybe he, or she, was afraid it would land next to the body on the riverbank, so they hid it."

"And not very well, at that," Derek said. "If they did indeed determine it was the murder weapon, the autopsy must have shown blunt force trauma to the head consistent with the size of the rock. Skull fracture, contusions, swelling, I would imagine. Even tissue and hair on the rock. Must have been quite a blow."

"Yeah, like the fall wasn't going to kill him," Jeremy quipped.

"I'm wondering if our police will be able to handle this," I said.

"I know. How many murders have they had to investigate recently?" Jess pointed out.

"Or ever, for that matter?" I added.

"Zippo," Jeremy concluded.

"They'll have plenty of help from the county crime scene unit," Derek noted.

"Well, the same goes for the county people, if you ask me," Jess observed. "They can't possibly have much experience with homicide investigations. I can't remember the last murder in the county either."

"Actually, Chief Hennessey and his people have an advantage over the county team," Derek explained. "They know just about everyone in town. And, they have a pretty good idea what's going on."

"Do they?" Jeremy asked.

"Somebody's going to have to solve this murder one way or another," I remarked.

"We probably have a better handle on what's going on in town than the cops," Jess said.

"That's true. I mean, who talks to cops? Unless they have to, I mean," Jeremy said.

"I was in my law office all day," Derek said. "But Ari told me the chief came by the town council offices and was asking a lot of questions."

"Like what?" I asked.

"It's no secret that Glenn had been seeing quite a bit of the council's secretary, Gina Velasco," Derek said. "Actually, more like all of her," he added under his breath.

"Seeing? You mean as in having an affair?" I asked.

"I suspected he and Gina were involved," Jess said. "They used to come in here after work quite a bit looking a little too cozy. Then, they seemed to have broken things off."

"How ticked off was Angela? I hope she has an airtight alibi," I said.

"Which one of them broke things off?" Jeremy asked.

"I think Glenn did when Angela threatened him with divorce," Derek said. "He couldn't handle it."

I was shocked. "So, Angela knew about it? Wow. I knew they were having problems, but I didn't know the extent of it."

"The secretary must have been pretty ticked off, too. She had a pretty good motive herself, didn't she?" Jeremy proposed.

There was an abrupt, awkward silence when the young barista brought our coffee. We conspicuously resumed talking when she returned to the service counter.

"You know, we should keep our voices down," I whispered. "The walls have ears in this place. Should we even be talking here?"

Jess shrugged. "What's the difference? Everyone must be talking about Glenn's murder."

Our powwow broke up at about five thirty. I walked across the street to pick up my dinner order and the cabernet before heading home. The moment I opened the door to the cottage,

Dylan jumped up to greet me. I swore he could smell veal through walls.

"Hey, Dyllie. You're the star of the day, aren't you? Don't worry, boy, we'll save you some leftovers."

I could tell that Aunt Tessa had arrived home before I had. The dining table was already set for dinner, complete with a charming centerpiece of rust-colored mums and pale peach roses, which she must have picked up from one of the local street vendors in the city. She wasn't much of a cook, but she knew how to make a table look beautiful. I never appreciated it more. A lovely, quiet dinner would be a welcome respite after my extraordinary day.

She must have heard me come in. She floated down the stairs, as elegant as ever, in beige cashmere lounging pants and a matching top.

"How was your day, Aunt T?"

"Better than Caroline Manchester's, I can tell you that. I've been playing her for years, but just when I think I've seen it all, the writers dream up another harrowing scenario for her."

"Can't wait to see it!"

I transferred our Caesar salad, veal, and eggplant parmigiana into serving dishes and the bread into a long, oval wicker basket. Aunt Tessa never allowed takeout containers on her table. I poured the cabernet generously into our crystal goblets, hoping it would help us both relax.

"Let's eat," I said. "Everything's still hot. Did Julien drive you home?"

"No, my usual driver did. Julien had a meeting with the Broadway people. He decided to pitch Sophie and Sebastian's saga to them as part of the show they're developing around *Edge*. It's certainly dramatic enough. Julien is fascinated by family drama, probably because he's adopted and never knew the truth about his own story."

"I didn't know Julien was adopted."

"The subject usually doesn't come up. His adoptive mother passed away less than a year ago."

"Sad. I wasn't aware."

"We certainly have enough of our own drama right here in town."

I brought her up to date on what was now the Glenn Hartman homicide investigation. She seemed to take it in stride, probably because she had been desensitized by years of outrageous soap opera storylines. But, because she was such a good actress, I never could tell what she was actually thinking.

"The eggplant is outstanding tonight," she raved and then paused, looking thoughtful. "You know, it's starting to sound more and more like *Edge* around here."

"It's worse, Aunt T. It doesn't end at three thirty with rolling credits and theme music."

"By the way, you should have ordered some filet mignon for our boy Dylan. Sounds like he was a true hero today."

"He knows he's a very good boy. But maybe next time. I think he'll be happy with a bit of veal."

Aunt Tessa's expression turned serious. "I don't know which is more catastrophic, suicide or murder," she said. "Both are devastating for the victim's family. But suicide has such a stigma. Hopelessness. Desperation. Madness. Now, in the Hartman case, the police are burdened with finding the murderer. The entire community will be involved. Frightening to think it might be someone among us right here in Willow Bluffs."

"I've been completely unnerved by all of this."

"If Hartman were involved in a love triangle, as you said, the truth will come out. I can't tell you how many love triangles have ended with murder on *Edge*. It's a very useful device when they want to write someone off the show."

"What if it was just some nut?" I proposed. "I'll be locking all the doors and windows from now on."

"Couldn't hurt. You know, dear, with Julien arriving and all, I didn't quite finish the story of Sophie and Sebastian this morning. Funny how history randomly repeats itself. Just to circle back a bit—from what I read in my mother-in-law's account—and she had done her research—many people who knew Sebastian had a hard time believing he would commit suicide, even though he was so absolutely distraught about being denied marriage to Sophie, the love of his life. It appeared to those who knew him that he had given up much too easily. He was much more volatile than depressive."

"So, you're saying he would have fought for her?"

"Absolutely. He did run out to the cliff. That is undisputed by all accounts. But he probably wanted to go there to think, get some air, get away from the conflict for the moment. It is also undisputed that Lucas followed him out there with the worst possible intentions."

"Do you mean he was going to kill Sebastian?"

"That's exactly what I mean, and according to the diary, Lucas most likely pushed Sebastian to his death from that treacherous cliff. He got away with murder. Dear Uncle Eduard, however, was so influential that he was able to make the whole scandal disappear with bribery, threats, who knows what."

"Unbelievable."

"The Vander Horns were rather diabolical back in the day. But don't forget, dear, they are only related to you and me by marriage, so don't fret."

"Does anyone else know this story?"

"Extremely doubtful."

I sighed. "Someone will dredge it up."

"Virtually impossible. I doubt that it's documented anywhere but family records. And, as I told you the other day, the only person I told was Julien, right after I found the diary in the library. Of course, he would be the last person to divulge that it's part of the Vander Horns's legacy. Bad public relations, you know. Something Julien abhors. But he does see it as a flashback sequence for the Broadway project. A backstory as a period piece to add to the play. Marvelous costumes and sets. I think it could work. He's almost compulsive about it."

"Maybe something about that cliff invites disaster."

"Of course it does, dear. By its very nature. It's geographical homicide."

Chapter Five

There was no denying that Gina Velasco was a dish.

Yet, as I showered and dressed that morning, I thought about Glenn Hartman's affair with her and still found it shocking. At twenty-five or so, Gina was a good fifteen years younger than he was and exceptionally pretty, with long, wavy red hair and an hourglass figure. Even though he wasn't the first man to fall victim to temptation, I thought he would have had more sense than to get involved with someone from the town council office. I wondered if besides threatening his marriage and career, he had set up his own demise. As preposterous as it seemed, I fleetingly considered Angela's and Gina's possible motives, but I immediately dismissed the thought. Nonetheless, hell hath no fury like a woman, or two, scorned. Time would tell.

I scanned the *Willow Bluffs Gazette* while I had a quick breakfast of cinnamon toast and coffee. Correcting its previous suicide story, the news of Glenn's murder filled the entire top half of the front page. Thankfully, the story stayed away from speculation.

Quotes from Chief Hennessey were noncommittal, citing his inability to comment on an ongoing investigation, which, to me, meant that he didn't know much anyway. Most of the account served as a glowing obituary of Glenn, reporting his years of loyal service to the town with gushing tributes from the mayor and fellow councilman. He was touted as a respected lawyer, a stand-up guy, dedicated, and forthright. Derek was quoted as saying it had been an honor to serve with him, even though they'd only been on the council together for a short time. It all sounded wonderful. Between the lines, however, was the unwritten, unavoidable fact that someone had wanted him dead. And it horrified me to think that I probably was acquainted with that someone.

Noting as I read the *Gazette* that the memorial service would be held the following afternoon at Carson's Funeral Parlor, I headed to Letter Perfect half an hour early to proofread and print the programs Angela had requested.

Jeremy arrived at the shop at nine on the dot, just as I had finished. He looked over my shoulder as I was packing them in a white Letter Perfect box.

"Nice job," he said.

"Thanks. I have to drop them off at the funeral home. I don't plan on staying long."

"Don't blame you. No worries. I'll cover."

If there was one thing that disturbed me more than heights, it was funeral homes, especially the Carson Funeral Parlor, where the service for both of my parents had been held. Only eight months had passed since they had perished in that horrendous crash in New York, and I wasn't certain I was ready to return.

I had vivid flashbacks as I drove along Willow Street, turning right up the steep hill on Pine Street where the sprawling white home sat, serving for years as a sanctuary for the community's bereaved. I relived the initial paralyzing shock I felt when

Aunt Tessa had arrived at my apartment late that night with the unthinkable news. I couldn't help feeling a twinge of the profound sadness that sometimes turned to numbness as scores of mourners, some strangers, offered their condolences in the unbearable weeks that followed.

I dreaded going inside. I grabbed the box of programs and sat in my car for a few minutes, staring ahead, frozen. When I finally mustered the strength to enter, I immediately noticed the familiar, overwhelming smell of flowers pervading the stuffy foyer, triggering yet another sorrowful flashback. At my parents' wake there had been flowers everywhere. Large sprays, arrangements on tables, vases, floor baskets. As I recalled, the overpowering scent had almost sickened me. I tried to turn off my senses. I slowly proceeded down the dimly lit hallway to the office, hoping no one would be there.

Mr. Frank Carson, a third-generation undertaker, seemed to move in slow motion as he got up from behind his desk to greet me. He looked exactly the same as I remembered him—depressing black suit; oily, black hair; and thick, black-framed glasses. He spoke in a hushed monotone, so as not to wake the dead, I supposed.

"Good morning, Miss Langdon," he droned. "How are you doing, my dear? And, how is your lovely aunt?"

"We're well, Mr. Carson. Thank you for asking."

"Wonderful to hear. Wonderful. My, you've endured so much."

"I'll always be grateful to you and your staff for your support."

"Is there something I can help you with today?"

"Yes, I have the programs for Glenn Hartman's memorial service tomorrow," I said, handing him the box.

He opened the box, took the top program in his hand, and read it carefully. "Beautifully done, Miss Langdon. The grey border is *exceedingly* tasteful. Exactly what we need. Of course, I would expect nothing less from Letter Perfect."

"Thank you. Will three hundred be enough?"

"Yes, indeed. Our Gardenia Chapel holds about two hundred, so these will be fine."

"I can easily print more, if necessary."

"No need." He carefully placed the box on his desk. "I have personally helped Mrs. Hartman . . . bless her . . . plan a most intimate service."

"This is such a difficult time."

"Oh, it is, it is. Especially with the newspaper stories and such," he pointed out.

"Yes," I agreed. "Those must be awful for her."

"We're doing our best to assist. As you know, here at the parlor, we do our utmost to go above and beyond the ordinary."

"Yes, Mr. Carson, you certainly do. You were a tremendous help to me and my family in our time of need."

"We strive to provide peace and comfort to our bereaved." He walked toward me to see me to the front door. "Will we see you tomorrow, Miss Langdon?"

"Yes, of course. I'll be attending with my aunt."

"Excellent. Until then."

"Good day."

I couldn't get out of there fast enough. I hurried to my car, loathing the idea of returning the next day. Feeling melancholy, on the way back to the shop, I took a detour past my old house on Maple Street, a cadet-blue, two-story colonial with a cedar roof. I made the difficult decision to sell it after my parents' accident. It was much too large for me, and I thought making a new start at Riverview Cottage would be therapeutic. As I slowly passed by, I noticed a red tricycle in the driveway. I hoped the new family with two young children would be as happy there as I had been with my parents.

I drove around my old neighborhood on the way back to the shop, remembering the houses where my friends lived, but I was ultimately glad I had moved to the cottage. I usually wasn't one to dwell on nostalgia. Letter Perfect had become my happy place. It had given me a connection to my mother, but at the same time it provided me with an opportunity to work independently while pursuing a new career, and for that I was most grateful.

I made a quick stop at Vinny's Deli to pick up a tuna salad and provolone wrap along with a bottle of spring water. I worked at the shop uninterrupted through lunch until mid-afternoon. I had promised Aunt Tessa I would meet her at the manor house at three o'clock to sort through the furnishings that remained.

When I arrived at the estate, exactly at three, Aunt Tessa was already there, along with Jim Barclay from Cliffside Builders. Cliffside planned to renovate the home for resale, but they had agreed to keep the historical authenticity of the home intact. Features like the ornate woodwork, six marble fireplaces, Corinthian columns, wide-plank chestnut floors, and elaborate curved staircase would be duplicated if they couldn't be repaired. It was going to be a costly job, but the builders knew the coveted Eduard Vander Horn House would fetch a stunning price.

As soon I walked in, I heard Aunt Tessa's voice echoing in the empty two-story entry foyer.

"Lacey, I'm so glad you're here," she said. "Jim has so kindly offered to assist us."

"More than happy to help. It's very generous of you, Miss Vander Horn, to leave some of the antiques to be sold with the house."

"Unfortunately, Lacey and I simply have no use for many of the pieces. Many of them are old and lovely, but not particularly valuable. Let's take a look."

Jim and I followed her down the hall.

She stopped at the sitting room. "I've already taken most of the furniture I want. But the more I think about it, I would love to move this blue damask club chair to the cottage. Sentimental value. I can't let it go."

I agreed. "I can picture Uncle Jonathan sitting there reading."

"We can arrange to move it for you," Jim said.

"You're welcome to the sofa and occasional chair."

"We'd love those. We'll showcase some of the old pieces in the interior when we put the house on the market."

"Who will be handling the sale?" Aunt Tessa asked.

"I believe you're familiar with Tom Pierce's company, Republic Investments."

"Yes, of course. Tom's been my financial adviser for years."

"His company has a real estate division," Jim told us. "He's referred one of their top agents."

"Tom takes good care of me. He'll make sure everything goes well."

We continued down the hall to the library.

"Lacey, please speak up if there's anything you'd like. I'd also like this mahogany library table for the cottage," Aunt Tessa said.

Jim looked happy to oblige. "We'll move that, too."

"And all of these books and personal papers. Oh, my."

"My people can pack everything and arrange storage for you," Jim offered.

"I'll take a few things now, if you don't mind. Lacey, would you give me a hand?" She noticed a couple of empty boxes in the corner, and we quickly filled them with photo albums and journals. "These are personal. I meant to take them last time I was here."

She grasped one of the journals, which I assumed was the diary that contained the story of Sophie and Sebastian. She placed it, along with a few additional items she'd collected from upstairs, in a small box.

"Lacey, we'll take this one ourselves," she instructed.

"I'll drop off the other boxes in front of your cottage before I leave today," Jim said.

"Thank you. Let's see, I've already sifted through the upstairs bedrooms. I suppose the dining room set should stay with the house. We have no room for it."

"It complements the house perfectly," Jim said. "Just needs a bit of TLC."

"You'll have to dispose of the junk in the attic."

"No problem. Leave everything to us."

"I'm glad the old place is in your hands, Jim. I know your renovation will be true to the home's history."

"That is our intention, Miss Vander Horn. The Willow Bluffs Historical Society insists on it."

I finally recalled something I wanted to bring to the cottage. "Aunt T, you know what I'd love? Didn't you mention that there's a portrait of Cousin Sophie in the attic? We could hang it in the cottage."

"Why, yes. Are you game for going up there?"

As much as I hated heights, I thought I could handle the attic. "Love to," I answered.

"You can take the back staircase off the kitchen. You'll see the pull-down stairs in the hall. You'll know the portrait as soon as you see it."

"I'll leave you ladies to finish up."

"Thank you for everything, Jim."

"Of course."

He headed to the library to retrieve Aunt Tessa's boxes, while I hurried up the back stairs to the attic entrance. Fortunately, the creaky, old pull-down stairs weren't terribly steep and not too high. I managed. I easily made my way into the dark, grimy space, and just as Aunt Tessa said, I saw what looked like a covered oval painting, leaning against a stud, sneezing when I removed the dusty sheet protecting it. There she was. Cousin Sophie. She was indeed an alluring beauty. She wore an exquisite Victorian white lace blouse, its high collar accented in the center by a unique oval blue and white cameo brooch with an intricate gold filigree border. She wore her glistening dark brown hair swept up with long tendrils falling to each side of her face. Her light blue eyes and pale porcelain skin made her appear delicate, almost vulnerable, with only a hint of a smile, yet as I gazed at the portrait, I felt as if I were under her spell. I wondered what had happened to that beautiful cameo over the years. I'd have to ask Aunt Tessa. I very carefully descended the attic stairs, grasping the painting tightly by the brushed gold frame with one hand. I met Aunt Tessa in the kitchen.

"Ah, I see you found it."

I was truly excited. "It's wonderful, isn't it? She's stunning."

"Absolutely. No wonder Sebastian and Lucas fell in love with her. Wait until Julien sees her!"

"Her brooch is quite something. I've never seen a blue cameo before."

"I believe that color was quite popular back in the day."

"I can carry it back to the cottage. No problem at all."

"Perfect. I've got the box. The painting certainly should be displayed. Sophie is part of our heritage, and the estate's as well, in her own special way."

As we left the house by the back door, Aunt Tessa and I were both surprised to see that the gate to the cliff was open.

"That's odd," Aunt Tessa said. "The gate was definitely closed earlier."

"Did Jim happen to mention if he was going out there?"

"No, I don't think so. Let's check it out."

We crossed the lawn and walked just inside the gate. I spotted the back of a redheaded woman in tight black jeans and a beige sweater standing near the cliff. She seemed to be looking out over the river.

I leaned the painting next to the fence and called to her. "Hello?"

The woman turned and slowly approached us. Once I saw her face, there was no mistaking her. It was Gina Velasco.

"Do we know her?" Aunt Tessa whispered.

"Vaguely," I said under my breath. "She was a *very* good friend of Glenn Hartman's, if you get my drift."

Aunt Tessa raised her eyebrows knowingly.

Gina stopped, looking surprised to see us.

"Something I can do for you?" I asked.

"No, no. I was just curious. The murder and all."

"Yes, terrible."

"I knew Glenn rather well," she explained. "We worked together. I wanted to see the cliff for myself. The whole thing is unthinkable."

"Yes, but I'm afraid this is private property."

"So sorry," she said, most unapologetically.

"Perhaps we should put up a no trespassing sign," Aunt Tessa said sardonically.

"I didn't mean to intrude. I'm just a bit overwrought."

"Everyone's been unnerved the past couple of days," I observed.

"Yes, of course. I'll be going now. I suppose I'll see you at the memorial service tomorrow."

She strode right past us, her head held high, as if nothing was amiss.

Aunt Tessa looked appalled. "Of all the unmitigated gall."

Chapter Six

If Glenn Hartman could have witnessed the standing-room-only turnout at his memorial service, he'd have wished he'd been that popular in high school. I had always figured he'd been the smart, nerdy type, the nebbishy kid who kept track of the baseball team's towels and water bottles rather than the slugger who scored the winning home run in the bottom of the ninth inning. No one seemed to know much about where he'd grown up or attended college and law school, but everyone seemed to agree that he'd become a well-respected professional in Willow Bluffs. Anyone who knew him, even if they didn't know him well, would have said he was a hard-working attorney and town councilman, who was devoted to his wife and two children. And, by all appearances, that was true. He'd kept a low profile, preferring to work behind the scenes instead of in the spotlight.

And yet, as things turned out, it was clear he had managed to fool us all, which explained the crowd of three hundred plus curiosity-seekers packed into the Gardenia Chapel at the Carson Funeral Parlor. The inquiring minds of Willow Bluffs, me included, wanted the whole story and all the salacious details.

After all, a quiet, unassuming family man didn't ordinarily have a hot, young mistress—or turn up mysteriously murdered at the bottom of a cliff.

Glenn's closed casket loomed large in the chapel. I sat quietly beside a very somber Aunt Tessa in the back of the room, hearing nothing but occasional whispers, sniffles, and sobs as the mourners waited for Mr. Carson to begin the memorial service. Julien, seated on her other side, had insisted on driving Aunt Tessa and me, and I had no objection. I knew I'd be distracted all day with memories of my parents' death. I found it difficult to concentrate. Perhaps I shouldn't have worn the same black linen suit I'd worn to their funeral. It only made my recollections more palpable.

Vignettes of my parents' service looped persistently through my consciousness, weighing on my mind like a black iron cloud. Even worse, I kept having visions of what their horrific, fatal car crash must have been like. I fought to stop my mind from going there, but I did not win. I shuddered, thinking of the terrifying seconds during the late-night ice storm as their BMW sedan spun out of control and slammed head-on into the guardrail on the Hudson Parkway in New York City. Aunt Tessa touched my hand from time to time, but there was nothing she could do except let me allow the darkness to play out. I knew she was distraught, too. After all, she had lost her nephew. But, as an actress, she was adept at masking her true feelings.

"Are you okay, dear?" she asked softly.

"I'm determined to get through this one way or another."

"You're a Langdon. You will."

Yes, that was true. I felt somewhat bolstered.

Frank Carson emerged precisely at ten o'clock, cutting a pathetic figure in his signature shiny black suit. He spoke painstakingly slowly in a hushed and garbled monotone as he began the service. "Good morning, ladies and gentlemen. I thank you all for coming today. As we remember Glenn Hartman, beloved son, loving husband, devoted father, dear brother, esteemed member of our community . . ."

Shifting uncomfortably in my seat, I tuned him out as he droned on. I tried to stop my persistent flashbacks by focusing on the mourners. The good citizens of Willow Bluffs had turned out en masse, and they provided exactly the diversion I needed.

The attendees sat apprehensively in the stuffy, dimly lit Gardenia Chapel, which was bursting with elaborate floral arrangements. Gold silk Roman shades covering double hung windows that hadn't been opened in thirty years, a faded navy blue and gold floral Aubusson carpet, mahogany side tables holding dusty brass lamps and cream-colored pleated shades added to the depressing ambience.

Angela Hartman, in a black linen suit, black gloves, and a hat with a veil that obscured her face, sat in the first row, facing the casket with her two children, six-year-old Emily and nine-year-old Glenn Jr. Glenn's brother and the extended family were directly behind them. I noticed Mayor Ariana Nikolas, Derek Conover, and the other town councilmen sitting together close to the front. A few rows back, Jim Barclay from Cliffside Builders looked impeccable in a stylish, double-breasted, blue pinstriped suit.

No one could have missed Gina Velasco, her flaming red hair with fresh auburn highlights cascading down her back. She sat on the aisle directly behind Derek. She'd poured her voluptuous figure into a tight black sheath with a plunging neckline that revealed a little too much décolletage for the occasion and accented, most curiously, with red patent stiletto heels.

She had clearly dressed to raise the dead.

Chief Hennessey stood in the back, deliberately conspicuous, observing. Glenn's older brother Dennis and Mayor Nikolas delivered touching eulogies, but they seemed to go on forever. At last, the soloist from the Willow Bluffs Reformed Church sang *Ave Maria*, accompanying herself on the organ behind the casket. I exhaled. It was finally over. We were all invited to Glenn's gravesite at Willow Hill Cemetery for a brief service before the burial, another situation I dreaded. Everyone rose and slowly filed out of the chapel.

"Are you going to the cemetery, Aunt Tessa?"

"Of course. It's the right thing to do." Tastefully dressed in a black wool A-line dress with a matching coat, her manners were always as refined as her appearance.

"We'll drop you at the estate afterward," Julien whispered, leaning forward.

I rode with Julien and Aunt Tessa, and Derek followed as we joined Glenn's long funeral procession rolling slowly through Willow Bluffs' suburban streets. We finally arrived at Willow Hill Cemetery and stopped along the narrow, winding service road by his gravesite. For the first time that day I noticed the cloudless blue sky and bright morning sun.

Each of us was given a red rose as we gathered around the casket. The committal service was thankfully brief. Angela sobbed quietly as Reverend Timothy McFadden, the pastor of the Reformed Church, solemnly recited several prayers, ending with, "Eternal rest grant unto him, O Lord, and let perpetual light shine upon him. May his soul and the souls of all the faithful departed, through the mercy of God, rest in peace."

And the souls of all the faithful departed, I repeated to myself.

"Amen," we responded in unison.

Rev. McFadden continued, "We therefore commit this body to the ground, earth to earth, ashes to ashes, dust to dust."

Angela, Glenn Jr., and Emily each placed a rose on top of the casket, and everyone else followed, single file, doing the same. There wasn't a dry eye among us. Just then, watching Glenn's two young children overcome with sadness, and knowing the grief they would face in the months to come, the burden of my own loss faded. And, with that, the celebration of Glenn Hartman's life, which had been taken so suddenly and so violently, had come to a close. It all seemed so senseless, and some strange force was compelling me to find out why.

As the mourners dispersed, Aunt Tessa abruptly spoke up. "Lacey, there's something you should see. Your young man can come along."

I glanced at Derek and shrugged.

I was about to remind her that Derek was not my "young man" when she quickly added, "Mr. Conover, isn't it?"

"Please, Miss Vander Horn, call me Derek."

"Very well, Derek. Please, bear with us. This is family history. Follow me."

Tessa led us down a leaf-strewn dirt path covered by a canopy of elm trees. I'd been to Willow Hill many times since my parents' death, but I'd never ventured this far into the cemetery. It had always seemed intimidating.

"Obviously, this is the oldest part of the cemetery."

"I didn't realize it dated back this far," Derek remarked.

The engraving had eroded on many of the sandstone and granite stones, but looking closely I could make out some of the dates—1784, 1852, 1885. Some of the names were familiar. I recognized the surnames of old school friends—Van Pelt,

Janssen, Baaker. Willow Bluffs had a long history, most of which I was unaware.

We approached an imposing, weathered, gray marble monument that towered over all the others with VANDER HORN engraved in large block letters.

"As you can see," Aunt Tessa pointed out, "Sophie's father Frits and her uncle Eduard and their wives are buried here. Uncle Jonathan's ancestors were rather pompous."

"This is actually fascinating," Julien said. "We should take *Edge* on location and shoot a couple of scenes here. We're already using the estate for the opening shots."

"Julien, really! The last thing the cemetery would want here is a stream of fans. You know how they track things down."

"Where's Cousin Sophie?" I asked.

"This way," Aunt Tessa said, gesturing for us to follow.

"Who's Cousin Sophie?" Derek asked.

"You can fill in your young man later, dear."

I didn't bother to correct her.

We followed Aunt T around the Vander Horn monument to the row of graves behind it. I immediately spotted Sophie Vander Horn Van Dyk's clay-colored sandstone marker. It was fragile, just like Sophie, tilting forward and looking as though it might fall over in a gusty autumn wind. A separate stone marked her husband Lucas's grave.

"Oh my. I didn't expect this," Aunt Tessa said.

A bunch of yellow roses had been placed next to Sophie's stone.

"How odd," I said.

"Is there a note?" Julien asked.

Derek leaned down and carefully combed through the flowers with his fingertips looking for a message. "No note. No card."

"It appears our cousin Sophie has a secret admirer."

"Look how wilted the flowers are," Derek observed. "The petals fall off to the touch. Must have been here for a couple of days."

"Most curious," Aunt Tessa said.

"I wonder if a local florist would have a record," Julien offered.

"No, I doubt it. They look like grocery store roses to me," Aunt Tessa replied. "Short stems, small buds. I'm afraid Sophie's secret admirer is a bit frugal."

"Yellow roses are a symbol of unrequited love." I pointed out. But that was apropos. Poor Sophie had spent most of her life without Sebastian, her true love. From Aunt Tessa's account, I was certain she would have preferred to be buried next to him rather than Lucas, but I suspected it hadn't been up to her. "What about Sebastian DesChamps, Aunt T? Is he buried here in Willow Hill?"

"Oh, no. The Vander Horns would never have allowed it. Not Lucas's rival. Never."

"Any idea where his grave is?"

"No."

Derek brushed off the dried mud that obscured parts of the inscription on Sophie's stone.

Here Lies Interred
For Eternity
Sophie Van Dyk
née Vander Horn
25th April 1898—27th September 1937

"Look at that," Derek said. "The anniversary of her death was just a couple of days ago."

"Perhaps that's when the flowers were left," I suggested.

"Well, *someone* is aware of her," Aunt Tessa said.

"And possibly her story." Julien pointed out. "And what an absolutely amazing story!"

"Indeed," Aunt T said. "Indeed."

"Agreed. This was no random act. What about Sophie's daughter, Aunt T? Is she buried here?"

"Annabella? You know, I'm not sure. I've never come across her grave, but some here are unmarked."

"This is getting awfully macabre."

Derek looked confused. "I'm clearly missing something. Would anyone like to fill me in?"

"There must be a way to find her," Julien insisted, his curiosity laser sharp. "And the rival as well. Did you say his name was Sebastian?"

"Sebastian DesChamps. French. That was his tragic flaw, according to the Vander Horns. I mean no offense, Julien."

"None taken, Tessa. We both know my heritage is above reproach."

"Sophie could have a great-great grandchild. Maybe my age. I'd love to find out," I said.

"Be careful what you wish for, Lacey. You never know what skeletons you might dredge up. Go ahead and tell Derek the whole lurid tale, my dear."

I took a breath. "Ok, Derek, here's the condensed version. I'll elaborate later. Sophie Vander Horn, actually my aunt's cousin by marriage—on my Uncle Jonathan's side—lived a life of sadness after the love of her life, Sebastian DesChamps, died by falling from the cliff behind the estate, and then she was forced to marry the suitor her family had selected for her, Lucas Van Dyk."

"I think I've got it. So Sebastian fell?"

"Or jumped. Or was pushed," I proposed.

"By the other guy?"

"Yes. Lucas. Or so I'm told, correct, Aunt T?"

"That seems to be the consensus."

"Whoa."

"Now you know," Aunt Tessa said to Derek.

"I had no idea."

"I suggest we leave it there," Aunt Tessa replied. "At least for now. Lacey, shall Julien and I drop you at the estate?"

"You're not attending the repast, Miss Vander Horn?" Derek asked.

"We have to be back in the city," Julien said.

Aunt Tessa turned to me. "I'll be back at the cottage in a day or two, dear," she said, brushing my cheek with a kiss. "Stay strong. I was very proud of you today."

"I'll take you home, Lacey," Derek said.

The four of us made our way back through the dirt path, across the lawn, and to our cars on Hillside Lane. Derek and I got into his Prius and headed away from Willow Hill, and it wasn't soon enough for me.

"Do me a favor, Lacey."

"Sure."

"Come to the repast with me."

"I wasn't invited."

"I was. It'll be fine if you're with me."

"Oh, Derek, I don't know."

"I need someone to hang with over there."

"Since when are you the shy type? You'll know people."

"I'd feel a little less awkward if you were with me."

"Just for a while."

"I know this has been a quite a lot for you today."

"Too much, actually." Sophie's generation would have called it melancholia. The day had been overwhelming, and it wasn't over. "I imagine the repast will be terribly sad."

"True. But it's also an opportunity."

"Opportunity?"

"Yes. To observe," Derek said.

"I'm not going to win this discussion, am I? Okay, then. You talked me into it."

"I'm wondering if the killer will show up. Might be tempting. Like returning to the scene of the crime."

"That's an interesting thought. You think he's been among us all morning?"

"Yeah, maybe. Or *she*," Derek suggested.

"She? Like Gina? She wouldn't have the nerve to show her face at the Hartman house, would she?"

"No. I think she made her statement at the service."

"Loud and clear."

"But I do think there's a good chance that the killer could be someone right here in Willow Bluffs. Actually, the mathematical probability is pretty good. I did some research."

"I'm not surprised." I smiled at him.

Derek gripped the steering wheel tighter as he launched into assistant professor mode. "I obviously don't have my notes in front of me, but here's the deal. According to the FBI's latest statistics, last year almost two thousand murder victims were slain by family members. Pretty sure I have that number right."

"Really? Wow. Is that part of tonight's criminology lecture at Oakdale?"

"Law and Justice in America."

"Okay."

"If I recall correctly—one hundred or so husbands were killed by their wives, and about five hundred wives were murdered by their husbands."

"Haven't these people heard of divorce lawyers?"

"Evidently, they wanted to take the fast track."

"Interesting stats."

"Hey, I've got more. Do you want to sit in on my class tonight?"

"Thanks, but some other time. I've had enough murder for one day. Anyway, Jeremy will tell me all about it."

From the number of cars parked along Quincy Street, it appeared that many guests had already arrived at the Hartman home, a gracious, white, two-story colonial with black shutters. From the outside it seemed like the perfect suburban house for the perfect suburban family, certainly not the home of a murder victim. The front door was wide open, and we walked right in, landing in the dining room, which was overflowing with family, friends, and many of the locals who had been at the funeral home.

Derek and I surveyed the large, elegant room amply furnished with a heavy mahogany china cabinet and buffet and an oval dining table covered with a simple, ecru lace tablecloth. Tasteful floral arrangements had been placed throughout the room.

"I'm guessing everyone has the same two things on their mind," I said. "Who killed Glenn Hartman and why."

"For starters," Derek offered, "the guy had two women ticked off at him—"

"That we know of."

"Yeah, go figure. A couple of councilmen. And probably Barclay and Valenti, the builders on the subdivision deal Glenn wanted to block, and who knows how many clients or adversaries from his private law practice."

"I guess it will come down to who had the strongest motive."

"Remains to be seen."

"I have to say, no one here looks particularly suspicious."

"Hard to tell," Derek said.

Angela crossed the room, stopping to acknowledge Derek.

"I'm very sorry, Angela."

"Derek, thank you for coming. Glenn was always saying how he loved working with you on the council."

"Thank you, Angela. Likewise."

"Wish I could say the same for all the members. But that's how it goes. At least they all had the decency to show up."

"Everyone who worked with Glenn feels the loss," Derek said.

"I highly doubt it," she retorted. She then turned to face me. "Nice of you to come as well, Miss Langdon. So many people I don't even know are here."

"I wanted to pay my respects," I said, feeling awkward that I hadn't been invited.

Derek came to my rescue. "I insisted Lacey join me," he said.

"I appreciate it. By the way, the programs you designed for the service were just right."

"I'm glad you were pleased."

"I thought the service went beautifully," she went on. "Glenn would have approved, don't you agree?"

"Yes. Very touching."

"Please, help yourselves to some refreshments." She turned and vanished into the crowd.

"Is it me or does she seem unfazed?" I observed.

"Completely. She's working the room. If she killed Glenn, she's pulling it off like a pro."

"You'd think she could have managed a few tears."

"Probably got a ton of life insurance to ease her pain."

I hadn't thought of that.

Only a few of the guests indulged in the beautifully displayed buffet of pastries, mini-quiches, and pasta salad. I was uncomfortable standing around.

"I'll get us some coffee."

"Thanks. Black."

When I returned, Derek was chatting with Jim Barclay. I handed Derek his and took a couple of welcome sips from mine.

"Unfortunately, Ron had to be onsite in South Jersey today," Jim explained. "He was sorry he would have to miss the service, but sometimes these things can't be helped. We have a big shopping center going up down there."

"I'm sure the family appreciates that you're here representing Cliffside," Derek said.

"Miss Langdon, please let your aunt know that we'll move the pieces she wanted from the old house to the cottage this week. I'll be in touch to schedule."

"I look forward to it."

"Good to see you both," Jim said, turning to speak to Ari Nikolas.

"Surprising that Valenti wasn't here."

"Not really. Seen enough?" I asked Derek.

"Sure have."

We had just descended the front steps and were on our way to Derek's car when we were suddenly interrupted by a young woman with a notepad. "Councilman Conover?" she asked, knowing it was he.

Derek was cornered. "Yes."

"I'm Elizabeth Gardener from the *County Record*. I wonder if you'd care to make a statement about your colleague."

"Of course," Derek said, pausing a moment. "Everyone in the mayor's office and on the town council is in utter disbelief. We'll miss Glenn terribly."

"Off the record, he tended to butt heads with the other members, no?"

I don't know why I was so surprised by her bluntness. She was a reporter. It just didn't seem like the right time and place.

"Off the record, no more than anyone else," Derek responded diplomatically. "And on the record, let me add that he served the community of Willow Bluffs diligently and selflessly for years."

"Let's get out of here," I said. We quickly moved on, heading for the car, making eye contact with no one.

"Thanks for coming with me," Derek said as we pulled away.

"Anytime you need a repast date for a murdered guy who went off a cliff, I'm your girl."

"I'll keep that in mind."

"Would you drop me off at my shop instead of home? I should touch base with Jeremy."

"Sure. Do you mind if I make a quick stop at Town Hall? I'm teaching tonight and my lecture notes are in my office."

Derek turned into the town hall side parking lot on Willow Street, just a quarter of a mile north of Letter Perfect.

"I'll wait in the car."

"Fine. I'll just be a minute."

Derek entered the building through the side door. While I waited, I stretched my legs as far as I could into the foot well and tried to relax. It had already been a long day, and it was only midafternoon. From the corner of my eye, I sensed movement. I abruptly sat forward to get a better look. I had a view of the front steps and the few parking spaces adjacent to the building's main entrance. It was unmistakably Gina Velasco, walking briskly and teetering on her stilettos. Ron Valenti followed close behind, carrying a large box. I watched as they both got into a black SUV and drove off.

That was out of left field. What were they doing together at a time when no one was around, and what had they taken out of the building?

Derek returned, tossing his materials for class in the back seat. He pulled out onto Willow Street.

"Did you see anyone inside?" I asked.

"No, it was kind of dead in there. Sorry, bad choice of words."

"Unless I was hallucinating, I just saw Gina Velasco and Ron Valenti leave the building together through the main entrance."

"Strange. I thought Jim said he was at a construction site in South Jersey today."

"He did."

"Besides, anyone he would want to see at Town Hall was at the memorial and then at the Hartman house. Are you sure?"

"Oh, I'm totally sure. Gina is totally recognizable."

"Yeah. You've got a point."

"The funny thing was that Ron was carrying a large box."

"I must have just missed them."

We were both perplexed. “I mean, what would he be carrying out of the town hall?”

“No idea. And what was he doing with Gina?” he asked, shaking his head. “I’ll tell you what—I’ll drop you off at the shop now. I was planning on going to my law office for the afternoon, but now I think I’ll go back to Town Hall. Maybe I can figure out what they were up to.”

“Let me know.”

“Of course.”

I sighed audibly. “A couple of days ago, Willow Bluffs was just a sleepy little town where nothing ever happened.”

“Yeah. That’s over,” Derek said.

“I hate change.”

“It’s inevitable.”

“All I can say is that someone, possibly someone I know, committed murder in my backyard, and I’m not going to rest until I find out who did it.”

Chapter Seven

I awoke Saturday morning to heavy, wind-driven autumn rain pelting the windows above my bed. Kicking away my gray silk comforter, I abruptly sat up, startled by a strange, distant sound. I realized I'd been dreaming about Sophie and Sebastian. At least, I thought I'd been dreaming, but I was still groggy and disoriented. It all seemed so vivid. I'd heard Sophie calling Sebastian's name from the ill-fated cliff again and again, her voice swirling in the wind, echoing across the Palisades and over the river. The desperation in her cries was palpable. I raised the shade and looked out the window. I had to convince myself that no one was outside. Of course, no one was. But I wondered how many times in her life Sophie had gone to the cliff futilely searching for her true love, hopelessly wishing he'd come back to her.

I threw on my go-to comfort clothes, a pair of gray sweatpants and my maroon Fordham University sweatshirt and cozy maroon wool socks. Yesterday, when I'd come home after the memorial, I'd felt compelled to find the perfect spot to display Sophie's stunning portrait. I'd placed it on the limestone mantel in the living room, leaning high against the fireplace. And then this morning, as soon as I walked into the living room, I stood before it, taking a long, critical look. I was pleased. It would do fine. In fact, the portrait seemed as if it belonged there, as if it had always been there. I didn't expect Aunt Tessa to return from the city until tomorrow, but I knew she'd approve.

I opened the front door to let Dylan out and grabbed the *Gazette* from the front porch before it got soaked. The story about the ongoing investigation of the Hartman murder didn't say much. In fact, it asked the public for more information than it gave with yet another plea for tipsters to call the anonymous hotline the police had set up. If anyone had leads, they were being very tight-lipped. The murderer was still at large, and that made me uneasy.

Dylan scampered back into the house quickly. I scratched the top of his head.

"If it wasn't raining, I'd take you for a long walk, Dyllie. Maybe later when I get home, but definitely tomorrow," I promised. "Okay, boy?"

He wagged his tail in agreement. Shaking off the rain, he ran into the kitchen and sat next to his bowl, intensely watching every move I made while I opened a can of Dog's Best Friend's Hearty Beef Stew for his breakfast. I decided I'd get something for myself later at Bean Around.

My dream had left me preoccupied with Sophie, Sebastian, and their story. I had a feeling that the painting would now be a constant, haunting reminder of the past. Now that it was a fixture in my home, I couldn't help but notice that there was something strange, even pervasive, about it. It was the eyes. Sophie had Mona Lisa eyes. Wherever I stood, her gaze seemed to meet mine. Was she trying to tell me something? Was she warning me? I was clearly under her spell.

I had to move on. I had a busy day ahead of me at the shop. I dressed quickly in designer jeans, black leather boots, and a beige turtleneck cashmere sweater and headed out the door.

When I arrived at Letter Perfect at ten, Jeremy had already opened the shop and was busy organizing the sample invitation books. Saturdays always meant a flurry of activity. Three brides-to-be and their mothers were coming in to select wedding invitations, and I had an appointment with a new client who needed help planning a fiftieth birthday party for her husband. And there would undoubtedly be walk-ins.

"Morning, Lace. Hey, is the county sheriff's truck still in front of the Bean?"

"I didn't notice."

"Crazy stuff. I wonder if they have any suspects yet."

"Doesn't sound like it."

"Conover's class was pretty cool last night. Got me thinking."

"Yeah, I know Derek did a lot of research."

"Derek? So you two are pretty tight?"

"Just friends. Acquaintances, actually."

Jeremy raised an eyebrow. "Uh huh. Whatever. Be sure to tell him what a great, hard-working guy I am, okay? I need to ace that class."

I laughed. "I'm sure you'll tell him yourself, Jeremy."

"So, according to FBI stats, Hartman was probably offed by a relative, or his wife maybe, or someone else who knew him pretty well. Friend, girlfriend, business associate."

"Sounds that way."

"He could have checked off every box. I mean, it's not like some random dude would bash the guy's head in with a rock and toss him over a cliff."

"You put it so delicately, Jeremy."

"Nothing delicate about murder."

"Nope."

"You know, the guy was just plodding along living his life and then—bam!"

"You never know what's going on in someone's life. So, what's happening here in our little shop, Jeremy?"

"The usual Saturday crunch. The appointments you booked last week are coming in, but nothing new," Jeremy said, walking toward the shop's side window. "The sheriff's truck is gone. I wonder where they're headed. Seriously, I'd love to be in on the investigation. I'm obsessed."

"We all are."

"Doesn't look like they even have a person of interest yet. Ridiculous. Today's story in the *Gazette* is pretty lame," Jeremy said.

"I'll bet the cops aren't telling all they know."

"Yeah, I watch a lot of *Dateline*, too," Jeremy quipped.

"Glenn's murder would make a pretty good story."

"Sure would. I pulled out the top wedding books for your first appointment. Mrs. Pierce and her daughter. They should be in any minute."

The Pierces had been associated with my family for as long as I could remember. While Julien LaFontaine managed Aunt Tessa's professional career, Thomas Pierce, president of Republic Investments, personally handled her portfolio. His company's real estate division and, of course, Tom Pierce himself, had earned a windfall on the subdivision of Aunt Tessa's seven-figure property with more to come once the sale of the manor house had been finalized. And, knowing Mrs. Pierce, she wouldn't hesitate to spend lavishly on their daughter's wedding.

A swath of rain blew in from the front door as Mrs. Pierce and her daughter rushed into the shop, eager to take cover.

"What horrendous weather. My umbrella is useless in this wind," Mrs. Pierce grumbled. Her demeanor quickly changed. "Lovely to see you again, Lacey."

"Likewise."

"You know Ava, of course. Newly engaged."

"Congratulations!"

Positively glowing, Ava flashed a stunning crystal-clear emerald cut diamond that must have been at least a carat and a half.

"Who's the lucky groom-to-be?" I asked.

"Jason Barclay. Jim's son."

"Oh, yes. Wonderful! All the best to both of you. Please, sit down," I said, gesturing toward the conference table. "Now, tell me, how do you envision the wedding?"

"I was thinking along the lines of a rustic theme," Ava remarked.

"Rustic-elegant, Ava," her mother insisted. "We have a hold on a date at the Saddle Creek Inn for six months from now. But first things first.

"I want to throw an intimate engagement party for Ava and Jason in a couple of weeks, and I desperately need your help. I know it's very spur of the moment, but we want to have the party as soon as possible. You did such a wonderful job with the groundbreaking ceremony last week. I was hoping you'd be available. What do you think? Doable?"

"Truthfully, it's a bit of a time crunch, but certainly doable if we handle the invitations by email."

"We'll need a caterer, florist, everything. It will just be family and the wedding party. Maybe a couple of business associates. I suppose we'll have to have Jason's father's business partner. I think his name is Valenti. I don't know him very well. Anyway, I'm thinking we'll be about thirty people or so. We'll have it at the house."

"I usually work with Classic Caterers. They'll handle everything from hors d'oeuvres to bar service to dessert to clean up. And I know they can put something together quickly."

"You'll help us coordinate everything?"

"Absolutely. Send me the guests' email addresses and all the details, and I'll get started right away."

"Oh, I'm so relieved. You're a godsend, Lacey. We'll be in touch soon."

"I look forward to it."

Just as the Pierces were on their way out, Jess breezed in with lattes for Jeremy and me.

"Coffee time," she announced.

"Thanks. Put it on my tab."

"Already did. Just wanted to tell you there have been a lot of press people sniffing around today. Again."

"Yeah? Anything new?"

"Not that I've heard. Mostly from the *Gazette* and the *Record*. That woman from *Soap Opera Weekly* was back. Natalie something," Jess recalled.

"Natalie Summers. I met her at the groundbreaking. I think she's doing a feature on my aunt."

"Or something," Jess said. "She's awfully interested in your family."

"Yeah. She was asking a lot of questions when I met her," I said.

"Has she come into your shop?" Jess asked.

"No. Not yet, anyway."

"I would expect her if I were you. She asked me if I knew you. Then, she was asking about the Vander Horns. Ancestors and all that."

"She must be doing an in-depth story," I proposed.

Jeremy laughed out loud. "For a soap rag?"

"She said something about going to the cemetery today."

"Who's she going to interview in the graveyard?" Jeremy added.

Jess laughed. "You know how those soap fans are. They're obsessed. Anything about Miss Tessa Vander Horn, the queen of *Edge of Darkness*, would be fascinating to them. We forget that Lacey's aunt is a huge star."

I was on my guard all day, but as it turned out, Natalie Summers never came into the shop. I wouldn't have had time to talk with her, anyway. I had one appointment after another with clients, and we were happy to close up a few minutes after five.

By the time I got back home to Riverview Cottage, the rain had stopped. The estate's longtime caretaker and gardener, Arthur Taylor, was high up on the extension ladder, making me nervous as he fiddled with something along the roofline. Close to seventy years old, I sometimes thought that he took on too much at the estate. But Aunt Tessa didn't have the heart to fire him.

"You okay up there, Arthur?" I called.

Dylan, aware of the intrusion, barked intermittently from inside.

"For sure. Nothin' to it. Some storm today, wasn't it, miss?"

"Awful," I agreed.

"Yup, this is what happens when it rains sideways. Wind blew the gutter right off. Could cause big trouble, you know."

"I don't know what we'd do without you, Arthur!"

"There. All fixed now. You won't have to worry about water leaking in the cottage." He slowly descended the ladder. "Sure glad things are getting back to normal around here. So much confusion last week. I don't cotton much to talking to the police."

"Did they interview you after the murder?"

"Sure did. I told that police chief that I saw someone early in the morning the day of the big ceremony."

"The day of the murder," I clarified.

"Yup. No idea who it was, though. Must have been before seven. It was still kind of dark."

"You told the police?"

"Oh, sure. Didn't help much. Funny thing was, I saw someone lurking around again yesterday."

"Did you report that?"

"Nah. Too dark. Couldn't see who it was. Figured it wouldn't matter much."

"Maybe I'll give the chief a call and let him know. Just for the record."

I suspected Arthur knew more than he was telling. He was loyal to the family to a fault, but for some reason he seemed reluctant to get involved.

"Hope he doesn't come around here again."

"If you don't mind, Arthur, let me know when you see something unusual happening around here."

"Sure thing, miss."

He collapsed the extension ladder and brought it to the tool shed on the edge of the east lawn.

After I let Dylan have a good run around the backyard, I called the Willow Bluffs police and spoke to Officer Jane Kowalski. She thanked me for the information and said she would pass it on to the chief. He would certainly check the estate's surveillance video once again but, ultimately, we both knew it was probably a dead end. Even so, I hoped a detective would speak with Arthur. Possibly, when pressed, he would remember something more, or something significant going forward. He had full access to the estate at all times.

I poured myself a glass of Pinot Grigio and sat on the floor in front of the boxes that Aunt Tessa had Jim Barclay deliver from the main house. I had nothing to do but relax and rummage through the collection of papers, photos, journals, and memorabilia. My curiosity had gotten the better of me. I hoped I would find some family treasures. I had just dug in when I heard my phone chime. Derek was texting.

you home
hanging with Dylan
doing anything tonight
not really
how about dinner at grimaldi's my treat
you wouldnt be asking me out would you
no not at all well maybe technically yeah I guess I am

I paused for about thirty seconds. *Well, I wouldn't mind going out*, I thought. And a nice bronzino didn't sound bad.

ok why not
pick you up in an hour

I suddenly felt unexpectedly concerned about what I should wear. I wanted to look nice, but I didn't want to look as if I'd tried too hard. I squeezed myself into a pair of skinny jeans and chose a simple black silk blouse and black booties, which magically elongated my legs, making me look taller than my almost five-feet-five frame. My hair and makeup were good enough. I simply brushed out my hair and refreshed my lipstick with cinnamon-colored gloss.

Dylan began to bark, signaling that someone had arrived, and then I immediately heard the doorbell. I checked my watch. Derek wasn't due for twenty minutes. It didn't matter. I was ready. But, on my way to the door from my bedroom, I looked out the living room window and noticed my regular United Shipping deliveryman was standing on the porch, package in hand.

"All packages for the estate are coming here now, right?"

"Yes, thanks, Bobby."

"Just one tonight," he said, handing me a small parcel wrapped in plain brown paper. "Take it easy."

I immediately noticed it had a handwritten address rather than a typed label. I looked closer and froze.

Miss Sophie Vander Horn
2265 Willow Street
Willow Bluffs, New Jersey

I very carefully removed the brown paper without disturbing the address to reveal a black velvet box, the kind that would hold jewelry. I gasped when I saw what was inside. Sophie's blue cameo brooch, without question. I was certain it was the exact pin that she wore in the painting, a carved silhouette in blue stone facing left on an ivory background, and it was clearly old. The clasp was tarnished, and the fastener was dull from use.

Inside the box, under the holder for the brooch, I found a small card, folded in half, faded and worn around the edges. I handled it gingerly, unfolding it slowly so it wouldn't tear. "Sebastian Des Champs" was printed in the center. It must have been his calling card, a popular nineteenth-century refinement. He had inscribed the card, in an ornate hand:

"To Sophie, with love forever, S."

Completely awestruck, my immediate reaction was that Aunt Tessa might have sent it, but I quickly realized that made no sense. She was due to come back to the cottage tomorrow, and she would have simply brought it. Unless, of course, her plans had changed. I picked up my phone and called her.

"Lacey?" she answered.

"Hi, Aunt T. Just wanted to confirm that you're coming back tomorrow."

"Yes, Julien is driving me over in the morning. Everything okay, dear?"

"Fine. Just double-checking. By the way, did you send a package to the house?"

"Package? No dear, nothing."

"Okay. It's not important. See you tomorrow."

I heard the doorbell ring again over Dylan's persistent barking. I peeked outside again, and this time it was Derek.

"Hey, what's up? You look rattled. Bad day?"

I showed him the package, the brooch, and the painting of Sophie. For once, Derek looked completely dumbfounded.

"You're saying that the guy who jumped off the cliff four centuries ago sent this pin to your dead cousin?"

"Yes, that's basically it. She's actually my aunt's cousin by marriage. But still family."

"Whatever. This is weird, Lacey."

"No kidding."

I could sense that Derek, always the voice of reason, was trying to apply logic to an absolutely illogical situation.

"I don't like it, Lacey," he cautioned. "First of all, who had access to the pin?"

"Actually, if the brooch was somewhere in the main house, I guess lots of people could have come across it. Construction crews, movers, realtors, the guests at the groundbreaking, caterers. Reporters. Could have been anyone. Is it possible someone found it and was returning it?"

"Why address it to a dead person?"

"Good point."

"Did you ask the delivery guy where it came from?"

"Nope. He was gone before I looked at the address."

"Okay. Is there a tracking number on the package?" Derek asked, taking out his phone.

"Yes. There's a sticker under the address."

"Read it to me."

"United Shipping. USTZ5P462."

Derek quickly entered the code. "It's coming up. Wait a sec . . . It was shipped from the United Shipping Store in Fort Lee. The address of the shop is the only return address. No help at all. Where's your aunt now?"

"In the city."

"Maybe we should pay her a visit. She should know about this, and I think we should tell her in person."

"This is too bizarre." My chest tightened. "Do you think we're in any danger?"

He took longer to respond than I would have liked.

"I don't know, Lacey," he finally said. "But someone went to a lot of trouble to send that package anonymously."

"I know," I said uneasily. "Really twisted. Derek, what if they're watching the cottage?"

Chapter Eight

"Is it valuable?" I asked Aunt Tessa.

"My dear, it's priceless!"

"Are you sure this is actually Sophie's pin?" Derek asked.

Holding the cameo tightly in her right hand, Aunt Tessa examined it closely. "Yes. No question about it."

I had called Aunt Tessa from the car to tell her we'd be stopping by her Manhattan penthouse. She was delighted, but she had no idea why. She had probably assumed we were having dinner in one of the restaurants in her Upper East Side neighborhood. She was shocked when we arrived and gave her the news about the disturbing delivery. The three of us sat in the overdecorated, traditional living room on overstuffed, white twin sofas, Derek and I opposite Aunt Tessa, mulling over what had happened.

Derek got up and took a few steps toward the wall of windows facing downtown. From the thirty-fifth floor, the breathtaking city lights and twinkling stars put on a dazzling show. "What an incredible view, Miss Vander Horn," Derek said.

Still holding the pin, Aunt Tessa got up and joined him at the window. Looking as elegant as always in beige cashmere palazzo pants and a matching tunic, she admitted, “You know, I’ve lived in this apartment for thirty years, and I have never once taken this spectacle for granted.”

“With good reason.”

Once they’d returned to the sofas, I concentrated on solving the mystery of the unexpected delivery. “What do you remember about the cameo, Aunt T?”

“Let’s see, first of all, my mother-in-law, Josephine Vander Horn, found it locked away in a dresser drawer about ten years ago. She brought it to Harrison’s to be appraised.”

“The jeweler in Willow Bluffs?” Derek asked.

“Yes, and as I recall, they determined the cameo had been carved from a type of quartz, blue agate, I believe, was the name of the stone. It’s only worth a couple of hundred dollars in monetary value, but of course, to us it is a precious heirloom.”

“Yes, of course,” Derek agreed.

“Apparently, blue agates were quite popular in France at the end of the nineteenth century,” Aunt Tessa explained, “so there was some speculation that Sebastian may have purchased it when he was abroad.”

“Interesting,” I noted.

With the cameo still in her hand, Aunt T took another close look. “You know, there’s another interesting thing about this piece. The silhouette is facing left. Josephine was told that this is quite unusual.”

“Does that have any significance?”

“I honestly don’t know,” Aunt T admitted.

"Would Josephine have told the people at Harrison's the story behind the brooch?" I asked.

"Oh, I'm certain she would have. The jeweler would have been interested in the provenance of such an old Vander Horn piece," she conjectured.

"Miss Vander Horn, I've been wondering, where did you last see the pin?" Derek asked.

"Ah, good question. I'm quite sure it was a couple of weeks ago. When I was in the manor house, I brought it downstairs to the library with some other things. Some old lace handkerchiefs, some cuff links of Jonathan's. A vintage marcasite watch, as I remember. Just a few small items. Nothing particularly valuable. I put them in the top desk drawer."

"In the library?" I clarified.

"Yes, I'm sure of it."

Her recollection made perfect sense. "And then, a few days ago when we were at the house with Jim Barclay, you put everything in a box and brought it to the cottage."

"Correct."

Derek suddenly spoke up. "Are you sure the pin was actually *in* the desk that day when you went back?" he questioned. "Maybe it had been taken sometime after you put it in the desk and before you retrieved everything. I doubt you would have noticed."

"Interesting," I said. "We *were* rather rushed."

"Oh my. I hadn't thought of that, but it's entirely possible. I couldn't swear that I saw it in the desk at that time. Stupid of me to have been so careless. It never occurred to me that anyone would have been interested in those items except us. I can tell you this, I'm fairly certain the desk drawer was still locked when Lacey and I were there."

"*Fairly* certain," Derek repeated, as the lawyer in him took over.

"Don't blame yourself, Aunt T."

"You know, it wouldn't be too difficult for someone to break into one of those locks," Derek proposed.

Aunt Tessa looked disturbed. "I just can't imagine why someone would do a thing like this. Sending the cameo to Sophie at the estate is completely bizarre."

"More like deranged," Derek retorted.

I shot him a disapproving look. I didn't want to alarm Aunt T any more than we already had.

"So many people were in and out of the main house," she said.

"Let's start with the obvious. Who knew Sophie and Sebastian's story?" Derek asked, now in full cross-examination mode.

"Anyone could have figured out they were in love by the note inside the box," I said. "And it was certainly reasonable to assume that Sophie had lived on the estate, since the cameo was found there, or at least now it belonged to someone who lived on the estate."

"Truthfully, I suppose I had told the story to a few people," Aunt Tessa confessed. "It made for interesting conversation."

"Absolutely," I said.

"As I've said, Julien and I passed the story along to the writers of *Edge* as an option for a backstory, a prequel of sorts. I'm sure some of the production people heard about it as well."

"Julien," I repeated.

"Yes, but you don't think—"

"I don't know what to think, Aunt Tessa."

"The staff writers do talk," she admitted.

"So, in other words, there were some people knew," I replied.

"Did anyone have an ax to grind, Miss Vander Horn?" Derek asked.

"With me? I don't think so."

"You know, someone who might want to harass you," he went on. "Either you or Lacey?"

"I can't think of anyone," Aunt Tessa answered.

"Neither can I. I mean, I'm in the party business. You know, happy occasions."

"What about your television show, Miss Vander Horn? How are things on the set?"

"*Edge of Darkness* is just one big happy family." Aunt Tessa laughed. "Truly. We have our little in-house squabbles, but certainly nothing to warrant a response like this."

"No one could possibly replace Aunt Tessa on *Edge*," I said, "if that's what you're driving at. She's been with the show for decades. She IS *Edge of Darkness*."

"Ok, I get it," Derek said. "So, no jealousy, competition . . . ?"

"None at all. Not with Aunt T's role as the beloved Caroline Manchester. Aunt T, have you had dinner?"

"No, dear, I was just going to fix something light. What about you two? I thought you said you were going out?"

"We had a slight change in plans," I said.

"I'll order from Jean Luc. It's just down the block. And they deliver. Lacey, would you mind opening the cabernet? Top shelf of the wine rack."

After we enjoyed a leisurely dinner, Aunt Tessa made another excellent suggestion.

"Lacey, why don't you stay with me here in the city tonight? You have everything you need in the guest room."

Derek nodded in agreement. "That's not a bad idea, Lacey. I know I'll feel better about you staying at the cottage once the Willow Bluffs police know about what happened."

"My driver can take us back to the cottage in the morning. Julien won't be around. He mentioned something about having lunch at Sardi's tomorrow with some prospective producers for the Broadway project."

"You know what? I'm exhausted. I think I'll take you up on it."

"I'll let you both get some rest," he said. "Brunch tomorrow, Lacey?"

"Sounds good to me. Hey, do me a favor," I said, reaching for my bag on the foyer console table. "Here's my key. Would you mind looking in on Dylan? Maybe a short walk, and he'll need some kibble and a little bit of whatever leftovers you can find in the fridge for dinner. Just leave the key under the flower pot next to the front door."

"Of course. Let me know when you get back tomorrow. Good night, Miss Vander Horn. Thanks so much for your hospitality."

"Not at all. I hope to see you again."

I should have known better than to check emails before bedtime. I noticed Mrs. Pierce had just sent me the details for Ava and Jason's engagement party, along with the guests' email addresses. Since time was of the essence, I decided to forge ahead and get busy, even though I was tired. Moreover, I thought working for a while might take my mind off the cameo debacle. I pulled up my go-to party planning website, celebr8.com, crafted a simple but elegant invitation, and emailed it to the thirty-five or so names on the guest list with a quick RSVP turnaround date of just a couple of days away. It was unusual, but I understood Mrs. Pierce's preference to have the engagement party so soon since the wedding was just six months away.

I noticed, along with family and members of the wedding party, several familiar names on the list. Aunt Tessa and Julien, of course; Jim Barclay and his wife; Ron Valenti and a guest; Mayor Nikolas and her husband. It would be a manageable number of guests for a party held in a home. If I really worked at it, I'd have enough time to finalize the menu and wait staff with Classic Caterers, plan the décor, and possibly breathe. Thankfully, I fell asleep with catering arrangements on my mind rather than ghostly deliveries.

* * *

The next morning, Aunt Tessa's driver Charles picked us up promptly at eight. With light Sunday morning traffic, we breezed across the George Washington Bridge to Route 4 West and sailed into Willow Bluffs in twenty minutes flat. I didn't express my concern to Aunt Tessa, but I was afraid of what we might find when we arrived at the cottage. Another strange surprise? Anonymous half-dead flowers? A break-in? I was relieved when Charles dropped us off and all was well. I think Aunt Tessa felt the same way, but neither of us uttered a word about it.

Derek, Aunt Tessa, and I all thought we should report the cameo incident to the Willow Bluffs police, just to have it on the record. I picked up my phone, wondering exactly what I would say. The whole thing sounded so preposterous. Were we making too much of it? Had it simply been some kind of weird mistake? The dispatcher transferred me to a patrolman who listened patiently, and said he'd relay it to the proper channels. I wasn't sure what he meant by that.

My phone lit up with a text from Derek.

pick you up about 10 for brunch
sounds good see you then

About a half hour after my call to the police, Dylan darted for the front door, barking wildly and clearly announcing the arrival of a visitor. I spotted Sergeant Martinelli on the front steps, and I ushered him inside, patting Dylan on the head to calm him. Aunt Tessa was seated in the club chair in front of the fireplace, beneath Sophie's portrait.

"Miss Langdon. Miss Vander Horn," the sergeant said, as he and I sat on the sofa opposite Aunt Tessa.

"I'll get right to it, Sergeant. I received this package yesterday evening," I explained, handing him the outer box. "You'll see it contains a jewelry case with a cameo pin that belonged to one of our ancestors."

"So I was told."

I took a breath. "The strange thing is that the package was addressed to my aunt's cousin, Sophie Vander Horn, who, according to her gravestone, died in 1937."

"I see."

"Extremely bizarre, isn't it?"

Sergeant Martinelli examined the outside of the shipping box and then removed the jewelry case and opened it, looking at the delicate cameo closely. He carefully removed the note from the bottom of the case. "What's this?" he asked.

"It's a calling card. A nineteenth-century refinement. From Sophie's suitor, Sebastian DesChamps. There's a note."

"Ah, yes," he said, carefully turning it over. "I see the inscription. What would you like us to do, Miss Langdon?"

"I'm not exactly sure. We can't understand why the cameo was sent to us."

"It is your family's property, is it not?"

"Of course."

"Doesn't that explain it?"

"No, not entirely."

"I would say someone found the pin and decided to send it back."

"But my aunt is certain she had locked it in a desk drawer in the library of the main house, right, Aunt Tessa?"

"I'm *somewhat* certain."

"*Somewhat,*" Sergeant Martinelli repeated. "Then, isn't it safe to assume that it was somehow lost or misplaced?"

"Or removed," Aunt Tessa offered.

"That doesn't quite make sense, ladies."

"How would someone have known to send it here?" I proposed.

"That is a good question, but it's likely it was found right here on the Vander Horn property and then shipped back to ensure security."

He sounded astoundingly logical. I was beginning to feel completely ridiculous and somewhat annoyed. "Sergeant, we're certainly not suggesting that Sophie's suitor came back from the dead to send the package, but we do feel that someone may have been lurking around the manor house who should not have been there."

"I can understand your concern, Miss Langdon. Everyone in town has been on edge since the Hartman murder. You have no idea how many craz—um, unusual reports we've had this past week."

At least he managed to stop short of calling us crazy, I thought. "It's just so odd."

"Odd? Perhaps. Criminal? Probably not. If you are reporting a *possible previous* theft or loss, and the item is now in your possession, I'm not sure what the police can do about it."

Aunt Tessa and I both looked at the sergeant blankly.

"I'll tell you what," he went on. "Just to be on the safe side, we'll take a look at the estate's security cameras again. And we'll send a patrol car around several times to keep an eye on things here at the estate."

"I appreciate it," I said, knowing he was merely placating me. "Thank you, Sergeant."

I accompanied him to the door.

"Good day, Miss Vander Horn. Miss Langdon. If there's anything else, don't hesitate."

"That went well," I said sarcastically.

"He thinks we've lost our minds," Aunt Tessa lamented.

"Good thing we didn't mention the yellow roses on Sophie's grave."

"Indeed."

Derek arrived at the stroke of ten, jolting Dylan out of his bed once again with the sound of the doorbell.

"Hey. All set?"

"I am."

"Care to join us, Mrs. Vander Horn?"

"No, thanks. I have a few errands."

"Lacey, grab the shipping box. Just the box. I have an idea."

I followed along. When we went outside to Derek's Prius, I tossed the box onto the backseat.

"I thought we'd have brunch in Fort Lee," Derek said. "There's a place overlooking the river I think you'll love. The International Cafe. But I want to make a quick stop at United Shipping first."

"Oh. Good idea. You think they might be able to tell us something?"

"It's worth a shot."

We pulled into a strip mall on Lemoine Avenue in Fort Lee and parked directly in front of the small United Shipping store. It was surprisingly busy for a Sunday morning, but after a few minutes a clerk approached us.

"I know this is a long shot," Derek said, "but we're trying to figure out who sent this package."

"It was definitely sent from this location," I explained, placing the box on the counter. "Check out the return address."

"Tough one," the clerk said. "That's a default address that we use when no return address is given." He scanned the codes affixed to the box. "Yeah," he said. "Just as I thought. This was dropped in the drop box out front. I can tell from the origination code. It's a flat rate shipping box. We have them in a few sizes. This one is nine ninety-five. Great deal. For a flat fee, the shipper can send whatever fits inside. Super easy. You can even order them online."

"So, you wouldn't have weighed the package," Derek confirmed.

"Nope. No need for the customer to come in and wait in line."

"Then, there was no interaction with whoever sent the package?"

"Most likely none at all. Works out great. We empty the drop box twice a day. Once around noon and again at the end of the day. We code the packages, and our trucks take them to the sorting facility in Newark. Last truck leaves around six."

"By the way," I asked. "How long would it take for a package to get to Willow Bluffs?"

"One day. Two tops."

Derek was about to turn to leave when he suddenly stopped. "One more thing. Do you have surveillance cameras?"

"There's one up in the corner," the clerk said, pointing to the ceiling. "But, like I said, the sender probably never came in. No cameras outside. Sorry."

"Okay. Thanks for your help."

We walked out, feeling less than satisfied.

"Dead end," I remarked to Derek.

"You've got that right," he answered. "Dead right."

Chapter Nine

After a leisurely brunch at the charming International Cafe in Fort Lee, Derek and I returned to Riverview Cottage to relax, or at least try. The delectable brioche French toast smothered in strawberries and whipped cream had eased our frustration, at least temporarily. But unfortunately, after hitting a wall at United Shipping, we still had more questions than answers. Dead flowers. Calling cards. Phantom packages. I felt compelled to learn more, but I knew our options were extremely limited, if not nonexistent. As Derek read the *Gazette* on the sofa, I sat on the floor next to Dylan and leaned against the hearth. Sensing the tension that had overcome me, Dylan rested his head in my lap and snuggled. I slowly stroked him behind his ears.

"We're missing something," I said, my thoughts wandering.

"Obviously," Derek agreed, looking up from the newspaper. "But what?"

I twisted around and gazed at Cousin Sophie's portrait. "I don't know. Something." I sighed. "Everything."

"Can you be more specific?" Derek teased.

"No. But, I have an idea. Actually, it may be more like a premonition. I'm feeling like maybe if we go back into the old house, we'll find some sort of clue to what's been going on." Something had been nagging me, frustrating me. I couldn't explain it, and I couldn't get it out of my head.

"You're not making a lot of sense."

"I know. Can't hurt to look around, can it?"

I wasn't sure if Derek actually disapproved or if he was simply too comfortable on the sofa to move. "Lacey, I thought the builders didn't want anyone in there. The house is about to go on the market, isn't it?"

"If you want to split hairs."

"I'm just being practical." Derek pointed out.

"Until they find a buyer and close a deal on the sale, the house is still technically in my family."

"That's a stretch. The builders own the place."

"Officially speaking."

Derek frowned. "All we need now is to find ourselves charged with breaking and entering."

"You lawyers," I scolded, shaking my head. "There's absolutely nothing to worry about," I assured him.

"No? I'm a member of the bar, you know."

"I'm well aware. We won't be breaking and entering. I have a key."

"Oh, well, in that case . . ." he retorted sarcastically.

I got up to retrieve the key Aunt Tessa kept in the junk drawer in the kitchen. I was all in on the idea.

"Come on. Let's go," I proposed.

"Now?"

"Why not? I won't rest until we do. Grab your jacket."

I managed to coax Derek off the sofa. "I can't believe I'm agreeing to this."

"It'll be an interesting experience for you, if nothing else. You've never seen the inside of the old place, have you?"

"No. Never."

"Then it'll be fun. Hey, Dylan, you watch the house, okay? You're a good boy." He barely opened one eye.

"Do they have surveillance cameras?" Derek wanted to know as we crossed the lawn, heading toward the carport.

"Yes. A couple. But just at the entries."

"Can we get in unnoticed?"

"Possibly," I said, looking up at the roofline and immediately spotting two cameras positioned toward the lawn. I quickly reconsidered. "Well, probably not. But if anyone asks, I'll say Aunt Tessa thought she left her gloves in the library the other day."

Derek laughed. "Sure, that's plausible. Hopefully, no one will ask."

"Let's go in the front door. We've got nothing to hide."

"Not much," Derek said, as we stood on the front steps. "Wow! Just look at this place," he added, taking in the beauty of the grand Italianate manor. "Must have been something coming here as a kid."

"I suppose. I took it for granted, though. I didn't even give it a second thought. It's always been in my life. And that's part of the problem. Besides all the weird things that have been going on, between losing my parents this past year and now with Aunt Tessa losing her wonderful home, I feel like my identity is slipping away."

"Listen, Lacey, I understand where you're coming from. Losing your parents was tragic. But you're dealing with it. You've faced everything straight on. And I can see that you're coming into your own. You know, you're establishing yourself as an independent woman."

"I've tried. But I'm still a little too vulnerable at times."

"Don't forget you've still got the cottage. And the cliffs will be here for an eternity."

"That's for sure."

I opened the front door to reveal the splendor of the grand foyer with its majestic crystal chandelier, richly paneled walls, and gleaming Carrera marble floor.

"This place is incredible," Derek said, taking it all in. "But I have to say, also a little eerie."

"That's because it's basically empty," I said. "You should have seen how Aunt Tessa had the place decorated. She has exquisite taste, you know. She always has. She married Uncle Jonathan when she was just nineteen, sixty years ago, right after she joined the cast of *Edge of Darkness.* As soon as she moved in, she hired a top-notch design firm from Manhattan and every room was done to perfection. From then on, the home was always a showplace, even more elaborate than the mansion in the *Edge.*"

"Losing it must be hard on her."

"She's such a good actress, we'll never really know for sure."

Standing in the expansive two-story foyer, I wondered if this would be the last time I would walk through the old place. I would always have my memories, even if I couldn't return. As long as the massive Italianate house existed, it would remain a part of me and would never cease to command the cliffs of Willow Bluffs. If only it would send us some clues or give us some of the answers we've been looking for. It was just a hunch, but something told me that the strange occurrences we'd been experiencing had something to do with the house, or perhaps the extended Vander Horn family. I had to find out.

I gazed up at the landing looming over the sweeping staircase. "Maybe we should start upstairs in the bedrooms," I suggested. "Follow me."

"Why not? You've managed to get me this far."

I grasped the elaborate railing supported by intricately carved corbels as we ascended the curved mahogany staircase and stood in the majestic hallway leading to the bedrooms.

"The primary bedroom is to the left," I said, my voice echoing throughout the foyer.

"I wish I knew what we were looking for," Derek said.

"Me, too. But whoever sent Sophie's brooch to the cottage must have gotten it from inside the house. Maybe they left some kind of clue."

"If only we knew who had access."

The empty primary suite looked barren without Aunt Tessa's palatial country French furnishings, overstuffed silk chairs, antique dressing table, and bucolic paintings. The floors and moldings had been freshly vacuumed.

"Aunt Tessa said that she had last seen Sophie's brooch locked in a desk drawer in the library. But what if she was wrong? Maybe it was up here. Take a look in the closet," I suggested, as I scoured the dressing area.

"Doesn't look like there's a sign of anyone. In fact, it looks like the whole place has been cleaned since the work was done on the house."

"I think you're right." I didn't see so much as a speck of dust anywhere. "As long as we're here, let's check the other five bedrooms."

Derek and I made a clean sweep of the entire upstairs. If anyone had come in looking for the brooch, or who knows what else, they left no indication. Not a footprint, a dropped handkerchief, a stray piece of paper. Nothing.

"Dead end," Derek said.

"I'm afraid you're right. Thanks for indulging me. Sometimes, you just have to follow your heart. Let's go downstairs to the library. If that was Aunt Tessa's best recollection of where she had seen the pin, then maybe . . ."

We made our way down the staircase back to the first floor, and Derek followed me through the main hall. Just outside the library we heard someone approaching.

"I was afraid of this," Derek mumbled.

Fortunately, it was only our caretaker.

"Arthur! I didn't expect to see you," I said with surprise.

"Didn't expect to see you either, miss." He looked Derek and me up and down. "Need something?"

"Yes, actually. My aunt thought she might have dropped a glove last time she was here," I managed. "I told her I'd take a look for her."

"A glove, you say. Yes. I'll keep my eye out. Usually make rounds twice a day, miss."

"I appreciate it, Arthur. This is my friend Derek."

"Yes, I've seen him on the property. Pleasure."

"This is his first time seeing the place. I thought I'd show him around. We'd like to look for the glove inside the library. Aunt Tessa remembers being in there recently."

"Ah, the library. The old place has its secrets, you know."

"Secrets? I suppose it does," I said.

"More than meets the eye, miss. More than meets the eye." Derek and I exchanged a puzzled look. "Just lock up when you leave," Arthur added.

"Strange guy. What was that all about?" Derek asked.

I shrugged. "Not sure. Sounded cryptic."

"Indeed. Do you think he could be in on any of the shenanigans? He could easily have had access to the brooch."

"Arthur? Never. He's been with the family forever. Let's go inside," I said, opening the door to the library, one of the largest rooms in the house.

Entering the library, I hardly recognized what was once a dark, sleepy, stuffy, cluttered retreat. Bright sunlight streamed in now that the heavy green velvet curtains had been removed. The floor to ceiling mahogany bookshelves had been cleared, dusted, and polished to perfection. The richly carved wainscoting that lined the walls had also been restored to look like new. I envisioned a sophisticated new owner decorating it with a transitional touch to bring it into the twenty-first century, perhaps an elaborate writing desk, intimate nooks for reading, traditional leather sofas with matching club chairs, overstuffed cushions, and cozy throw blankets.

"Imagine what it would cost to build something like this today," Derek remarked, taking it all in.

"Absolutely prohibitive," I speculated.

"For sure. This entire house is incredible, but the workmanship in this library alone is incredible. I've never seen millwork like this before." He ran his hand along the bottom bookshelf in the center of the room. "Look at this. The outer edge of each shelf is hand carved. And if you look up, you can see that the underside of each shelf has been finished as well. Smooth as silk," he said, reaching underneath.

"You're right," I said, feeling the satin finish for myself.

"Wait a minute . . ." Derek added with hesitation. "This is odd."

"What?"

"I can feel something protruding from under the bottom shelf." He knelt down and craned his neck to try to see what was there. "I can't make out what it is," he said, standing up again. "I wish I had a flashlight. It feels like it has some movement. Could be a lever of some kind. Metal maybe. Long and narrow." I could see him tugging on whatever it was. "Yes, it definitely does move." He pulled the lever toward him forcefully. With that, the bookcase began to move slowly backward, opening up to what appeared to be a doorway. Derek, moving with it, continued to apply pressure until the bookcase fully opened inward, revealing what looked like a secret room.

Derek stepped back and gasped. Completely stunned, I simply stared in disbelief.

"Whoa! I had no idea," I said.

"This is an architectural quirk if I've ever seen one. Let's go in," Derek said, thoroughly intrigued.

"I don't know." A touch of claustrophobia came over me. "Do you think the bookcase could close on its own?"

"No, I don't. It was too difficult to open. Besides, there must be a way to access the door from inside."

"Yes, but how?" I wanted to know, hesitantly following Derek inside.

"What do you suppose this is all about?"

"Honestly, I've been visiting this house my entire life and I never knew this room was here," I admitted.

"I don't think it's been cleaned in the past hundred years."

"I would have to agree with you. I guess the renovation crew didn't know it was here either."

"Maybe Arthur did, though," I said, recalling his words. "I believe he said 'there was more than meets the eye' or something like that."

"He was right. Did they have safe rooms back in the nineteenth century?"

"Safe rooms? No clue. Might be worth researching, though."

"All this might make a bit of sense if the Vander Horns needed protection from something. Or someone," Derek concluded.

"Do you think that's what this is about? Protection? I don't know. Would the family have needed that? Maybe old Uncle Eduard just wanted a quiet place to enjoy a cigar."

"There's always that possibility, but this would be taking things to another level, don't you think?" Derek pulled out his phone and began snapping photos. "In case no one believes us," he said, capturing the room and the secret entrance from all angles.

Feeling a bit more comfortable, I slowly made my way into the center of the room. It wasn't large, maybe about fifteen feet by fifteen feet, which made me feel more like the walls might close in on me at any moment.

"This is awfully austere compared to the rest of the house, isn't it? Quite a contrast," I said.

It was obvious from the abundant cobwebs that the room hadn't been touched in years. The white paint on the walls had turned greyish, and the dusty, wide-planked, wooden flooring looked well-worn and scratched. There were no finishing touches, no area rugs, paintings, accessories, or decorative wallpapers to give the room character. The space was as basic as it could be. Open oak shelves, much simpler than the elegant bookcases in the library, lined two walls. A clumsy, plain, towering armoire dominated the room. The only other furnishings were a nondescript table, which might have doubled as a dining and work area, and a few random, mismatched chairs that had been pushed against a wall.

My curiosity was piqued. I wondered if Aunt Tessa would be able to shed any light on this mystery. If she had known about this hidden chamber, she had never mentioned it. In fact, she never even hinted about it. Given its exclusive, concealed entry from the library, it had to have been built as part of the original house. Anyone who had lived there had to have known about it.

"Interesting. The armoire is unlocked. Let's see if there's anything inside," Derek said, pulling the double doors open.

I crossed the room to join him. "Anything good?"

He scanned the contents. "Hard to say. Looks like some old business records," Derek said, brushing the dust off a stack of leather folders. "Very old." He picked one up and glanced at the papers inside. "All of this must have had something to do with the family business. Silk manufacturing, right?"

"Yes. The company is still operating in Paterson, though on a much smaller scale."

Derek continued to look through the records. "At first glance, there doesn't appear to be anything meaningful here. Just some old balance sheets. Bookkeeping records. Typical business stuff."

"What do you think, Derek? Should we take everything with us?"

"I don't see why we shouldn't. Whatever papers are here would belong to your family and to your aunt most definitely."

"You don't think we have another mystery on our hands?"

"Nah. Not at all."

I couldn't tell whether or not Derek was being completely truthful with me. He knew I had a lot on my mind, and if he did indeed think something was askew about these business records, I'm not sure he would have wanted to worry me further. But for now, I took everything at face value.

"Let's hope so. I'm certain Aunt Tessa would want to know about all this. That is, if she doesn't already," I added with some hesitation.

"Don't overthink it. Could be nothing more than an oversight. But I have to say, it's hard to believe she wouldn't have known about it."

"You're right," I agreed,

"Help me unload this stuff, please," he asked.

As I grabbed a stack of folders, I noticed something had been placed behind them, all the way to the back of the shelf.

"Hold on. There's something else."

I placed the folders on the floor and reached for what appeared to be a lovely, antique wooden box. I sat down and placed it on my lap. "What do you make of this?"

"I don't know, but this place is full of surprises."

"Beautiful, isn't it?"

"Indeed," Derek said, removing a handkerchief from his pocket and then brushing the dust from the top of the box.

About ten inches square, it appeared to be made of finely polished burled walnut in rich amber tones. "It feels rather heavy."

"Let's see what's inside," I said.

Derek attempted to remove the lid. "Not so fast. It's locked."

"Just our luck. Can you force it open?"

"No idea," he replied, inspecting the lock. "I don't want to damage the box, but I think I can slide a knife under the cover to release the lock."

"Certainly no knife in here. Maybe a letter opener," I said, scanning the armoire's shelves. "We may have to take it back to the cottage to get into it."

"Maybe not. I just need something hard and thin."

"Well . . . how about a credit card?" I suggested.

Derek reached into his pocket and removed a card from his wallet. "Don't leave home without it."

Turning the box on its side, he managed to slip the credit card into the narrow opening under the lid, sliding it over the locking mechanism until its pin was successfully released.

"Genius," I said.

"There you go." Derek handed the box back to me, and I carefully removed the lid. The box was filled with handwritten letters on fine personal stationery that had yellowed with age and turned the color of parchment. Rifling through them, I could see they were letters from Sebastian to Sophie, perhaps a chronicle of forbidden love. Most of them had never been posted, indicating that they had been hand delivered either by Sebastian himself or by a trusted member of the DesChamps household. I wondered if Sophie had a confidante in her home who intercepted Sebastian's letters and then passed them on to her. A loyal maid, perhaps. Maybe even her mother. Aunt Tessa had said nothing of Sophie's mother's opinion of Sebastian as a suitor for her daughter. But from what she had told me, Sophie's father, Frits, and her uncle, Eduard, despised Sebastian and would surely have confiscated his letters if they'd had the opportunity.

"I cannot wait to read these. This is a veritable treasure trove! I have to take a look at just one right now."

"Don't you think we should be going?"

"Just one." I carefully removed the top letter from its envelope. The folds were worn through, bare, and ready to break apart, indicating that the letter must have been opened, read, reread, and closed many, many times before. "It's dated April fourth, nineteen-twenty. Listen to this. 'My Dearest Sophie, Meet me in Washington Park this Thursday afternoon at four o'clock. I will be sitting on our favorite bench under the weeping willow tree, which must be weeping, indeed, for us, my darling. The situation is becoming impossible. Until I see you. We must find our way. Yours forever, Sebastian.'"

"That beats an email," unromantic Derek said.

"I've never heard anything so romantic. And this is just the tip of the iceberg." I held up a postcard of what appeared to be Lake Como, Italy. The cerulean lake water glistened beneath the snow-capped Alps. "Cernobbio" was printed across the bottom. "Another keepsake, I assume. It's blank though. I wonder if Sophie traveled to Lake Como. And look at this." I showed Derek a blurry, faded picture of a young woman sitting on a deck chair with the lake in the background. "Annabella?"

"Your imagination is running away with you."

"Perhaps. I could sit here all day going through these."

"No doubt. But we really need to get out of here. Take as much as you can carry from the armoire."

We managed to take about half of what was there, along with the antique box. We'd have to come back for the remainder at some point. I had a terrible thought. "Derek, what if we can't close the secret door?"

"Then, I guess it won't be much of a secret anymore," he assured me as we exited the interior room and returned to the library. "I don't think it will be a problem."

I stood by nervously as Derek put down the records he was carrying and reached under the bottom bookshelf for the lever that operated the door. As he forcefully pushed it away from him, the heavy bookcase slowly closed inward until it was flush with the wall.

"Closed right up. No one would guess," I said.

We made our way out the front door, down the porch steps and across the lawn to the cottage.

Back inside the cottage, we dumped everything on the floor, and then I let Dylan out to run around the yard. I threw my jacket over the couch, sat down on the floor, and dove right into the box of letters. Derek, more interested in the business ledgers, sat on the sofa trying to organize them chronologically.

"Hmmmm," I said. "Odd that she saved this. Take a look."

Derek leaned down and read a newspaper clipping over my shoulder.

The Paterson Herald. April 12, 1920

Mr. and Mrs. Frits Vander Horn of Willow Bluffs are pleased to announce the engagement of their daughter Sophie to Lucas Van Dyk, son of Mr. and Mrs. Hendrik Van Dyk, also of Willow Bluffs. A summer wedding is planned. The couple will make their home in Willow Bluffs.

"Must have been the equivalent of doomsday to poor Sophie."

"What was the date of the letter you read before?" Derek asked.

"I forget. Let me look. Here it is. April fourth, nineteen-twenty. Sebastian must have known that Sophie's engagement to Lucas was imminent."

"Do we know when Sebastian fell, or was pushed, off the cliff?"

"No. Not really. But I'd sure I like to find out."

The bell summoned me to the door.

Aunt Tessa and Julien appeared on the porch, shopping bags in hand. As soon as I opened the door, Dylan scooted inside right behind them.

"Sorry for ringing, darling, but I simply couldn't manage my key. We picked up a few things at that little boutique I adore in Englewood."

"I see," I said, taking their coats.

"Good to see you again, Lacey," Julien gushed, oozing with charm, as always. "And you, Derek.

"What's all this?" Aunt Tessa asked, glancing at everything we'd brought from the old house.

"A few things that were left at the house."

"You've been exploring. Looks like you've done some research in the library."

"You could say that," I said.

She noticed the antique burled box on the floor. "Why, that box belonged to Cousin Sophie. Haven't seen it for years. How did you manage to find it?"

"It was a purely accidental discovery, I can assure you. We went over to the house to take a last look."

"Ah, I see."

"By the way, do you know if Cousin Sophie ever visited Italy?"

Aunt Tessa raised her eyebrows and shrugged.

"You never said a word about the secret room, Aunt T."

"You are correct. I did not. But I suppose now is as good a time as any."

"Indeed it is," I said, my curiosity aroused.

"My dear, I think this calls for a bottle of cabernet, if not something a bit stronger," Aunt Tessa directed.

I slipped into the kitchen and uncorked a bottle of one of my favorite California reds, a vintage Black Hawk cabernet sauvignon. I placed it on a tray with four sparkling, long-stemmed goblets and carried it into the living room, setting the tray down on the coffee table.

"Gather round," Aunt Tessa instructed.

I sat on the hearth, Julien and Derek made themselves comfortable on the sofa, and Aunt Tessa, positioned herself on the club chair facing us.

Aunt Tessa appeared ready to break into a soliloquy. I reached for the bottle of cab. "Generous pours, if you don't mind, Lacey," she told me.

Chapter Ten

"To the Vander Horns," Aunt Tessa proposed, raising her wine glass, "but with a caveat. As you all know, we can't choose our ancestors."

Julien and Derek sat on the sofa across from her, looking intrigued. I shifted to the very edge of the hearth, cabernet in hand, anticipating a colorful saga, as only she could relate.

"Lovely to have you all here," she began. "First of all, I'm so pleased Lacey and Derek found Sophie's long lost keepsake box. I hadn't seen it for years. I hope you'll all have the chance to look through the contents. You'll find that the letters from Sebastian are heartfelt. Yes, they had a love that was true but, sadly, not meant to be. If only we had the letters she wrote to Sebastian. They are surely lost forever."

Aunt Tessa glanced down at the pile of folders on the floor. "The remainder of what's here, the stash that Lacey and Derek found, however, is another story. I must confess, I was terribly remiss in not removing all of it from the house myself. But, as you all know, the sale of the family property has taken an overwhelming toll on me," she explained, reaching for her wine glass and taking a sip. "You see, Sophie's uncle Eduard, also my husband Jonathan's great-great-uncle, was an opportunist and a shrewd businessman, if not a scoundrel at times. The tale I'm about to tell you had been passed down through generations of Vander Horns. I can't vouch for its complete accuracy, but I can tell you that it's the best account we have. Let me begin by saying that the year 1920 brought a unique challenge to our country."

Derek caught on immediately. "1920. Prohibition?" he asked.

"Exactly."

"The Eighteenth Amendment," Derek said. I shot him a sidelong glance. "Sorry. American History major here. A fascinating time. Prohibition didn't work out precisely the way it was supposed to."

"Indeed. Evidently the great state of New Jersey didn't want Prohibition," Aunt Tessa explained. "Banning alcohol seemed senseless to so many. And, of course, Uncle Eduard and his cronies agreed. Like many others at the time, he vowed to find a way around Prohibition, skirting the new law any way he could. Never one to let an opportunity pass him by, he put his mind to work. Frits, Sophie's father, wasn't much of a schemer but always followed his brother's lead. They found a way to make their mark in a most unusual era. Our dear uncle and his brother became rather notorious bootleggers in this part of the state. Prohibition was so hated here at the time, I believe they felt they were providing a necessary community service."

"That's a new one," Derek quipped.

"Aunt Tessa, wasn't bootlegging a mob thing?" I asked.

"Not entirely. As the story goes, Eduard wasn't affiliated with the mob per se, although from what Jonathan told me I don't think he was completely clean in that regard. It wasn't only bootlegging that was going on. Smuggling had also become rampant."

"This is what we stumbled upon in the old house?" I asked.

"Regrettably, yes."

"My parents would have been shocked," I said. "I don't think they had any clue at all."

"I never spoke of it, and that was probably just as well. No one wants to think of their ancestors as bootleggers. If someone had asked me about it, however, I wouldn't have denied it."

"I don't know. I'm finding this rather fascinating. A little notoriety adds some spice to the past."

"So much more than spice, my dear," Aunt T said with a sly grin. "As far as we can ascertain, this is how it all happened: The E. and F. Vander Horn Silk Company owned a number of trucks that they used to distribute fabrics to their clients. According to my husband, Eduard found these trucks to be very useful in the transportation of, shall we say, contraband, from Wildwood in South Jersey."

"Why Wildwood?" Julien asked.

"It's Jersey folklore," Derek explained. "Anyone who has spent any amount of time down the shore has probably heard about it. During that time, rumrunners coming in from the Bahamas on schooners would unload their smuggled booze down the shore, all along the Jersey coastline. It was open season."

"That's right," Aunt Tessa acknowledged. "The Coast Guard couldn't possibly patrol the entire coast all the time. In fact, they were something of a joke. No match for the smugglers arriving daily. They had limited resources, and they were constantly being outsmarted."

"And many times, they would just look the other way," Derek said.

"Yes. Trying to stop the rumrunners was an exercise in futility," Aunt Tessa agreed. "The bootleggers were always one step ahead of the law. Eduard's people would purchase alcohol from smugglers at a base price. His company's trucks would transport the cargo up here, and then he would warehouse the goods in the secret room behind the library. Eduard would sell it at a premium to discreet buyers, speakeasy owners, and who knows who else."

"Hard to believe. No one on the estate was wise to it?" I asked.

"I think the family and servants knew enough to look the other way. If others were aware of it, they must have kept their mouths shut. Keep in mind, this was rampant in the twenties."

"Why didn't they simply store everything at the silk factory in Paterson?" I wondered.

"Think about it," she explained. "The estate really was the perfect cover. Quiet. Private. Tucked away in a sleepy little town. I mean, even if someone had suspected, no one would ever have discovered the secret room inside the library. They must have brought everything in late at night. They had designed the perfect covert operation."

"Amazing," Derek said. "Must have been a nice side business. I guess the brothers never got caught."

"From what I understand, it was easy enough to bribe the law and town officials to be blind to what was happening. Many of them were in on the action."

"Everyone was on the take at that time," Derek said.

"This is where things get a bit dicey," Aunt Tessa said. "Purely conjecture, however. My husband thought Sebastian might have known what Eduard was up to. And Sebastian was already on shaky ground. Both Frits and Edward despised his family, the DesChampses, originally from France. The brothers considered some of their business dealings to be unscrupulous, alleging that they copied the Vander Horns's textile designs, undercut prices, and stole clients. All hearsay, but who knows? Sebastian wasn't involved, of course, but in Frits and Eduard's eyes he was guilty by association. That might have explained Sebastian's untimely demise."

"You mean Eduard and Frits may have had something to do with Sebastian's murder?" I asked.

"Yes, I think I may have mentioned that once before, Lacey. Of course, there's no proof of that. They were dead set on Sophie marrying Lucas Van Dyk, for their own business reasons. Again, there's very little proof of any of this. But the story's been passed down through the generations."

"If the brothers were involved in murder, that would make the bootlegging seem like child's play in comparison." Derek pointed out.

"Yes, I suppose it would," Aunt Tessa agreed. "Again, we'll never know for sure, will we?" She took a long sip of cabernet. "Ah, family!" she added.

Julien, who had been listening intently, finally spoke up. "Amazing that this was kept so quiet."

"Only his partners in crime were in on it, and they kept everything hush-hush. There are no written accounts of Frits and Eduard's operation, none that we've been able to find, anyway. It's oral history and may have been embellished over the years. So, we just have to take the story at face value."

"What about the newspapers? They weren't suspicious?" I asked.

"Are you joking, my dear? The editors and reporters wanted in on the action. Besides, the press was lobbying to repeal the wildly unpopular Eighteenth Amendment."

"Still, this all could have ended badly for Eduard and Frits," Derek said.

Aunt Tessa nodded in agreement. "That is very true. I've been told that protection became more and more necessary. Competition was increasing. And the mob's activity became far-reaching. Eduard's truckers were forced to carry guns."

"I've read that it got to be like the Wild West down the shore near Atlantic City in the Roaring Twenties. A free-for-all. Speakeasies, brothels, gun fights in the wake of all the booze smuggling. The whole Prohibition debacle completely backfired."

"Yes, it did, Derek. You know your history," Aunt Tessa said. "Leave it to Uncle Eduard to capitalize on everything he could."

Julien was beginning to look uncomfortable. "Tessa, I had no idea about all of this."

"Not something I was eager to share."

"For good reason," Julien said.

"We all have our skeletons, I suppose. Especially where family is concerned."

"You've got that right," Derek acknowledged. "How long were Eduard and Frits involved with all of this?

"For about five years, I believe."

"And then, the 21st Amendment repealing Prohibition was passed in 1933," Derek said.

"So then, it was all forgotten," I put in.

"I wonder how much money the brothers made," Julien pondered.

"Maybe there's a clue in the business records," I suggested.

"I'd like to take a look," Derek said.

"It's all yours," I conceded. "This place certainly has its secrets. You know, when we ran into Arthur earlier today, something he said made me think that he knew about the hidden room."

"That's certainly possible," my aunt said. "You know his family has been with the Vander Horns for a couple of generations. His father and grandfather were both caretakers here. I'm sure he doesn't know the full extent of things, however. In any event, Arthur is completely loyal to the family."

Julien, his face ashen, had hardly spoken throughout Aunt Tessa's revelation. "I would hope so."

"Oh, stop, Julien," Aunt Tessa scolded. "It's ancient history."

"Nonetheless, we absolutely cannot let any of this bootlegging scandal leak out," Julien insisted. "Your reputation is at stake, Tessa."

"Julien, don't you think you're overreacting?"

"Hardly, Tessa. Your fans idolize you. This would be a black mark. You're not only Tessa Langdon Vander Horn, you're also Caroline Manchester, matriarch of an upstanding family."

"On a *soap*, Julien darling. I don't know. A little gossip never hurt anyone."

"You know I've always shielded you, Tessa."

"That you have."

"I can't imagine what the gossip rags would do with a story like this."

"Perhaps a little notoriety would do me good. 'Tessa Langdon Vander Horn, bootleg empire heiress.' You know what? I like it. You know what they say. There's no such thing as bad publicity."

Julien wasn't amused. "I'm not ready to go there. Lacey. Derek, you must promise that this story will never leave this room."

"My lips are sealed," I vowed.

"Same here. I'll take it to my grave," Derek agreed.

"Come on, Julien. How can I convince you to lighten up? If you were to actually use some of this on *Edge*, you would have to admit that a little colorful family history might add some interest to the Manchester family's backstory. Everyone loves a little dirt, especially in a soap."

He shifted in his seat, uncrossing and then crossing his legs. I could see the idea of using the bootlegging story in the *Edge* was beginning to intrigue him. "You know, you may have something there."

"But when all is said and done," Aunt T reminded us, "let's not forget dear Cousin Sophie in all of this. Not to mention poor, suffering Sebastian."

With that, I picked up the beautiful antique box that was resting on the floor between me and Aunt T. "I think there may be enough in here for another soap," I mused. "I plan to go through everything."

I opened the lid and began sifting through the old, fragile faded letters. I noticed some newspaper clippings along with other keepsakes.

"Yes," Julien said, thinking out loud. "A backstory to the Manchester clan. Flashbacks. This could indeed be interesting. Something fresh."

"Yes. A period piece woven into the story. None of the other soaps are doing it. In fact, I don't think it's ever been done before."

"Actually, Sophie—I mean Tessa—it has," Julien recalled.

Aunt Tessa looked puzzled. "Your mind is wandering, Julien."

"So sorry. Remember *Dark Shadows*, way back from when you were starting out? Very successful."

"Why, of course."

"Okay, you've changed my mind. Let's bring the idea to the production meeting next week. In fact, historical flashbacks could work for the Broadway production I've been developing as well. I like it. Gives the project a multidimensional quality. Depth."

"We may end up being indebted to great-great-Uncle Eduard." Aunt Tessa grinned.

"I'd love the chance to look through the letters when you've finished with them, Lacey," Julien said.

"Of course."

Sophie's portrait had been looming over us all afternoon. What, I wondered, would she have added to the story?

"This has been quite a day!" Derek said.

"So it has," Julien agreed.

As I continued to fidget with the contents of the box, I noticed an envelope that was crafted of heavier paper than the others. Picking it up, I carefully removed what was inside—an elegant formal invitation engraved on weighty white stock with a navy blue border.

I placed it on the coffee table. "What do you all think of this? How sad this must have been for Sophie! I can't even imagine."

Aunt Tessa, Derek, and Julien gathered around to take a look.

Mr. and Mrs. Frits Vander Horn
Cordially Invite You
To a Reception at Their Home
2265 Willow Street, Willow Bluffs
To Celebrate the Engagement of Their
Daughter Sophie

To Mr. Lucas Van Dyk
The Twenty-Seventh of April
Nineteen Hundred and Twenty
At Eight O'clock in the Evening
RSVP

"Sophie's parents didn't waste any time moving her engagement to Lucas along, did they?" Derek observed.

"And Sebastian sure exited in a hurry," I reminded everyone.

"Didn't he, though," Tessa remarked. "Right off the cliff."

"The question remains: Did he fall, jump, or was he pushed?" I mused.

"Has anyone ever read his obituary?" Derek asked.

"Sebastian's? I don't think anyone in the family has ever looked for it," Aunt Tessa said. "Not recently."

"Interesting," Derek said, looking thoughtful. "Did you find anything else on the engagement party, Lacey?"

"No, but I'll keep looking."

"I'll bet they had booze." Derek laughed.

"Very funny," I said.

"How about the wedding?" he asked.

"I'll let you know. I intend to go through every single item. I wish there were photographs."

"Let me know when you've finished with them," Julien said. "I'd love to take a look myself. Well, my friends, this has been most enlightening, but I must be on my way. Tonight, I'm meeting with the executor of my mother's will. It's finally out of probate. He has some personal effects to give me."

"I'm so sorry, Mr. LaFontaine," Derek said.

"Ah, thank you. She passed eight months ago. Ninety-six."

"Marie was a remarkable woman," Aunt Tessa commented. "You know, the LaFontaines moved here from France and built up quite a silk import business. They were close colleagues of the Vander Horns."

"True," Julien added. "We came from Lyon, the silk capital of France."

Lacey looked surprised. "I had no idea."

"The Vander Horns took over our silk business about twenty years ago," Julien noted.

"Small world," Derek said.

We all got up, and Aunt Tessa and I said good-bye to Julien and Derek. We were all left with a lot to think about.

"Poor Sophie," I lamented.

Aunt T stared at her portrait.

* * *

Monday morning felt like a new beginning, although Aunt Tessa's revelation had stayed with me in a quietly haunting way. As she'd said, you can't choose your relatives. At times we all had to overlook the dark moments in our family's past. But this was more than anyone could have imagined. A secret room. Bootleggers. Star-crossed lovers. If Julien hadn't been considering using the story on *Edge of Darkness*, I might have been tempted to write a book. In any event, I decided it might not be a bad idea to write it all down. I hated to think about it, but at seventy-something, Aunt T wasn't getting any younger. She was my only living relative, and one day all I would have left would be memories. A depressing thought.

On the way to my car, I noticed Arthur walking toward the cottage coming from the community park construction site on the South Lawn.

"Good morning, Arthur," I called.

"Find what you were looking for yesterday, miss?"

"Yes, I suppose I did."

"Mrs. Vander Horn's glove? Maybe you found somethin' you weren't looking for as well. Never know what to expect around here."

"I'm beginning to believe that, Arthur."

"Wish I knew what was goin' on with the field house."

"What do you mean?"

"Haven't you noticed? Things are pretty much at a standstill, if you ask me. No new deliveries for a while now. They're not gettin' very far."

"Really? I haven't been paying much attention. I'm at my shop all day. But now that you mention it, the work does seem to be stalled. Any idea why?"

"Nobody tells me much of anythin', miss. I just pick up on things here and there. I can tell you this. Everyone was so hell fired up about building this thing. Somethin's not right."

"I'll have to look into it."

"Yep. Mr. Barclay was coming by every day for a while there. Haven't seen him in some time now. One of those reporters from the *Gazette* was nosin' around there this morning first thing. Takin' pictures. Trespassin' if you ask me. That's why I went over there."

"What did he want?"

"Don't know. But I got rid of him. That's still my job, as I see it."

Once again, he had left me with the feeling that he knew more. "Thanks, Arthur. Good thing you're around. I guess I should be paying more attention. Let me know if you see anything else unusual."

"For sure, miss. Will do. Here's Mr. Barclay now," he observed, pointing to a black SUV pulling into the carport. "I called him this morning. That's why I'm here, you know."

"Lacey. Always a pleasure," Jim Barclay said, as he exited his SUV and walked toward us. "I understand we had a visitor," he said to Arthur.

"Yes. From that newspaper. Got rid of him fast."

"I'll have to call the *Gazette*," Jim said. "No one has contacted me."

"How's the construction going?" I asked.

"A bit slower than I'd hoped."

"If you'll excuse me, gentlemen."

I made a mental note to speak to Derek about the community park. Jim Barclay certainly hadn't revealed anything, but there was undoubtedly more to the story than what he had indicated. Little, if any, progress had been made on the field house. Hopefully, the holdup was nothing more than a supply chain issue or something like that. Ever since they had broken ground, the feeling around town was to have the field house and the new community park completed as soon as possible. I hardly ever noticed whether or not crews were working. There had to be an explanation.

So much of my life revolved around the estate, the Vander Horns's legacy, and Sophie and Sebastian. Their story intrigued me to the point of distraction. Driving into town, I wasn't sure why I'd brought Sophie's one-hundred-year-old engagement party invitation with me. Maybe I wanted to remind myself of the beauty of true love when it goes right and the tragedy of ill-fated love when it goes wrong. I hoped to experience the former someday. I related to Sophie's vulnerability. Although she still had her parents when she was my age, they were not much use to her. It was almost as if I was adopting her as my alter ego.

As I parked my car in Letter Perfect's small lot, I saw that Jeremy had already arrived. I hurried inside; it promised to be a busy week.

"Hey! You're early," Jeremy said.

"My aunt left for the studio first thing. I thought I'd get a jump on work. Tons to do. I have to get in touch with Classic Caterers."

"What's up?"

"Ava Pierce's engagement party."

"Right. You had a couple of calls already. A fortieth birthday and an anniversary party. Both are looking to book full-service venues."

"Shouldn't be a problem. Call them back and get as many preliminary details as you can and tell them I'll get back to them tomorrow at the latest. I'm beginning to stress about the Pierces."

"On it."

As a summer bartender at a posh Cape Cod resort the previous summer, Jeremy knew the ropes of the catering business. He was the perfect assistant for event planning, pinch-hitting for me whenever I needed him.

"I'll be in my office."

I reached into my bag for the invitation to Sophie and Lucas's engagement party and propped it up on my desk. Engraved invitations were meant for happy occasions. I wondered if the guests who attended the Vander Horns's affair had known about Sophie's love for Sebastian. She must have felt trapped. And doomed.

Jeremy breezed into my office with his notes on the latest party inquiries. He picked up the old invitation. "What's this?"

"Just an old piece of memorabilia from my aunt. I thought it would be fun to keep for old time's sake."

"April 1920? I think you missed the RSVP deadline."

I finally turned the old relic face down on my desk. It was beginning to depress me.

I spent a hectic but productive morning lining up Classic Caterers for the Pierces' party, and I substantially narrowed down the menu options for the buffet. Mrs. Pierce and Ava would make the final selections. I had my recommendations for china, flatware, crystal, and table linens ready for them to approve. I left detailed messages for our two new clients, saying I hoped to meet with them during the week. I also assured them that they had plenty of time to finalize their arrangements. Ready for a break, I headed next door to Bean Around. I hadn't seen Jess in several days.

"Hey, bring me an Americano," Jeremy called as I headed out.

I hadn't bothered with my coat. The brisk autumn air invigorated me as I hurried across the sidewalk to the coffee shop.

Jess greeted me as warmly as ever. "Hello, stranger! Where were you all weekend?"

"Oh, you know, family stuff. What'd I miss?"

"A couple of things, actually."

"I'm starving."

"You're in luck. We have your favorite—melted brie and black forest ham on a croissant today."

"Amazing."

"Take a seat. I'll bring one right over with a latte."

"You're the best, Jess!"

Everyone said that something was always brewing at Bean Around, and they didn't necessarily mean the coffee. No matter what was happening in town, people were talking about it at the coffee shop. It had become the central nervous system of Willow Bluffs, the place to go for the 4-1-1. It wasn't that the townsfolk were a bunch of gossipmongers. It was just that we were a lively, friendly bunch happy to keep our fingers on the pulse of the community. And we did just that. Every single day. We took pride in our town and resented anything that would make it change for the worse. And we talked about it.

Jess returned to my table with the most fabulous looking croissant sandwich and a piping hot latte. She wasted no time bringing me up to date.

"I'll say this much. If Gina Velasco and Glenn Hartman had been, shall we say, involved, and we know they were, she certainly got over him fast."

"Ok. What do you mean by that?"

"She was in here with Ron Valenti twice over the weekend," Jess recalled.

"And . . ."

"They were looking pretty cozy at a table for two in the corner."

"Seriously? I wonder what's up with that?" I took a bite of the ham and brie croissant. "Oh, my! This is absolutely decadent, Jess."

"Yeah. Tell me about it. I had two of them, regrettably. Delicious, but they won't look great on my thighs."

"Oh, come on, Jess. You have nothing to worry about. Actually, I saw the two of them coming out of the town hall the other day. We thought it was odd. We couldn't tell what they were doing, though. Made me wonder."

"I've been wondering, too," Jess said. "I mean what in the world is a babe like Gina Velasco doing with a schlub like Ron Valenti?"

"Good question. I mean the woman gets around. But at least Glenn was a good-looking guy. And the two of them worked together and all, so that kind of explained their relationship."

"I don't know," Jess said, shaking her head. "I'm sure a lot of people still don't get it."

"Especially Glenn's wife," I said.

"Maybe it was simply all over between Glenn and Gina."

"It was all over for Glenn. That's for sure. For good."

"Gina could have been the one who helped him off the cliff," Jess offered. "For that matter, Angela had a strong motive as well."

"I'll say. The scorned wife. I wonder if the police are tuned into any of this."

"They must be," Jess noted. "But every time I see Chief Hennessey, he's completely tight-lipped on the investigation. He hasn't revealed a thing. I'm sure the *Gazette* is honing in on it, too."

"Oh, Jess. I almost forgot, I'd like an Americano for Jeremy."

"Right away. Pick it up at the counter. I'll put it on your tab."

"You're the best."

Just as I was about to leave, Derek came in.

"Hey," I said to him. "I was going to call you this afternoon."

"What's up?"

"Have you heard anything about the construction on the new park?" I asked.

"No. Not a thing."

"I saw Jim Barclay earlier today."

"At the estate?

"Yes. Arthur called him to let him know a reporter from the *Gazette* had been checking things out."

"Investigative reporting?" Derek asked.

"I don't know."

"Ron wasn't with him?"

"Nope.

"There hasn't been much activity on the construction site," Derek pointed out. "The new field house is completely stalled. These projects tend to ebb and flow. Could be a hold-up with a permit. I'll ask around."

That seemed to have come out of the blue. "You'll check it out personally? Why?" I asked.

"Curiosity," Derek admitted.

"Careful. You know how that turned out for the cat."

Chapter Eleven

"I loathe that place," I said to Derek, switching my phone to speaker so I could type.

"I realize nobody's dying to go to a funeral parlor . . . then again, I guess they are. But the place has been around for generations. They just might have what I'm looking for."

"I don't know."

"A favor. Just this once. You know Mr. Carson pretty well."

I paused a moment, looking up from my laptop. I was having a hard time saying no to Derek. An outing to Carson's Funeral Parlor was not what I had in mind, but he'd been standing by me as a true friend recently. And I'd been through some tough times. "Ok. If you insist," I conceded.

"I knew you'd come through. I'll pick you up at the shop in ten minutes."

I gathered my purse and jacket and promised myself I'd finish typing the Pierces' guest list the minute I returned. Ava's engagement party wasn't going to arrange itself but, on the other hand, I knew I still had ample time.

I had one eye on the window when I spotted Derek's Prius parked out front.

"Back in about an hour or so," I called to Jeremy, as the door closed behind me.

"You're the best," Derek said, as I got into the car.

"Dead right," I quipped. "No pun intended."

We drove north on Willow Street and then up the hill on Pine Street to Carson's Funeral Parlor, clearly no one's favorite place to be.

"Really, thanks for doing this, Lacey. For whatever reason, I've had a hunch that we should take a look at Sebastian Des-Champs's death certificate. The more I thought about it, I realized this would be the most likely place to find an archived copy. I'm curious, that's all."

"I'll say one thing for Frank Carson, he's as meticulous as he is weird. If anyone has records that old, it would be him."

We pulled into the circular driveway to the sprawling, white clapboard home. Set on a hill, it must have dated back to colonial times as one of the oldest structures in Willow Bluffs. The leaves on the surrounding trees, recently rich shades of red and gold, had turned brown and shriveled. Most had already fallen, making the place completely depressing. We crossed the expansive wraparound porch, an odd feature for a funeral home. I wondered if it served as a gathering place for the spirits at night.

"Did you call ahead?" I asked, as we entered the foyer.

"No. I was afraid Carson would put me off and I wouldn't even get my foot in the door."

"What makes you think they even handled Sebastian's funeral?"

"It's a pretty good bet. They've been the only game in town for years. Actually, a couple of centuries, I think."

Frank Carson greeted us as soon as we walked in. "Ms. Langdon. What a surprise. At your service," he said in a hushed monotone, as if his clients could actually hear us. Wearing an ill-fitting, shiny, black suit and heavy, black-framed glasses that had slid down his nose, he looked half dead himself, and his greasy black hair looked like it hadn't been washed since the last time I saw him.

"Mr. Carson, have you met my friend Derek Conover from the town council?"

"Of course. A pleasure. Is this official town business?" Mr. Carson wanted to know.

"No, nothing like that, sir," Derek replied. "We're looking for a copy of a death certificate from 1920."

"Oh, my. More than a hundred years ago. For whom?"

"A friend of Ms. Langdon's extended family," Derek clarified.

"Most unusual. May I ask why?"

"We'd like to confirm the date of his death. There seems to be some discrepancy about the date. And also, how the gentlemen died."

"How he died? He is gone, is he not? And he has been for some time now. Does it matter?"

"It could. For the sake of family history. Especially Ms. Langdon's family. Her Aunt Tessa."

"I see. For Tessa Vander Horn, that's another matter entirely. Remarkable woman. And the name of the departed?"

"Sebastian DesChamps," Derek said.

"Ah, yes. Sebastian DesChamps. The DesChampses go way back," he recalled. "Another prominent family in the silk business from long ago, if I recall my local history. I believe my grandfather, or even my great-grandfather, may have served the DesChampses."

"Excellent memory, Mr. Carson," I said.

"Do you know what became of the family?" Derek asked.

"No, sorry. I assume they relocated. I haven't come across the name at all in recent years."

"If you have any records, Mr. Carson, anything at all, we'd love to take a look," Derek continued. "The death certificate would be a big help. Or even an obituary."

"I'm expecting a client momentarily, but I may have what you're looking for. I'll be happy to take you downstairs if you don't mind doing some searching yourselves. I have records going back to the mid nineteenth century. I wouldn't say they're complete, but you never know."

"We'd appreciate it," Derek said.

"Follow me."

"Um, wait a minute. What else is down there? Or who else should I say?"

"Not to worry. You won't wake the dead. A little funereal humor." He smirked.

Neither Derek nor I laughed.

Mr. Carson led us down a dimly lit staircase and through a long, dark hallway to a storage room.

"Our records room." He pointed it out. "Dead files, so to speak."

Derek and I exchanged a sidelong glance.

"Feel free to search. I'll be upstairs on an appointment."

"This place is giving me the creeps," Derek said.

"Hey, I don't want to hear it. This was your idea." A loud bang made me jump. "What was that?"

"The upstairs door closing. Probably Carson."

"Okay. Hope it's not locked. All this research the past couple of days is giving me a bad case of claustrophobia."

"We're fine," Derek assured me. "The stiffs won't hurt you."

"So delicately put. But what I want to know is, how many more dusty rooms filled with old files are in my future?"

"Are you suggesting that I don't take you to the finest places?"

I had never seen such a damp, dirty, mildewed mess. Boxes everywhere, about fifteen decades worth. Some were labeled, some were on metal shelving, and others were just stacked one on top of the other.

"They aren't in chronological order." I pointed out. "We'll just have to look through everything."

"Nothing's easy, is it?"

"Nope. Let's start at opposite ends," I suggested. "Meet you in the middle."

We both dove into the mountain of boxes.

"What exactly are you hoping to find?" I asked.

"It's just a shot in the dark but maybe a clue about his cause of death. I don't know. Maybe we can get some closure. Did the guy jump off the cliff, or was he pushed? Wouldn't you like a proper ending to the story? Especially now that Julien plans to use the family history in your aunt's soap opera. I think we should make it real."

"Okay. I get that."

We plodded along for over an hour, ruling out the boxes that were labeled with their year, and looking inside the ones that weren't for some clues. Slowly but surely, we were making headway.

"Hey, I found something," Derek called out, pointing to a grimy handwritten label that had been affixed to a large file box. Opening it, Derek added, "Jackpot! It looks like everything in here is from 1920, but the individual files aren't in alphabetical order."

"Of course, they aren't. Give me a bunch."

We each meticulously plodded through the copious files.

"Here it is," Derek said excitedly. "DesChamps, Sebastian. Let me see what's here. Funeral expenses. Embalming, details of the service, hearse, burial."

"Too much information."

"Ah, jackpot again! The death certificate. Talk about a needle in a haystack." Derek stopped to read the document. "Listen, it says 'immediate cause of death subarachnoid hemorrhage and subdural hematoma.'"

"What's that?"

"A really bad whack on the head. Also says 'due to a consequence of impact from fall.'"

"How do we know he wasn't hit on the head *before* he fell? Like Glenn."

"We don't. But we do know he went off the cliff."

"Or he was pushed. So, we're back where we started from."

"At least we have confirmation of the fall. The doctor who signed the death certificate couldn't make any further determination either. There must have been an autopsy, but I don't know where we'd find a record of that report at this point in time. Even if the medical examiner's office had it, they would never release it to us."

"Yeah. Let's quit while we're ahead."

"This is something," Derek observed. "He's buried in the cemetery right here in town. There's a map that shows the location of his plot. I hope there's a copy machine upstairs."

He took out his cell phone and snapped a couple of photos of the documents just in case there wasn't one.

"You're so practical. This is downright depressing. I mean, that someone's life is reduced to this, a dusty file in a cardboard box in the basement of a funeral parlor."

"At least, people still care about the guy. That's something. Maybe we should visit his grave. Pay our respects. He's probably been spinning, the way we've been talking about him lately."

"Sure. Why not? Like the afternoon hasn't been enough of a downer."

On the way out, we stopped in Frank Carson's private office to say good-bye and thank him for his help. As strange as he was, he had been most accommodating in giving us access to what we were looking for, even making photocopies of Sebastian's death certificate and the cemetery lot map for us to take with us. He didn't ask what we planned to do with them. Apparently, he didn't care.

Once outside, the overcast afternoon sky and brisk autumn breeze made me shiver. The chill went beyond that. I'd had enough of old houses, dusty storage rooms, and funeral parlors. I was relieved we were on our way out of there.

Derek drove south on Hillside Lane so we could stop at Willow Hill Cemetery on the way home. We were both oddly curious enough about Sebastian to pay him a post-mortem visit.

"Funny, but I'm beginning to feel like I know Sebastian," Derek said.

"He's intriguing," I acknowledged. "If not a bit of an enigma. But, you know, I think I would have wanted him for a friend if I had been his contemporary back in the day."

"Me, too," Derek agreed. "Sounds like he was an upstanding guy. Maybe back in the day, I could have helped him out as far as Sophie was concerned."

"Like how?"

"You know, guy stuff."

I laughed. "Yes, you would have figured it out, for sure."

"You don't give me enough credit," Derek said, laughing.

"Sebastian truly loved Sophie. But what a tangled web it became, thanks to Sophie's father and uncle. I'm glad Julien finally decided to use their love story as a plot line in *Edge of Darkness*. I have a feeling it will catch on. That and the Prohibition thing."

"I know what you mean. I may have to watch a soap for the first time ever." He laughed again.

"If I know Julien, he will personally make sure it's well done. Most people don't know that he contributes to the writing on the show quite frequently."

Derek looked surprised. "Really?"

"Yes. They call him 'the script doctor.' He's always editing Aunt Tessa's lines. Everything must be perfect for her. He's adamant."

"He's quite a manager."

"Mega-manager is more like it. He always gets his way."

"That's what you would want in an agent."

"Julien really is extraordinary. There's a rumor that he's even written a couple of romance novels under a pseudonym."

"Julien? No way. I would never have guessed. He looks like the quintessential country gentleman."

"I can't get Aunt Tessa to confirm that, though."

"We must investigate." Derek laughed.

"Aunt T's been lucky to have him all these years," I said.

"It'll be interesting to see what they do with the Prohibition storyline. A little history never hurt anybody." He turned left onto Hillside Lane. "Here we are."

As we got out of the car, I dreaded spending time wandering around Willow Hill Cemetery, especially when I should have been at the shop catching up on work, but on the other hand, I was most interested in seeing Sebastian's grave. If nothing else, I hoped it would make everything seem real, or maybe even give me closure, proving once and for all that Sebastian did, in fact, exist. Did he jump off the cliff because of ill-fated love, or did Frits and Eduard arrange for his untimely demise after he stumbled upon their Prohibition scheme? We would never know, but the cemetery visit would bring us as close to him as we could possibly get.

Derek, studying the map we'd found, got his bearings. "This way," he directed, pointing up a hill. We walked a long distance until we found him on the eastern gate of Willow Hill.

"He's about as far away from Sophie as someone could get," Derek said. "Probably the Vander Horns's doing."

Sebastian's modest, limestone grave marker, weathered but still legible, was practically flush against the cemetery's black, wrought iron fence.

"Any further back and he'd be off the property. Maybe that's why Aunt T thought he wasn't buried here," I said.

I stood silent and motionless, staring at all that was left of poor, tragic Sebastian DesChamps. A simple grave marker, a small plot, reasonably tidy. Nothing remarkable. A feeling of sadness washed over me. If only he'd been permitted to pursue his love for Sophie, his life would have taken a completely different tack. At that moment, I felt the connection to him that I had been hoping for, empathizing with his tragic life. Derek and I quietly studied his gravestone.

"You and Sophie are together, now, Sebastian. Rest in peace," I whispered.

Here Lies
Sebastian DesChamps
In Eternal Rest
Born August 14, 1894
Died April 29, 1920

"'DesChamps,'" I read slowly. "That means 'of the fields' in French. Sad, but it looks like that's where he ended up. Gone too soon."

"Futile life."

"He died just a couple of days after the engagement party for Sophie and Lucas." I pointed out.

"I just noticed that, too."

"The party was on the twenty-seventh," I recalled. "The shock of that alone would have been enough to kill him."

"Isn't it odd that no one else from his family is buried here?" Derek asked.

"Yes. Although Carson did say the family moved away."

"No doubt. After a suicide or murder, I imagine the family would have wanted to make a fresh start."

"Not sure which would have been worse for them. Suicide or murder."

"A lose–lose situation," I supposed.

"Look around," Derek said. "Notice anything else? Isn't it strange that Sebastian's grave is the only one that's being tended to?"

He was correct. The other graves in that remote section of the cemetery were overgrown with weeds. The headstones were covered with enough dirt to obscure the engravings. Sebastian's plot, however, was perfectly manicured, and his grave marker, although old, was pristine.

"Odd. Someone is taking care of Sebastian."

"Very weird," Derek noted. "Could it be the same someone who sent that antique cameo to the cottage?"

"I have no idea but that would make sense. I doubt we'll ever know. Too much to process. Do you think any of this has any bearing on Glenn Hartman's murder?"

"It doesn't seem like it," Derek reasoned.

"There are too many crazy things going on in this town."

"Let's go," Derek said.

A chill ran down my spine. "I wish I'd worn a warmer coat."

"We'll be back in the car in a couple of minutes," Derek assured me. "Let's just make a quick stop to see Sophie," Derek said, glancing at the map. "It's sort of on the way."

"Wow, you're really into this."

"We're here, anyway," he replied. "And I've never heard a story quite like this one."

I had to agree with him. Something felt right about being here.

"We have to follow this path toward Hillside," he noted, pointing to the map. "Should only be a few minutes."

We started walking toward Sophie's grave. Granted it was a Tuesday afternoon, but Willow Hill was eerily quiet and remarkably empty. Not even a caretaker was in sight. Graveside services would have been performed much earlier in the day, so there were no lingerers, and no one seemed to be visiting loved ones. It had to be the loneliest place in Willow Bluffs.

As we approached Sophie's resting place from a distance, something looked off. I noticed an object of some kind lying over Sophie's grave. It clearly wasn't scattered flowers or hay covering newly seeded grass or windblown debris. "What is that?" I asked, as we edged closer.

Derek walked right up to the grave, looking puzzled. "It looks like a coat," he said, bending down to pick it up. "It is. It's a man's coat."

"Maybe it belongs to one of the caretakers?" I wondered.

"I don't think so. It's not just a coat. Look at it. It's a fine, vintage coat. Authentic." He held it up. Navy blue wool, cinched waist, double breasted, with brass buttons and velvet trim on the collar and pockets. "What do you think?"

"I don't know. Nice quality. Early twentieth century maybe?"

"Looks that way," Derek agreed. "Must have belonged to someone of substance."

"Is someone trying to spook us?" I asked in disbelief.

"If they are, they're doing a pretty good job."

"Who would do a thing like this?" I asked, half in frustration, half in horror.

"It would have to be someone with access to the family history."

"Obviously."

"How about that handyman? Arthur?" Derek proposed. "He's awfully tuned in. Knows everything. Not to mention that he's a little out there."

"Never. He's loyal to a fault."

"Julien?" Derek threw out. "He's gone berserk over that Sophie and Sebastian business."

"No, not Julien. Not on your life. He would do anything for Aunt T."

"Wait, how about that reporter from the soap magazine?"

"Oh, right. Natalie something? Summers. I couldn't imagine why."

"Also, the builders have had full access to the house," Derek mused.

"You're certainly full of suggestions."

"At least I'm thinking. You simply dismiss everything at hand."

"Not really. As far as the builders go, Ron Valenti is a little weird. Especially now that he's been running around with that dish Gina. But how would that be connected to this and the brooch? And Glenn's murder also? Doesn't make sense."

"Maybe it just doesn't make sense *yet.* We don't know everything."

"I think you've accused all of Willow Bluffs. But what about you, Derek? You've had plenty of opportunity," I kidded.

"Nah. No motive for me," he said with a smile, examining the coat more closely. "Hold on," he added. "There's something in the coat pocket."

My heart sank to my feet. It was as if I were living in a nightmare, and I couldn't wake up. "I'm not sure I want to know."

"It's a note."

"Of course, it is. From the dead, I presume. Again. This is getting much too crazy for me."

"Actually, it's one of those calling cards," Derek said.

"So, it must be from the same person who sent the cameo to the cottage," I said, grimacing.

"Take a look," Derek said, holding it in front of me. "You decide."

My dearest Sophie,
Something to keep you warm,
on these cold autumn nights.

—S

That pretty much did it for me. I knew I couldn't handle much more. This had been a deliberate act that required considerable forethought. Someone not only had gone to the trouble of buying a vintage men's coat and placing it on a grave but had also included a personal note suggesting he, or she, knew a little too much about these two desperate lovers. Not an easy task. *Who would have known enough to pull something like this off?* I asked myself.

"Someone around here has become seriously unhinged," I said.

"We have to find out who did this before it gets completely out of hand."

"If you ask me, it already *is* out of hand. It's almost as if someone knew we'd be here today."

"Impossible."

"Is someone watching us?" I asked.

"I think we would have noticed by now. At least no one's been harmed," Derek reasoned.

"Not yet," I warned. "I'm a mess. And the police are useless."

"Somewhat. It'll be all right."

"I wish I was as certain as you. Should we take it?" I asked.

"The coat? Absolutely. Why don't you throw it over your shoulders if you're still cold?" Derek said, draping it over me.

Sidestepping him, I shot him a look that said, *I'd rather freeze to death.* "Let's get out of here," I insisted.

"You've got it."

I was eager to get back to the shop to distract myself in work. Feeling overwhelmed, we barely spoke on the way back.

"I'll be busy with the Pierce party all afternoon," I said.

Pulling into Letter Perfect's lot, Derek said, "I'm swamped, too. We have a town council meeting at five. Ari wants everyone there."

"What's up?"

"For one thing, we have to nominate an interim member for a temporary term to replace Glenn Hartman. Voters will choose a permanent member in the next election."

"Do you have anyone in mind?"

"Not really. Interested?"

"No, thanks."

"Just thought I'd ask. I think Ari wants to go with a woman."

"Thanks for thinking of me, but I'll leave Willow Bluffs politics to you pros."

"Talk to you later, Lacey. Thanks for coming."

"We made some progress."

I rushed inside.

"Hey, stranger. Glad you made it back," Jeremy quipped.

"What did I miss?"

"A few retail customers buying stationery. Mrs. Pierce called. She's getting nervous about the party."

"I'll call her back."

"She added someone to the guest list. I have the name here somewhere."

"Would you bring it into my office?"

"Sure. And someone called Natalie something."

"Summers?"

"That's it. She's very anxious to talk to you."

I decided diving into my work was the best medicine to help me recover from all that had happened. I planned to make Ava and Jason's engagement party a spectacular event, but I would have to tend to every detail. For a moment, I wondered if I'd ever have an engagement party of my own. I had to admit, Derek and I had been getting along famously. I didn't want to go there. I immediately put it out of my mind. Derek and I were friends. And that was fine. So I told myself.

I couldn't believe I'd actually considered Derek a suspect, even in jest, in the strange shenanigans that were going on. I hoped he hadn't taken it the wrong way, but he struck me as being very easygoing. If I'd gone so far as suspecting Derek, I had a feeling I was going to be suspicious of everyone who was close to the Vander Horns.

As soon as I sat down at my desk to organize my thoughts, Jeremy breezed in. “Here’s that addition for the Pierce party guest list,” he said, placing a note in front of me.

I raised my eyebrows as I read it. + 1 for Ron Valenti, Gina Velasco, Pierce engagement party.

“Wow. Really?”

“Yeah. That’s the name she gave me. Something wrong?”

“No. Just surprised.”

It took a couple of hours, but I brought the arrangements for the Pierces’ party up to date, the buffet layout, floral centerpieces, linen décor, and the complete guest list, which would be indispensable in helping Ava and Jason keep track of their gifts. I had just finished speaking with Mrs. Pierce to let her know what had been arranged, when I received a text from Derek.

meet me for a drink at grimaldi’s
now? why don’t you just come to the cottage later
will your aunt be there
probably but why
id rather talk privately im at grimaldi’s now
ok wrapping up give me 15 minutes

Grimaldi’s, bright, bustling, and everyone’s favorite old-school Italian place, was crowded for a Tuesday night, but as soon as I walked in, I spotted Derek at a high top table in the far corner of the bar.

“Hey! I was working on the Pierces’ party all afternoon. God is in the details. You’ll be attending, right?”

“Wouldn’t miss it.”

"What's going on? Your text sounded urgent."

"Not really urgent," Derek clarified. "Just sensitive."

"I see."

The bar waitress brought two glasses of cabernet to our table.

"I took the liberty of ordering." He took a sip. "We got a disturbing piece of news tonight at the town council meeting."

"Oh, no. Something about Glenn Hartman?"

"No, no. Nothing like that. But, listen, this is strictly between us."

"Sure."

"It seems that Cliffside Custom Builders, now the sole owners of the Vander Horn property, defaulted on this quarter's property taxes."

"Probably just an oversight," I suggested.

"Hardly. As Ari understands it, Cliffside doesn't have the funds to make this quarter's payment. And it's a hefty one, all that prime acreage on the cliff."

"Wow. I don't understand. I thought they were doing great."

"None of us get it. Again, this is hush-hush," Derek reminded me.

"Of course."

"The town gave Cliffside a break on the taxes last quarter because they had agreed to build the community park and all. But this time, full payment was due."

"How late are they?"

"Over two months," he said.

"I guess that explains why construction on the field house has stalled."

"Exactly. I never would have guessed that they were having financial problems," Derek said. He suddenly grimaced. "Oh, wouldn't you know? Don't look now. Speak of the devil."

I instinctively turned my head.

"No, no, don't look," he repeated.

"Who is it?" I wanted to know.

"Ron Valenti and Gina Velasco. Together. Very together."

"Can we hide?"

Derek grimaced. "Too late. Ron saw me."

"They sure have no problem being seen together. I mean, her lover just died. Unreal."

"Oh, no. They're coming over."

"I'll try to act nonchalant."

"Yes, do that."

"I'll let you do the talking."

"Just smile and nod."

"I'm good at that," I said.

"Derek, Lacey. Mind if we join you? You know Gina, I presume?" Ron asked.

"Of course," Derek said, smiling.

"Our table isn't quite ready," he explained.

"Please, sit down," Derek said graciously.

"Thanks," Gina said, looking like she didn't mean it.

"We were looking at some real estate in Fort Lee today," Ron said. "Exhausting."

"To buy or sell?" Derek asked.

"Possibly to represent and sell. Gina's looking into getting her real estate license."

"The market is hot," Gina chimed in.

"Sure is," Ron agreed. "Our table may take a while. Should we order an appetizer while we're waiting?"

"Whatever you'd like," Derek said.

I smiled and nodded. I was getting good at it.

"How about calamari with marinara sauce?"

"I stay away from that stuff," Gina said.

"She's always watching her figure," Ron joked.

So is everyone else, I said to myself. In fact, wearing a tight black V-neck sweater, black skinny jeans and black suede stiletto boots, no one could possibly have missed her.

The hostess came over. "Your table is ready, Mr. Valenti."

"That's that, then. Thank you."

"We'll talk another time," Derek said.

"Yes," Ron said agreeably. "Gina and I will see you at the party for Ava and Jason, right?"

"We'll be there," Derek replied. "Lacey's handling all the arrangements."

"Perfect." Ron smirked. "It'll be drop dead incredible."

Chapter Twelve

I wasn't sure I was in the mood for Natalie Summers early Wednesday morning, but I returned her call first, anyway. She was coming to the cottage right away. Whatever she had to tell me was urgent enough that she had to do it in person. Then again, every encounter I'd had with Natalie required considerable urgency.

Aunt Tessa had already left the cottage to head to the studio. When Julien came by to pick her up, he insisted that I sit in on the *Edge of Darkness* production meeting at noon. He planned to pitch the future "Sophie and Sebastian" story line to the team of executive producers, and he wanted me there beforehand to run it by me to make sure he had everything right.

I was actually intrigued, and I had a couple of hours to spare, especially since I had worked until late last night after I got home from Grimaldi's, so I planned to drive into Manhattan right after breakfast. Jeremy would be meeting with a new client first thing with the idea of taking the lead on planning an event himself. We were getting incredibly busy, but if he could take on a few small parties, it would lighten my load considerably. And the Letter Perfect clients loved his charm and wit.

When Aunt Tessa and I chatted over breakfast, she didn't seem to be aware of Cliffside Custom Builders' tax default on the estate. I kept it under wraps, as Derek asked. I saw no need to worry her. She would have hated to learn that there were problems. Ron Valenti had certainly appeared carefree at Grimaldi's. I hoped that meant a remedy was on the way and the financial mishap would resolve itself before it became public knowledge. The same could have been said for Jim Barclay when I saw him the day before. I saw no indication that the company was in trouble. I hoped to get a text from Derek saying that it was all a misunderstanding and everything was fine.

I expected Natalie at any moment, and I hoped she'd be brief. Fat chance of that, though. At least my trip to the city would give me an excuse, if I needed one, to break away.

Dylan sprang to the door the second the bell rang.

"Good morning, Lacey. Thank you sooooooo much for seeing me on such short notice," she gushed. "I brought some Vermont hot chocolate from the Bean. Jess says 'hi,' by the way."

"Thanks. I just had coffee, but I can't resist this stuff. Come in."

We sat down at the kitchen island. The steaming white hot chocolate with a mound of whipped cream floating on top looked and smelled incredible. Meeting with Natalie had just gotten easier. "This is absolutely decadent," I said.

"Right? Can't get enough."

"What's going on?"

"I've been dying to tell you. As you know, I've been doing research for my article on your wonderful aunt. You remember, for *Soap Opera Weekly*. It's turning out to be an in-depth biographical piece. I'm going back as far as I can. Our readers want to know! I've been looking into her family background, and her late husband's background."

I cringed at the thought of what she might have discovered about Eduard and Frits.

"Anyway, my magazine wants the story on your aunt to be nothing less than complete. And the last thing I want is to get scooped by that rag *Soap World*. They make stuff up. But I digress. So, I've been working like crazy."

"Good for you."

"Did you know that *Soap Opera Weekly* is owned by the Entertainment Today Television Network?"

"No. I had no idea."

"I'm hoping to sell the story to them as a biopic. It would be perfect for their viewership."

"Aunt Tessa would love that, and her manager Julien would, too."

"It would be epic. I've been doing some research. And let me tell you, the *New York Times* has got nothing on *Soap Opera Weekly* when it comes to getting a story. We can do research with the best of them." She laughed. "We leave no stone unturned."

"I'm sure," I said, wishing she'd get to the point.

"So, hopefully, you won't mind that I've been asking a lot of questions."

"Of course not," I replied, surprised she was just mentioning this now. "I'd be the same way."

"I've always felt that close *personal* contacts are the best sources," Natalie insisted.

"Yes, I imagine they would be."

"Wow. I've already done the standard searches. I went down to the archives at the Department of State, you know down in Trenton, to retrieve documents. Fascinating. I got your Aunt Tessa and Uncle Jonathan's birth certificates, along with your

Uncle Jonathan's parents'. It means a lot to me to have those. I have to say that holding those documents in my hand gives me a certain connection to them. As if they were a part of my own family."

"Wow. I'd love to see those myself."

"Oh, of course. They're in my office right now, but I'll make copies for you. Anyway, this is what I've been so anxious to tell you. A few days ago, I took a ride around town. I didn't see your car in the Letter Perfect lot, so I thought you might be here. I drove over to the estate, but you weren't around. Too bad. I had even brought some hot chocolate for you. I thought it was worth a shot."

Was she a stalker? I said to myself. Somewhat flattered and somewhat alarmed, my heart pounded.

"But," she continued, "your charming caretaker Arthur was here removing dead mums from the patio, and I stopped to chat with him. Oh, and he loved the hot chocolate, by the way."

"No doubt."

"Long story short, we sat together on the patio overlooking the cliffs, chatting about what it takes to keep a place like the Eduard Vander Horn House in tip-top condition, inside and out. Not only today but decades ago. Arthur's just full of information."

"True. He's been around a while."

"Yes. His whole family. And I love this. He mentioned that his father and grandfather had also worked here as caretakers. But, listen to this, way back in the day, the Vander Horns employed a butler and two housemaids and a cook, if you can believe it."

"Fascinating."

"Incredible, right? But this is where it gets really amazing. Arthur's father became very friendly with the last cook who was employed here, James Olivieri. The master of the house at the time, your uncle Jonathan's grandfather, if I'm not mistaken, Ruben Vander Horn, became especially close to James, a gifted chef. Afraid he'd be stolen away by another family, Ruben treated James very well. He remembered him in his will and gifted him some items from the estate."

"That was very generous of Ruben. He was well known as a philanthropist, I believe, donating to Oakdale College and Cliffside Hospital."

"Exactly right. I was able to verify that. The best part is that James's daughter Genavieve now lives in Brooklyn Heights and owns a restaurant in Manhattan. East Side. Arthur gave me the name. Olivieri's. I called her yesterday. Lovely woman. We spoke at length."

I had no doubt about that.

"I told her about the story I'm doing on Miss Vander Horn, and that I knew you, and she insisted I come into the city to meet with her. The upshot is, she has some old photos that her father had given her, some taken by him and others given to him by Ruben as a reminder of events he catered for the family."

"I've been looking for old photos. That's the one part of our family history that's missing."

"She was so gracious. She even said I could borrow them to make copies."

"Wonderful. I hope I get to see them someday."

"That's the amazing part. I mean why I'm here. I'm on my way to meet her at her restaurant. Why don't you come along? I'd love the company. I promised her I'd do my best to get you to join me."

"Actually, I'm heading into the city myself this morning. Why don't you ride with me? I don't mind driving."

"Oh, perfect. I know she'll be absolutely delighted to meet you."

"What time are you expected?" I asked.

"Anytime after ten."

I glanced at my watch. Nine thirty. "We may as well head out now, then."

I took a couple of last sips of hot chocolate, gave Dylan a treat, and we were out the door, on our way to the carport. I thought Natalie had missed her true calling. CIA operative might have been more up her alley. But I had to hand it to her. She was getting her story in a big way.

"I love your yellow Beetle," she said.

"Thanks. Easy to park in the city."

I turned on the GPS as soon as we got in the car.

"What's the address?"

She reached into her purse for a notebook. "Here it is. One twenty-four Sixty-Seventh Street. Between Lex and Park."

"Nice."

We were making the trip at just the right time, as the commuter rush had ended. We sailed over the George Washington Bridge, admiring the glistening city skyline in the autumn sun. I easily merged onto the FDR Drive, exiting at Seventy-First Street.

I grabbed a coveted parking spot right on the street, just off Third Avenue. We walked two blocks west and then four blocks south to Sixty-Seventh Street toward the restaurant in the bustling Upper East Side neighborhood. We weren't far from Aunt Tessa's apartment, and it was obvious from the manicured properties and swanky boutiques that we were in the midst of an extremely high rent district. We spotted Olivieri's in the middle of the block on Sixty-Seventh between Park Avenue and Lexington. The restaurant's entrance was elegantly marked with a burgundy awning with "Olivieri's" written in flowing white script across the front.

"We're both in jeans and casual sweaters. Do you think we're okay?" I asked.

"Too late to worry about that now."

As we entered, we found ourselves on the garden floor of a stately, five-story brownstone. A handsome, forty-ish man, most likely the host, greeted us somewhat reluctantly as he looked us up and down. "Sorry ladies, we don't open until eleven thirty."

Natalie spoke right up. "We're here to see the owner, Genavieve Leigh. I'm Natalie Summers from *Soap Opera Weekly*, and this is Lacey Langdon. Ms. Leigh is expecting us."

Natalie had a way of making *Soap Opera Weekly* sound like it was the *Wall Street Journal.*

His demeanor instantly mellowed. "One moment. I'll let her know."

Natalie leaned over and whispered in my ear, "Kind of snooty. Goes with the territory, I guess. I hear it's almost impossible to snag a reservation, unless you're a regular."

Once I took everything in, the reason was obvious. The long, narrow eatery, tastefully appointed with intimate, gray leather booths, gave off a sleek, contemporary vibe. Chrome and crystal chandeliers hung from the ceiling like jewelry, and tables in front of the gleaming walnut bar looked out into the brownstone's stunning garden, undoubtedly open for dining in warm weather.

Genavieve Leigh appeared wearing a white apron over a simple, black, turtleneck knit dress. She must have been in her mid-sixties.

"Ms. Leigh, I'm Natalie Summers from *Soap Opera Weekly*, and this is Lacey Langdon, Tessa Vander Horn's niece."

"Pleasure. Do call me Genavieve. Lacey, I'm so glad you came along. I feel like you're family. I'm so happy you came in. As I told you on the phone, Natalie, my family has so many memories from the estate in Willow Bluffs. Come, let's sit where we can talk."

She led us to a booth in a corner. Natalie and I sat facing the courtyard garden.

"My grandfather, James Olivieri, served as a cook on the estate for the Ruben Vander Horn family for years," Genavieve said. "I even visited years later with my father two or three times when I was a young girl. A beautiful place, as I recall."

"Indeed," Natalie said.

"My grandfather passed down many recipes to my father, who, fortunately, wrote them down. We're well known for our pasta, a favorite of Ruben's, apparently, and our veal dishes. Many of our specialties were inspired by James's original recipes. That's why the restaurant bears his name—my maiden name. You must come dine with us. I'm afraid we're already overbooked for lunch today, but I'd love to have you both come to dinner sometime. As my guests, of course."

"Thank you," I said. "So gracious of you."

"Just give Michael a call. Your aunt comes in from time to time with a very distinguished gentleman, Lacey."

"Aunt Tessa lives nearby. And she's definitely not one to cook."

"We're trying a new special today. Michael," she called to the host, "would you bring some gnocchi for our guests?"

He disappeared into the kitchen.

"In fact," Genavieve went on, "many members of the cast and crew dine with us. We're always thrilled to have them. But our guests can never seem to get them to divulge any secrets about the plot."

"They are sworn to secrecy," I told her.

Michael appeared with two sumptuous plates.

"Sometimes the simplest dishes are the best," Genavieve explained as he placed them in front of us. "Our gnocchi, homemade, of course, with freshly chopped imported San Marzano tomatoes, basil from our herb garden outside, a hint of garlic, extra virgin olive oil, and the finishing touch, a sprinkling of freshly grated asiago cheese."

Natalie and I took a bite.

"What do you think?"

"Oh, my. Absolutely delicious. And so fragrant," I observed.

"Wonderful," Natalie agreed. "Melts in your mouth."

"Ahhh, thank you. A good dish should be a feast for sight, smell, and taste," Genavieve said. "But on to the business at hand. I have something for you. I'll be back in a moment." She excused herself and slipped into the back of the restaurant, returning to our booth with what looked like a photo album and a small box. "I think you'll enjoy these old pictures my grandfather had saved," she said. "Not very many here, maybe a dozen or so. You'll see there are descriptions on the back of some of them. You'll recognize the beautiful shots of the estate, of course, inside and out. Oh, those cliffs. Magnificent. Please, go ahead and keep the album for a while. I'm so happy to share it."

"I'll have copies made of the photos and get it back to you pronto," Natalie promised.

"My Aunt Tessa will love these. Thank you so much."

"Truly, my pleasure. That's why we save mementos like these, isn't it? One day, we hope we'll be able to do something meaningful with them."

"The cliffs and the house certainly haven't changed much," I noted.

"I've seen shots of the house in the opening credits of your aunt's soap, *Edge of Darkness*, correct? Stunning," Genevieve said.

"Yes. In the show, the old place looks a little ominous," I said.

"That's what makes it so wonderful. I love it," Natalie said. "Can't get enough."

"Before you go, I have something else. This is for you, Lacey." Genevieve reached for the small box she'd brought to the table and handed it to me. "Go ahead and open it."

I opened the vintage, black velvet box to reveal a delicate pair of cameo earrings. "Genevieve, these are lovely, but I couldn't possibly accept."

"I insist. One of the former Mrs. Vander Horns, Mrs. Ruben Vander Horn to be exact, gave them to my grandmother as a gift, and they've been passed along. I can't wear them, you see. The posts must be made of nickel. I'm allergic. But even if I weren't, I would want you to have them."

"The cameos can be reset," I suggested.

"I'm not one to fuss with jewelry like that. I don't believe they're terribly valuable, but they're priceless from a sentimental point of view. That's why I'd love for you to have them. After all, they are family heirlooms."

"Thank you so very much. This means a lot. I wish there was some way I could reciprocate," I gushed, my heart full.

"They belong with the Vander Horn family," Genavieve said.

"Do you have any idea how old they are?" I asked.

"No, not exactly. I don't have any idea who originally purchased them."

I wondered if Sebastian had originally gifted the earrings to Sophie, and that was why they had been given away to a staff member. "You know, this really is quite remarkable. Aunt Tessa has a cameo brooch that matches these earrings exactly. She'll be so thrilled to have a complete set."

"How interesting," Genavieve commented.

"I wonder if any of your relatives knew Sophie Vander Horn, Eduard's niece. She's a distant cousin. We only recently discovered a portrait of her wearing the brooch. The cameos are carved from blue agate, a common stone at the time. As you said, not terribly valuable, but beautiful nonetheless."

"I certainly recognize the name Sophie," Genavieve recalled. "I believe her wedding photo is in the album." She opened the album and immediately found the picture of a solemn looking Sophie in an intricate, ivory mantilla with her groom, Lucas Van Dyk.

"This is just the sort of thing we've been looking for. I can't thank you enough."

Natalie's phone buzzed. "Pardon me. My editor. I must take this." She slid out of the booth and headed for the entrance.

Genavieve quickly spoke up. "As long as we're alone, there's one more thing I have for you. Strictly for you and your aunt. It's something your family should have."

She hurried to the back and returned with a faded yellow envelope marked "Western Union." I carefully removed the telegram and scanned the message:

HEALTHY BABY BOY—ANNABELLA IS WELL—
LAFONTAINES EN ROUTE
LUCIA OLIVIERI
CERNOBBIO

I looked up at Genavieve. "I don't understand. This would be from Lake Como, correct?"

"Yes, my family once had a home there. Villa Olivieri. Your aunt will explain."

Very confused, I put the telegram in my purse. I recalled the postcard and photo I had found in the box of keepsakes. I thought there must be some connection.

Natalie returned. "So sorry for the interruption."

"I must say, I've enjoyed meeting you both, but the lunch crowd will be coming in soon and I must get back to work. We'll be full before long."

She walked us to the door as Michael placed a delicate bud vase holding a single, perfect white rose on each table.

"Delightful meeting you," I said.

"I hope to see you both again," Genavieve replied.

"I'll messenger the photo album back to you ASAP," Natalie assured her.

"Call Michael. We can do lunch or dinner!"

I suppose one never knows what a day will bring. I had dreaded calling Natalie earlier in the morning and then ended up having the most heart-warming and meaningful experience, thanks to her. I couldn't wait to tell Aunt Tessa all about it. And I knew Julien would be thrilled to have the old family photos. We had just enough time to get to the studio.

I was afraid this was going to send Natalie spinning into orbit, but one good turn deserved another. "Listen, I hope this isn't an inconvenience, but I have to stop at the *Edge of Darkness* studio for a few minutes. Would you mind?"

I thought Natalie would fall over on the sidewalk. "Mind? Are you kidding? This is fantastic. I mean, truly fantastic. I've been trying to get in there for two weeks. It's impossible. I can't even tell you . . . You have absolutely made my day! Week! Year! What a coup! My editor won't believe it. I mean, I can hardly believe it."

I got the impression she was okay with it.

It could have simply been my state of mind, or the glow emanating from Natalie, but the city was shining in the midday sun. We walked east on Sixty-Eighth Street down to Lexington Avenue and then south to the corner of Fifty-Ninth and Lexington where Landmark Productions was located. We took the elevator up to the twenty-fourth floor, the home of the studios for the *Edge* and a newer daytime series, *Tomorrow's Light*.

"Ms. Langdon, we've been expecting you," the receptionist acknowledged. As soon as we approached her desk, she picked up the phone. "Ms. Langdon's here for Miss Vander Horn," she announced. "Please, have a seat," she said to us. "Claire will be right out."

Before we could even get comfortable in the Art Deco reception room, Claire Collins came to retrieve us. A young and ambitious production assistant on the show, Claire wore many hats, including part time script girl, wardrobe consultant, gopher, therapist, and all-around miracle worker.

"Julien said you'd be coming in. Please, come this way."

She walked us through a long corridor lined with blow-ups of the *Edge's* stars, dressed in full character. Tessa as Caroline Manchester, the show's matriarch, was the most recognizable.

"I know every single one of these *Edge* actors," Natalie boasted. "I've been watching ever since I can remember."

"We love all of our *Edge* fans," Claire said.

"The place is a treasure trove," Natalie told her.

We stopped in the conference room, where production meetings and table readings took place. "Your aunt and Julien will be right with you. I have to get back. We're always a little crazed before tapings," she explained.

We sat down at the long, black, rectangular Art Deco table. "This is the nerve center," I told Natalie. "Apparently, all the big *Edge* decisions are made right here. Who lives, who dies, where the story lines go, marriages, births, divorces, love stories, back-stabbing. Everything."

"Amazing."

Julien and Aunt Tessa entered the room together, Julien in a dapper, pinstriped suit and my aunt in black wool stovepipe trousers and a beige cashmere sweater.

"Lacey, just in time," Julien said.

"Julien, this is Natalie Summers from *Soap Opera Weekly*."

"I'd love to have a word with you, Mr. LaFontaine, for my story," Natalie said.

"Delighted."

"Natalie is doing an in-depth piece," Aunt Tessa told him. "Great exposure for us."

Claire returned, looking down at notes on her clipboard. "Just to review, you have the production meeting right after lunch and camera blocking immediately after that. After blocking, we'll do a complete run-through. Hair and make-up at two and then taping."

"A long day," Tessa said. "I've been running lines with Julien since nine."

"Do not fret, Claire. We're laser focused," Julien said.

"Lacey, there's time now for you to look at the treatment I prepared. Your aunt has already approved. I just want to be sure that you do as well. I certainly don't want to get anything wrong, and you've been right there on the front line."

While Aunt Tessa, Julien, and Natalie chatted at the conference table, I read through Julien's summary of the proposed "Sophie and Sebastian" subplot, and it sounded to me like it would be a big hit, complete with flashbacks and period costumes. From what I knew about daytime TV, it had been decades since anything along those lines had been done.

"This is going to be sensational, Julien," I said. "You nailed the essence of the story. I'm very impressed. I'm so glad you decided to go with this."

"I hope the producers and writers share your enthusiasm," he said.

"I'm sure they will," I replied. "You have something innovative here. I think it will take off."

Julien smiled. "I have a vision. I plan to give the *Edge* a new dimension. It's going to be big."

"Bigger than Luke and Laura," Aunt Tessa mused, with a twinge of sarcasm.

"Yes, *General Hospital* in its heyday. One can only hope. From your mouth to the soap opera gods' ears!" Julien exclaimed. "Tessa, I ordered a Cobb salad for you. Ladies, can we get you anything?"

"Thanks, but we're fine," I said.

"Please, join us, anyway," Aunt Tessa.

"We've had a most unusual morning, Aunt T. Thanks to Natalie, we visited a woman who is a descendant of someone who was on the staff at the estate. You may actually know her, but I don't think you're aware of her connection to the Vander Horns. Genavieve Leigh, the owner of Olivieri's."

"Yes, I love that little place. I've met her. What a small world!"

"Her grandfather, James Olivieri, was a cook for Ruben Vander Horn. She lent us some of her photos." I reached into my bag for the album of a dozen or so photos and slid it across the conference table to Aunt Tessa. "What do you think?"

"These are marvelous," she said, curiously turning the pages.

"Indeed," Julien agreed, leaning over her shoulder.

"Oh my. Look at Sophie." She sighed, stopping for a moment. "Her melancholy wedding day. I've never seen this before. The saddest bride I've ever seen."

"We could certainly use these for research," Julien said, promptly calling to Claire in the hallway. "Claire, would you have the graphics department make copies of these photos right away?"

"May I be so bold as to ask for a set for myself?" Natalie requested.

"Of course," Julien said. "Three copies of each, please. Tessa will want a set for herself, I'm sure."

"And there's something else." I took the small, velvet box from my bag, opened it, and placed it in front of Aunt Tessa.

"Will you look at these!" she said, shocked. "Uncanny. Why, they match Sophie's cameo pin exactly. The same blue stone. They must have been purchased together."

"Yes. Blue agate," I clarified. "Genavieve insisted upon giving them to you. She said they belong with the Vander Horns."

"How exceedingly gracious!" Aunt Tessa gushed.

Julien's steely blue eyes flashed with enthusiasm. "Tessa, we must use those earrings on the show," he said, admiring them over Aunt Tessa's shoulder.

"Yes, they'll do nicely," she said.

"Of course, no one but you will wear them, Tessa. Along with the brooch. I mean, no one but you *could* ever wear them. Make sure you lock them up for safekeeping. We don't want any mishaps."

Aunt Tessa and Julien discussed *Edge of Darkness* all through lunch, careful not to reveal any key elements.

"Of course, Natalie, you won't divulge anything plot related," Julien instructed.

"I'm a vault," Natalie assured him. "You know I want to continue working with you."

I was eager to talk with Aunt Tessa. "Julien, why don't you show Natalie the script library. As a writer, she'd be very interested."

"Yes, I'd love that," Natalie replied.

"We'll be just a few minutes," Julien said, leading Natalie down the hall.

"You two go ahead," I said, closing the conference room door after they left.

Finally alone with Aunt Tessa, I pulled the telegram from my purse and handed it to her.

"What's this?" she asked, quickly reading it. She appeared stunned. "Oh my. I knew everything would come out eventually."

"I'm baffled."

"I'll get right to the point. Pardon me if I'm rather blunt. Annabella Vander Horn Van Dyk, the only daughter of Sophie Vander Horn and Lucas Van Dyk, got pregnant. As she was unmarried at the time, her uncle Eduard, the head of the Vander Horn family, insisted that she be sent away from Willow Bluffs to save the family from shame."

"Aunt Tessa, this sounds archaic."

"It was. Eduard arranged for her to stay at Villa Olivieri in Cernobbio on Lake Como, the home owned by the family of the Vander Horns's private chef. Annabella gave birth to a baby boy there."

"What happened to the baby boy?"

"This is the part that is truly unbelievable. Eduard knew of a colleague in the silk business from Lyon, France, Anselme LaFontaine, and he and his wife were desperate to adopt a baby. They arranged for a very, very private adoption. Anselme and his wife picked up the baby in Cernobbio just a couple of days after birth. They named him Julien."

"Our Julien?"

Aunt Tessa nodded.

I was absolutely floored. "Please go on."

"My mother-in-law painstakingly researched this. She was the family historian. The adoption has, of course, been a closely guarded secret. It's uncanny that the telegram from Genavieve would surface now. Her family must have had it for decades."

"Very odd indeed."

"Julien just learned the truth about his past the other night when he met with the executor of his mother's estate. He gave Julien a letter that she had left with her will. It explained to Julien the details of the adoption and how Eduard Vander Horn was connected to the LaFontaines. She finally disclosed that Annabella was his birth mother. After decades of searching, Julien finally had his answer. When he told me a couple of days ago, I didn't let on that I already knew. He would never have forgiven me. Now I'm afraid that the whole business might put him over the edge once and for all. Everything's getting twisted in his mind. He was even babbling about being entitled to a piece of the Vander Horn estate, which was settled long ago. Now he's even more consumed with Sophie and Sebastian. I'm hoping he settles down."

"I'm trying to sort everything out. Julien is actually Sophie's grandson."

"Correct."

"And if Annabella is Julien's mother, then that would mean that he and Uncle Jonathan are distant cousins."

"Correct again."

"Wow, Aunt T. Just wow. What a family saga!"

"A lot to digest."

A knock on the conference room door ended our conversation. Claire had come back with copies of the photos, and Natalie and Julien had returned from the script library.

"Natalie, there's one more thing you must see while you're here. Claire, why don't you show our guests around the glorious town of Manchester Hills?" Aunt Tessa suggested. "Upstairs, where the magic happens."

"Really?" Natalie exclaimed. "Wait. The actual sets?"

"It's all an illusion, my darlings," Aunt Tessa said, grinning. "Smoke and mirrors. But, somehow, it all works."

"Yes, follow me," Claire said. "There's just enough time before the meeting."

"I'll join you," I said as we walked up the back stairs to the twenty-fifth floor, the true home of *Edge of Darkness*.

"Mind if I take a few pics with my phone?" Natalie asked. "Maybe a few behind-the-scenes shots."

"Go right ahead," Claire replied.

I'd been on set at Landmark Studios many times, but it never ceased to amaze me. The expansive taping area covered the entire floor with dedicated sets throughout, some of which were temporary. Claire stopped at the most familiar set and threw open the stately double doors that led to a beautifully appointed drawing room. She invited us inside.

"Welcome to Manchester Manor," she said. "Where your fondest dreams and worst nightmares come true."

"I cannot believe I'm actually here," Natalie said, snapping away with her cell phone. "Funny though, the room looks so much larger on TV."

"It's all about camera angles," Claire explained. "Our cameramen can do wonders with wide angle shots. And some members of our crew have been here for decades. I think they could practically shoot blindfolded."

"Pinch me," Natalie said. "This can't be real."

We had walked straight into the Manchester clan's world where Aunt Tessa starred as Caroline Manchester. The drawing room, the show's command post, was beautifully decorated with dark mahogany wainscoting, an opulent burgundy and cream Persian rug, the royal blue velvet Chippendale sofa where Aunt Tessa often held court as matriarch pouring tea from a sterling silver pot. The room also boasted inlaid accent tables, an ornate writing desk, and oil paintings of the Manchesters' forebears, who seemed to be watching our every move.

Natalie suddenly stood frozen, staring toward the double door. Actors Allison Hart and Jason Cacio, scripts in hand, stood just outside. The pair played Caroline's gorgeous but frivolous daughter Eliza and her charming, ladykiller fiancé, attorney Alexander Mason, two of the most popular characters on the show.

"Hey," Jason called to Claire. "We're looking for a quiet place to run lines."

"Try the hospital room set," Claire suggested. "Nobody ever wants to go in there."

"Ah. Will do."

"Don't forget, blocking after the meeting."

"We're on it," Allison reassured her.

Natalie looked like she might keel over. "Wait," she beckoned. "A quick selfie?"

She rushed toward them, quickly posed and snapped a photo, the souvenir of a lifetime.

"Thank you so much," she said, bubbling over with excitement. "You have no idea."

I had a feeling they did.

"We only have a few more minutes," Claire said, glancing at her phone. We checked out Manchester Hills's bar and eatery, the Cozy Spruce, where the town's best and worst secrets were often revealed, and the law office young Alexander Mason shared with his father Spencer, Manchester Hills's most formidable attorney.

"I'm afraid we'll have to wrap it up," Claire said. "Time is getting tight."

"We can't thank you enough," I said.

"This has been absolutely unforgettable," Natalie cooed.

"Come back to *Edge* any time."

I had a friend for life. Natalie gushed like Old Faithful on our walk to the car and all the way back to Willow Bluffs. It had been worth enduring her constant over-exuberance. I knew she'd write a good story. I also knew she had a nose for the news and was tuned into the Glenn Hartman's murder investigation. Maybe she'd come up with something.

It was two o'clock by the time I dropped Natalie off at the estate to pick up her car. Then I headed straight to Letter Perfect. Jeremy was on the phone when I walked in. He gestured hello and ended his call.

"Hey. Jess was just here. Wanted to know what you were doing with that Natalie person."

"Nothing gets by her, does it?"

"Derek Conover wants you to call him right away, and I left messages from a couple of clients on your desk. Also, the RSVPs are coming in on the evite for the Pierce party. Only a couple of regrets."

"Good. Mrs. Pierce will be happy."

"Hey, did you see this?" he asked. He grabbed a copy of the *Willow Bluffs Gazette* from behind the counter and pointed to a headline.

"No, I didn't have a chance to look at the paper this morning."

Trouble in the Park as Builders Default on Tax Payment

"Wow. I guess the cat's out of the bag," I blurted out.

"You knew about this?"

"No comment."

"So that's why Conover has been calling."

"Still no comment."

I was surprised to see Angela Hartman, the grieving widow, walk in dressed exclusively in black, looking as though she was mourning her husband's brutal and untimely death.

"May I help you, Mrs. Hartman?" I asked.

"Where might I find an engagement card? I need one for Ava Pierce. I prefer your selection to the drug store variety."

"We have some lovely cards right here on the rack," I said.

"I won't be attending the party, of course. Way too soon after losing Glenn. I do want to send a gift, though."

"Very thoughtful of you."

"Incidentally, I hear Gina Velasco is going to the affair. Ha, no pun intended. She certainly doesn't seem to be in mourning for her close friend, my husband, does she? No shame at all. Odd, considering she made such a spectacle of herself, carrying on with Glenn for a couple of months."

Both speechless, Jeremy and I avoided meeting her eyes.

Mrs. Hartman pulled a card from the display. "I'll take this one," she said, placing her selection on the counter in front of Jeremy.

"Anything else?" Jeremy asked.

"I don't think so." She paused, shaking her head. "Too bad that tramp didn't go off the cliff with my dear departed husband."

Chapter Thirteen

Just breathe, I told myself. After a couple of weeks of organized chaos and more drama than Broadway, everything was finally set for Ava Pierce and Jason Barclay's engagement party.

The Pierces' home was decorated, the caterer was ready to serve, and the guests were expected within the hour. I welcomed the silver lining in the frenzy of frantic planning. I hadn't had a moment to obsess about the recent occurrences that had haunted me—the mysterious flowers and vintage coat on Sophie Vander Horn's grave, the bizarre package from a dead man to my cottage, or the inexplicable murder of Glenn Hartman. The arrangements had fallen into place beautifully, and I was confident that after all of my meticulous work, the party was at the point where it would practically run itself.

That was true until five thirty, when catastrophe struck.

The caterer's staffing director called with the devastating news that the bartender we'd hired had come down with the flu. I scrambled to find a replacement, not an easy task for a Saturday night on extremely short notice. As I suspected, every bartender on Classic Caterers staff was already booked. I tried a few local restaurants and bars, hoping to find a stand-by, or at least borrow someone for a few hours, but no one was available. I imagined myself pouring wine and champagne all evening, or rather spilling wine and champagne all evening, and then I remembered Jeremy. He had told me he'd worked as a bartender at the tony Chatham Beach Hotel on Cape Cod the summer before. I immediately called him. He came to the rescue, assuring me he could be at the Pierces' home in an hour.

I ran over and hugged him the minute he walked into the Pierces' home. "Jeremy, you absolutely saved my life tonight. Best pinch hitter ever!"

"Yup. And I won't let you forget it," he said, laughing.

"I'm sure you won't."

"You owe me big time."

"Don't overdo it, Jer."

He glanced around the Pierces' great room approvingly. "Looks like a party, Lacey. Just what we need around here, too. Cool for people to be doing something besides wondering who killed Glenn Hartman."

The Pierces' sprawling Federal style home, set on one of the most picturesque bluffs along the Palisades, was magnificent in its own right, and its stunning great room boasted a beamed, vaulted ceiling and expansive Palladian windows overlooking the Hudson River, the George Washington Bridge, and Upper Manhattan. I'd placed fifteen high top tables covered with glimmering gold tablecloths around the room, which would be ample for the forty or so expected guests. Jeremy was stationed at the built-in mahogany bar in the back of the room, and waiters and waitresses would pass hors d'oeuvres until the buffet dinner was served.

A masterpiece of a custom cake, a red velvet and cream cheese frosting replica of the neoclassical Butler Library at Columbia

University where Ava and Jason first met, was displayed on a gold serving cart next to the buffet. The stunning confection was clearly the piece de resistance. Gold and white balloon garlands adorned the perimeter of the ceiling, and glowing votive candles generously placed around the room completed the look. I hoped the additional high tops I added to the bluestone patio would lure some of the partygoers through the double set of French doors to enjoy the crisp, moonlit autumn evening.

The valets in the circular driveway in the front of the house handled the steady stream of cars as the guests began to arrive. Derek was among the first, approaching me as soon as he came in.

"You did it," he said, taking a good look around the room.

"Don't ask me how."

"No, really. Everything looks perfect. Like it took months of planning."

"It certainly *felt* like months of planning."

"Hey, is that Jeremy behind the bar?"

"Last minute sub. Don't ask."

"I wasn't going to."

Ava and Jason looked radiant, Ava in a white, lace, off-the-shoulder frock and Jason in a blue, pinstriped suit accented with a gold pocket square. They looked like they could have headed straight to the altar. I had to admit I was a tiny bit envious. Ava seemed to have her life completely in place with a degree from Columbia in economics, a lucrative job on Wall Street, and a fiancé. I felt like my life was still a work in progress and would remain so indefinitely.

Tom and Cynthia Pierce were beaming, as were Jason's parents, Jim and Anne Barclay. If Jim's company was indeed having tax issues with the town, he was hiding it well. The room quickly filled up with resplendent guests as the wait staff circulated with trays of artistically crafted canapés—miniature quiches and kabobs, caviar and bruschetta, baby shrimp, and sliced filet mignon on toast points. I had given the party all I had. After all, Tom had taken excellent care of Aunt Tessa's finances for years.

Even though I knew they would be attending together, it seemed odd seeing Jim's partner, Ron Valenti, arrive with Gina. I had seen them coming out of the town hall together the week before and together at Grimaldi's. Rather an unlikely couple, I thought. Ron, middle aged, paunchy, balding, and a good two inches shorter than Gina, looked like the typical suburban guy you might run into buying a plunger in the hardware store on Saturday morning. At least he was single, unlike his predecessor.

Gina, on the other hand, was a veritable bombshell. She certainly worked quickly, having moved on from the departed Glenn Hartman in no time at all. Never a shrinking violet, she wore a skin-tight, flaming red sheath with a deep, plunging neckline that left little to the imagination. I was certain I wasn't the only one wondering why they were together. What did she have on the guy? Something seemed off about it, but I did my best to look like I was taking it in stride.

I noticed Jeremy pouring glass after glass of champagne. I walked over to the bar with a suggestion. "Jeremy, just fill some flutes with champagne and leave them on the bar, and then guests can help themselves. That will free you up to make mixed drinks."

"You're right. Good idea."

Ron greeted me with a smile as he and Gina approached the bar. "Miss Langdon, I believe you know Gina Velasco," he said, presenting the eye candy on his arm.

"Of course. We met at Grimaldi's," I said. "Nice to see you both again."

"Gina, what would you like?" Ron asked.

She turned to Jeremy. "I'm dying for a Bloody Mary. Must be this red dress," she quipped. "But, no clam juice, please. I'm allergic."

"No clam juice. You've got it. I can make a killer Bloody Mary without it."

"Oh, and no shrimp garnish either," she added.

"No worries. I don't have any."

"Scotch on the rocks for me," Ron said.

Thankfully, Jeremy had the bar service well under control. As a matter of fact, everything was going according to plan. Once the buffet was served, I hoped to spend some time catching up with Mayor Ariana Nikolas. I hadn't seen her at all since the ill-fated groundbreaking ceremony. And I wanted to circulate as much as possible to spread the word about my party planning business as part of Letter Perfect. But I still had some work to do before I could relax; however, on my way to the kitchen to speak with the catering manager, I spotted Aunt Tessa and Julien, who had just arrived. I stopped to chat for a moment.

"Lovely party, Lacey," Julien said.

"Thank you. I hope everyone is having a good time."

"My goodness, that cake!" Aunt Tessa said, looking fabulous in a black lace Chanel original. "It's the eighth wonder of the world."

"It is a work of art," I agreed. "A replica of the library at Columbia, Butler Library, I'm told, where Ava and Jason first met."

"Most unusual. I see your young man is here, Lacey. Your date for the evening, I presume?"

"Oh, Aunt Tessa, you are incorrigible."

"Truly I am, darling."

"Derek's not my young man and certainly not my date."

"Why not, dear? You don't want to end up terminally single, do you?"

"Aunt T, what will I do with you?"

Julien took Tessa's hand. "Come along, Sophie," he said.

Aunt Tessa looked aghast. "Sophie? Julien, what are you thinking?"

"Oh, Tessa, I must be working too hard."

How bizarre, I thought. "Sophie" had rolled off his tongue so naturally. But *terminally single* had struck me hard. I repeated the words to myself as I headed for the kitchen. It sounded rather bleak, like something that would haunt me. I was only twenty-eight. I wasn't exactly an old maid yet, but I certainly wouldn't have minded a stable relationship. I had to admit, I did enjoy Derek's company. We'd both come a long way since Willow Bluffs High School, and here we were virtually thrown together when I moved back to town. His offbeat personality had been growing on me the past couple of weeks, and I couldn't deny that he was awfully good-looking in a casual, roguish way. But this certainly was not a date, I kept telling myself.

A commotion coming from the bar suddenly interrupted my soul-searching. A few people had gathered around Gina and Ron. I hurried over.

"Is something wrong?" I asked.

Gina was seated on a barstool, hunched over, looking dazed, her lips and eyes swollen. Ron held her by her shoulders to prevent her from falling forward.

"She's developing red welts all over her arms and chest," someone said.

When I looked at her closely, I became immediately alarmed. "Yes, and she's swelling dramatically," I said. "I've seen this before. I think it's some kind of allergic reaction."

"She's allergic to shellfish," Ron said. "But I don't think she's had any."

"Jeremy, phone the paramedics and police. Right away." I knew we couldn't wait to take action.

"I'm on it."

"Dr. Nash," I called out, running toward him. "We need you by the bar immediately," I said, taking his arm. We rushed to Gina's side.

"What's happening?" the doctor asked, quickly assessing her facial swelling. He reached for her wrist to take her pulse.

"Everyone, step away and give Dr. Nash some room," I demanded.

"This looks like anaphylactic shock," he declared. He closely examined her eyes and lips and palpitated her throat. "Does she carry epinephrine?" he asked Ron.

"Purse," Gina gasped. "Car."

"What did she say?" the doctor asked.

"She wants her purse," I said.

"I believe she keeps a dose of epinephrine in her purse," Ron said. "But I think she left it in the car. Can someone go? I don't want to leave her."

"Does anyone have an epinephrine pen?" Dr. Nash shouted into the room.

No one responded.

"Anyone? Epinephrine?"

Still, no one came forward.

"This is an emergency," Dr. Nash pleaded.

Jim Barclay was in earshot. "I'll go to your car, Ron," he said. "Did you use the valets?"

"Yes, they have the key." He reached into his pocket for the valet's stub and handed it to Jim. "Hurry!"

"She has a known allergy?" Dr. Nash asked Ron.

"Yes, like I said before you got here. She says she's allergic to shellfish, but she didn't consume any."

"There could have been cross-contamination. Or it's possible she's deathly allergic to something else as well. This is a classic case of anaphylactic shock," the doctor observed.

Gina wheezed and gasped, struggling to breathe. Ron moved aside and Dr. Nash tried to steady her on the barstool as he held his arms around her, but her body writhed, and she ultimately slipped off the stool and collapsed to the floor. Dr. Nash knelt next to her, once again checking her heart rate. She lay motionless.

"Her breathing seems to have ceased, and she's lost consciousness. I'm not getting a pulse."

He placed one hand over the other and began compressing her chest rhythmically to administer CPR. He continued for several minutes, stopping occasionally to give her rescue breaths, but it was futile. Her face had turned bluish. She was slipping away.

After what seemed like an eternity, Dr. Nash pulled away for a moment, pausing the chest compressions to check her pulse. "I'm sorry," he said. "There's not much more I can do." He resumed CPR. "I'll stay with it until the paramedics arrive."

I saw that the Willow Bluffs paramedic team had arrived, and Tom Pierce quickly ushered them into the great room to Gina.

"What's the status?" one of the paramedics asked.

"I'm an M.D. We have cardiac arrest caused most likely by anaphylactic shock. She'll need the AED stat. Three minutes since cessation of breathing."

Unfortunately, there was no sign of Jim returning with the epinephrine. While Dr. Nash continued the rhythmic CPR, the paramedics quickly unpacked the defibrillator. They attached two electrode pads to Gina's chest, above and below the heart. One paramedic remained with Gina, and the other monitored the defibrillator.

I noticed Derek heading in my direction. "The police just arrived," he said. "Tom is bringing them in. How are they doing?"

"We'll need a miracle."

"Everyone stand back," Derek said to the onlookers. "Give the paramedics some space. Please."

"Clear," the paramedic called. Then the machine administered a massive electric shock to Gina's heart. Gina remained motionless. To my untrained eyes, it seemed as if the shock had had no effect. The paramedic continued CPR for two additional minutes while his partner studied the defibrillator, waiting for it to analyze Gina's heart rhythm. Another shock was needed. My own heart raced.

"Clear," he called again, administering the shock and then initiating CPR for a second time.

His partner looked up from the defibrillator and shook his head. "No heart rhythm has been identified."

"We've running out of options, Doctor."

"One more shock," Dr. Nash instructed.

The two paramedics worked on Gina tirelessly and efficiently, but no response.

"We've lost her, Doctor."

Dr. Nash glanced at his watch. "Time of death, seven forty-two."

Seconds later, Chief Hennessey rushed in, with Sergeant John Martinelli and Officer Jane Kowalski following close behind him.

"Everyone, guests and staff, remain on the premises but move into the living room. We may want to speak with some of you," Chief Hennessey said.

Jeremy had turned ghostly white. "I feel like I killed her."

"Don't be absurd," Derek offered. "The autopsy will show the cause of death."

"That's just great. What are they going to say? Death by Bloody Mary?"

"Jeremy, don't blame yourself," I said.

"Gina Velasco came in contact with something that caused anaphylactic shock. It's that simple," Derek stated matter-of-factly.

"Or there was something else wrong with her," I said.

"You're the bartender?" the chief asked Jeremy.

"Yes, Chief."

"Your name?"

"Jeremy Ellis."

"You mixed her drink?"

"I did."

"What was in it?"

"Just a typical Bloody Mary," Jeremy explained. "You know, tomato juice, vodka, Worcestershire sauce, a dash of tobacco, fresh pepper, and a garnish of celery."

"She specifically said no clam juice," I recalled. "I was standing right there when she ordered."

"You're sure you didn't put clam juice in it?"

"Absolutely no clam juice in the drink," Jeremy said, reaching down under the bar. "See, the bottle is still sealed."

"Yes, I see that. Curious," the chief noted. "Is shellfish being served tonight?" he asked me.

"Yes," I answered. "Crabmeat mini-quiches and shrimp."

"Who was with her tonight?"

Ron spoke right up. "I was. I suppose she could have eaten one of those things with the crabmeat in it. She wouldn't have known what was in it. They were being passed around. I don't know. I guess she could have grabbed one off a tray when we were walking over to the bar. I really can't be sure one way or the other."

"But no shellfish near the bar?" the chief asked.

"None at all. I'm certain of it. Only on the servers' hors d'oeuvres trays," I explained.

"Chief, I swear—"

"Don't worry, Jeremy," Derek assured him. "This isn't your fault."

Jeremy looked terrified. "I sure as hell hope not."

"If there's any problem whatsoever, I'll represent you."

"Jeremy, there's no way it will ever come to that," I insisted.

"I want to talk to whoever's in charge of the catering staff," Chief Hennessey demanded.

"I'll get her, Chief," Officer Kowalski said.

"But first, pack up what's left of that Bloody Mary, Kowalski. Get it over to the forensics food lab ASAP. Let's see what they turn up."

Chapter Fourteen

Another killer party. Two events, two corpses. Not a stellar stat.

Certainly, death by Bloody Mary was a circumstance that no event planner had even remotely imagined. And the more I thought about it, the worse it seemed. Ava and Jason's engagement party the night before, the party that was supposed to have been such a glorious occasion, had all but turned into a repast for Gina Velasco, and in spectacular fashion. From the moment I woke up, the image of her keeling over from anaphylactic shock kept replaying in my head. It had been a full out disaster for the Pierce family, my business, Jeremy, and, of course, tragic for Gina.

Understandably, some of the guests had left after the party took its devastating turn, but we decided to serve the buffet dinner, albeit rather solemnly, to those who remained. The bridal party and close family members did their best to console the prospective bride and groom. What a way to begin their engagement. The wedding was only six months away. I hoped to be involved in the planning process, but I wouldn't have blamed the Pierces if they steered clear of my services. I was beginning to feel like the Typhoid Mary of event planning. More like Typhoid Bloody Mary.

* * *

The early morning sunlight streamed in through the cottage's living room windows. I sat alone at the kitchen counter, sipping a cup of coffee with a clear view of Sophie's portrait over the fireplace. Julien had insisted that Aunt Tessa return to her penthouse after the party to ensure she'd be well-rested and ready to shoot six new episodes of *Edge of Darkness* during the week. Sophie certainly wasn't very good company, and neither was Dylan, who napped in his bed next to the hearth, snoring occasionally. I had gone to sleep last night hoping things would look different in the morning, but they didn't. My thoughts had been drifting to the macabre, and with good reason. One death at my first event was unbelievable. Another one was unthinkable.

I wondered how Letter Perfect Events would recover. Maybe change our slogan from "Perfection to a T" to "Drop Dead Amazing." Once again, my mother's mantra haunted me: *Give it all you've got, no matter what.* I had to admit that the "give it all you've got" part was getting harder and harder, and "no matter what" was becoming more complicated every day.

As awful as I felt, I knew it was much worse for Jeremy. No good deed goes unpunished, another familiar old adage, tended to ring all too true. Well-meaning Jeremy, such a dedicated and loyal assistant, had stepped up to bat to save the party at the last minute, only to find himself in the middle of a mess. I was relieved that Derek had offered to help him out with any legal issues if he needed it. He was such a great, hard-working kid. He didn't deserve this.

My phone suddenly buzzed with a text from Derek. I wasn't surprised to see he was checking up on me after last night's debacle. We were all beyond rattled.

you ok
pretty much
good meet me at town hall at 11
whats up
not sure but Ari wants to talk to us
me too?
yeah something about the sale of your aunt's estate
ok interesting yes I guess I can be there
great later

The sale of the estate was a done deal. I couldn't imagine what the mayor would want to discuss at this late date, but I'd know soon enough. Perhaps something about Cliffside Custom Builders' default on their municipal taxes? Did she want to consult Aunt Tessa? I glanced up at Sophie. I had the feeling she was watching me. Her eyes were always upon me, as if she wanted to tell me something. "What is it?" I said out loud. "Are you warning me?"

If talking to a painting and hoping for an answer wasn't proof that I was going certifiably batty, then I didn't know what was. It was already ten fifteen. I ran to my room to change into skinny jeans and a burgundy turtleneck sweater. I pulled on a well-loved pair of dark brown leather riding boots, grabbed my black wool jacket, and headed for the door. I stopped by Bean Around on the way to the town hall to pick up coffee for all of us. Jess greeted me as soon as I walked in.

"Hey, Lacey. What can I get you?"

"Three pumpkin spice lattes. And maybe a new life."

"Uh, oh. Three?"

"Meeting."

"Scott, three pumpkins for Lacey," she called to the barista. "How are you holding up? Everybody's talking about last night."

"Okay. Just unreal, isn't it?"

"Never heard of such a thing."

"Yeah, tell me about it. Another Lacey Langdon drop dead amazing event."

"Look who just walked in," Jess whispered, leaning in.

With a sideways glance, I caught a glimpse of Ron Valenti stepping up to the counter right behind me. I hadn't had much chance to speak directly with him last night with all the commotion from the paramedics and the police. I thought I should offer condolences at the very least.

"Ron," I said, turning toward him. "I'm so sorry about what happened."

"Yeah. Thanks."

"How are you doing?"

"Not so good," he muttered.

"What a freak accident," was about all I could manage.

"Yeah. I felt so helpless."

"There was nothing you, or anyone, could have done."

"I should have been more careful."

"Careful?"

"I never should have let her into the party without her purse."

"You mean because of the epinephrine pen?"

Fidgeting with the change in his jacket pocket, he explained, "Yeah. Exactly. She was carrying the gift, you know, and I was taking the ticket from the valet. Just didn't notice that she left the damn purse in the car."

"Why would you?" I didn't know him very well. I'd only met him socially a couple of times, but he seemed agitated. I guess under the circumstances it was understandable. Come to think of it, I would have been a basket case.

"Fact is, she was allergic to bee stings and shellfish. Almost always carried the pen."

"It certainly wasn't your fault."

"Hope the police agree. I just came from there. Hennessey wanted to go over my statement one more time."

"Lacey?" Scott called out. "Three lattes."

"Oh, they're probably just being thorough. Following procedure, I'm sure."

"Yeah, whatever," he lamented. "Doesn't change anything. It is what it is. Can't believe she's gone. It's all a blur. If I'd only had that purse of hers."

"You've had quite a shock."

"Gone in a matter of minutes. It makes you think."

"Yes. Yes, it does."

I picked up the lattes and headed for my VW. As I drove the short distance down Willow Street to the town hall, a flashback of Gina's dramatic collapse played in my brain over and over again. I knew the disturbing imagery would take time to fade. For now, I hoped talking with Ari and Derek would provide a much-needed distraction. When I arrived, they were already in Ari's office. A copy of the Vander Horn property's proposed site plan submitted by Cliffside Builders was spread across Ari's desk.

"I brought some pumpkin spice lattes. Extra whipped cream."

"Thank you. Amazing," Ari said.

Derek eagerly grabbed a cup and took a sip. "Just what I needed. Thanks!"

I glanced over Ari's shoulder at the site plan. I was somewhat familiar with it from the blow-ups I'd made for the groundbreaking ceremony. "Actually, when you look at all of the proposed homes and the community park on paper it looks great, but I imagine when all of that is actually built, it could look congested."

"Exactly," Ari said. "That's what I've been looking at. And Tom Pierce suggested that the builders are going to petition the planning board so that a commercial zone be included for a small strip mall."

"That would be a tough sell," Derek said.

"Especially after their default on the property taxes. This is not something I'd like to see on the bluffs . . . oh, this latte is amazing. I hope you've put last night behind you, Lacey."

"Not quite, I'm afraid. I just ran into Ron Valenti at the Bean."

Derek looked shocked. "He's out?"

"Yes. Said he had just spoken with the police. Again."

"Probably looking for inconsistencies in his story," Ari noted.

Derek nodded. "Good. Then, I'm not the only one who thinks Gina's death is suspicious."

"Suspicious, indeed. Or maybe convenient," Ari suggested.

"Interesting," Derek surmised. "I wonder what she knew. She was the town council's secretary *and* Glenn's ex-girlfriend."

"Well, she's very ex now," I pointed out.

"Coincidence?" Derek asked.

"Doubt it," Ari said. "And why did she show up last night with him? The Vander Horn property developer of all people. I don't get it. I mean, let's face it, what was Gina Velasco doing with a guy like Ron Valenti?"

"That's the question on everyone's mind," Derek remarked. "Maybe it wasn't the shellfish thing that killed her. We'll have to wait for the autopsy results."

"You know, something seemed off with Ron when I saw him earlier. I know he's been through an awful ordeal, but he was incredibly defensive."

"Defensive? How?" Derek asked.

"About Gina not having her purse."

"In all fairness, you did say he'd just come from the police, right?" Ari stated.

"Yes, he was definitely nervous, but still. The way he was harping on it struck me as odd. Almost as if he needed to convince himself."

"Something is clearly amiss," Ari proposed. "I came in this morning to take a closer look at the entire deal. I wanted you to know what's going on, Lacey. We may need to be in touch with your aunt. Kind of under the radar if you get my gist. The property tax issue is problematic."

"She usually stays at the cottage a couple of times a week, if her taping schedule permits."

"Perfect."

"She's well insulated by her agent, Julien, and also Tom Pierce and the real estate people, but don't be fooled, she's sharp as a tack. She always has a handle on what's going on, even if she's reluctant to admit it."

"Derek, you're much more computer savvy than I am," Ari admitted. "Maybe if you comb through Glenn's files they'll tell us something."

"Sure. And Gina's. I can read their emails, too."

"This may be completely extraneous, but there's a reporter whose been doing an in-depth story on Aunt Tessa. She's from

Soap Opera Weekly, but she seems to be going above and beyond, if you know what I mean. I think she's probably harmless, but she's been hanging around a lot," Derek mentioned.

"Worth checking into. Another thing I want to do is revisit the entire subdivision proposal with the planning board."

"I'm with you on that," Derek said.

"Good. We're all on the same page. I guess that's it. And by the way, this is just between us. For now, anyway."

"Of course," Derek agreed.

Derek and I walked into the hallway. He planned on remaining in his office to go through the computer files on the Vander Horn property transaction, and I looked forward to going home to relax in front of the fire with Dylan.

"Is Ari making too much of all this?" I asked.

Derek shrugged. "I don't know."

"You have to admit, a lot of weird things are happening."

"I agree with you there. One hundred percent."

"Anaphylactic shock, murder, phantom roses, and a vintage coat on a grave, a package, and notes from a dead guy. And now the builders want to put a strip mall on a beautiful estate. What's going on in this town?"

"No idea. It will take some sleuthing to find out."

"Listen, let me know if I can be of any help," I offered.

"Will do."

"But not today." I laughed. "I'm half dead."

"I know. Go home and get some rest."

The minute I got into my car my phone buzzed once again. Now what, I thought. A text from Jess. As much as I wanted to, I couldn't ignore it.

you should come over here
whats wrong
that reporter is here
natalie?
yup
shes sitting alone with her coffee and her laptop looks like she'll be here for a bit
ugh half dead but I do want to talk to her again she's been amazing
this is your chance
okay on my way

I headed down Willow Street wondering how I'd approach Natalie Summers, but once I got to the Bean, that was a moot point. As soon as I came in, she got up from her table and approached me.

"Oh, Lacey. So nice to see you again."

"Likewise. What brings you into town?" As if I didn't know.

"Won't you join me? I've been hoping I'd run into you. I've been polishing up my feature story about your aunt. My table's right over there," she said, pointing.

"I'll bring your coffee over," Jess said with a knowing smile.

"The focus is still an in-depth bio of her and how her role as Caroline Manchester on *Edge of Darkness* has evolved over the last forty years or so. I keep adding more personal background and local color, too. There's so much out there."

"I'm sure your readers will love it."

"Oh, yes, you have no idea. No soap star is more beloved than Miss Tessa Langdon Vander Horn. I'm giving this feature all I've got, as you know."

"If there's anything more I can do to help . . ."

"As long as you brought it up, I'd love to come by the estate and take a few current photos, if you don't mind."

"Sure. Just let me know when you'd like to come."

"Is there anything wrong with right now?"

As tired as I was, I thought it might be best to get it over with. "That would be fine."

As soon as the words were out of my mouth, I hoped I wouldn't regret them. I was physically and emotionally exhausted, but ever since I'd met Natalie Summers at the groundbreaking ceremony, I had a nagging feeling that she could be useful. I wanted to know what she had found out since our visit to the city, which was undoubtedly plenty. She was friendly enough. And she had always seemed harmless.

We left the Bean, and Natalie followed me back to the estate. I parked under the carport, and Natalie pulled in behind me.

"Any chance I can go inside the main house?"

"I guess that would be okay. I'll have to stop at the cottage for the key."

"Fantastic."

"No photos of the interior, though, I'm afraid. The property is under new ownership."

"Oh, I know. I just want to learn as much as I can for background."

Natalie strolled beside me to my front porch and then followed me inside before I had a chance to ask her to wait outside. As soon as we walked in, Dylan greeted us with his usual exuberant barking and tail-wagging, excited to have met someone new.

"Hey, there! You remember me," Natalie said, patting his head as she surveyed the living room. Turning to me, she continued, "Such a lovely place! We were so rushed last time I was here I didn't really have a chance to appreciate it." She walked around the room. "So, this is where Miss Tessa Vander Horn lives when she's not in New York. Just beautiful!"

"Her rooms are actually upstairs."

"Very elegant, yet incredibly charming. What a stunning portrait!"

"Yes, I told you about her. That's Sophie Vander Horn, my aunt's distant cousin on her husband's side. If you notice, she's wearing the cameo brooch that matches the earrings Genavieve Leigh gave me."

"So she is. Beautiful. I'm so glad those heirloom earrings found their way back to the family." She stood before the painting, taking it in. "But, you know, there's something about Sophie. It's in her eyes. Rather forlorn, I'd say."

Forlorn. Exactly. Abandoned. Lonely. Was it that obvious? Sophie's eyes, a window to her soul, revealed that there was a story to tell. I wondered if Natalie was extraordinarily perceptive or if she had uncovered something in her research. If she had somehow discovered that Julien was Sophie's grandson, she didn't let on.

I found the key to the main house in the junk drawer in the kitchen and called Dylan. "Come on, boy. Let's go out."

Dylan led us across the South Lawn to the front porch of the main house. As I unlocked the front door, Natalie bent down and pulled something out from under the doormat. When she handed it to me, I gasped. It was one of Sebastian DesChamps's calling cards, exactly like the one that had arrived with the package to Sophie last week. I must have looked startled.

"Something wrong?" Natalie asked, craning her neck to see what was in my hand. "Sebastian DesChamps," she said slowly as she read the card. "I don't think you've mentioned Sebastian's surname before. Why, I'm certain I came across that name in my research. Yes, I remember now."

"Really?"

"I thought it was such a beautiful name! DesChamps. From the fields. I speak a little French, you know."

Yes, I recalled. From the fields. Haunting. Even ironic. "Do you? That's great!"

"Spent a semester at the Sorbonne," Natalie clarified. "I'll have to check my notes when I get back home. The DesChamps name may have had something to do with the silk business in Paterson."

"Yes, I believe you are correct."

"I've learned a lot about the Vander Horns. They had quite a reputation in silk manufacturing. Fascinating stuff. My readers will flip. I even visited the graveyard here in town about a week ago. I was looking for some family history."

"About a week ago?"

"Actually, more like a week and a half," she clarified as we entered the foyer. "This is amazing," she said. "How old is the house?"

"Built at the end of the nineteenth century."

"The marble is just gorgeous. Looks like Carrera. The best. They don't make them like this anymore, do they?"

"No. Definitely not. Natalie, let me ask you this. Did you by any chance notice a bouquet of yellow roses on one of the old graves?"

"Funny you should mention that. I did. Someone left them and then disappeared very quickly."

"You saw the person?"

"Barely. I can't even be sure if it was a man or a woman. It was dusk and kind of hazy. Hard to see."

"Too bad."

"Yes. I wanted to talk to whoever it was. I thought it might have been a relative who could have given me a little more depth for my story. Our readers want to know all there is to know."

I had no doubt that Natalie would have considered waking the dead for a story, and if she had unearthed anything about Annabella's banishment to Italy or the adoption she wouldn't have been able to contain herself. "As far as I know, my only living relative is my Aunt Tessa."

I showed Natalie the morning room, study, library, and sunroom before we ventured outside so she could take exterior photographs from every angle imaginable. She was thrilled she was able to accomplish everything she wanted in the name of her loyal readers. Relieved she'd completed her mission, I could go home to unwind. Dylan and I walked her to the carport, and we finally said our good-byes.

Yet on the way back to the cottage, an eerie feeling crept over me. How did that calling card get to the front door of the main house? Had someone been lurking around the cottage as well?

Back at home at last, I gave Dylan a treat and collapsed onto the living room sofa. I gazed up at Sophie. "This must have something to do with you. Talk to me."

Dylan nudged me with his nose and jumped up to snuggle next to me.

I reached into my pocket for Sebastian's card and examined it closely. The upper right hand corner was folded inward toward the front of the card, not just accidently dog-eared. It had been sharply and deliberately creased. I wondered what that was all about. Someone had either found a stash of Sebastian's cards, or he or she had gone to an awful lot of trouble to reproduce them. I had no idea why.

I couldn't resist the temptation to grab my phone and search the Internet for information on "calling cards." I scanned the first *Cyberpedia* article I found. "Popular in the 1800s . . . cards were exchanged to facilitate personal visits." It sounded to me like they were the nineteenth-century version of social media. "The tradition carried over to the early twentieth century among well-to-do families." Then, I came upon a fascinating footnote: "If the corner was folded in, the card had been left in person and not by a messenger or servant."

As if I hadn't been distressed enough already, I had to worry about a crazy person who had come calling, and there was nothing I could do about it. I couldn't call the police. Chief Hennessey already thought I was half nuts after the cameo incident.

My unrelenting phone vibrated once again. This time, a text from Derek.

i think i found something talk tomorrow

Chapter Fifteen

"Good thing I'm not a suspect or anything," Jeremy growled as he rushed into the shop.

He arrived at Letter Perfect twenty minutes late Monday morning, most unusual for him, and he seemed to be in an uncharacteristically bad mood. With a frustrated look, he dropped his backpack next to the cash register and took a seat on the stool behind the counter.

"What's wrong?" I asked.

"Chief Hennessey questioned me," he grumbled. "Again."

"This morning?"

"Yup."

"Did you call Derek?"

"No time. The chief just showed up at my parents' house."

"You could have asked to have a lawyer with you, you know."

"Wouldn't have made much difference," he replied, shaking his head in frustration. "It was supposedly unofficial. Anyway, all I could do was tell him what happened."

"How'd it go?"

"He asked a bunch of questions about Ron Valenti, which was kind of weird. You know, about what was going on when Gina died. Like, was Ron close to the bar? Was he there the whole time? And then, did I notice if he picked up the drink and gave it to Gina?"

"Interesting."

"Yeah. Something's definitely up with that."

"Well, did you?" I asked him.

"Did I what?"

"Notice if Ron handled Gina's drink."

"Oh, well, I couldn't be certain. But I said he might have. I mean, he *was* right there the whole time. Everything was pretty crazy."

"It was. I'm not completely sure about everything that happened either."

"I know, right. It's all a blur."

"I ran into Ron yesterday at the Bean. He was awfully nervous."

"Yeah, well, sounds like he should be. One thing I told Hennessey for sure, there is no way I put clam juice in that drink."

"The police know that, Jeremy. You showed them the bottle behind the bar. It was completely sealed."

"I got the feeling he doesn't think Gina's death was an accident."

"I wonder what else they've got."

"No clue. But I can tell you this. I've never been involved in anything like this before. I have to say, it's not cool."

"You have nothing to worry about," I assured him. "Listen, you're a witness. Nothing more. That's way better than being a suspect."

"Well, yeah. There's that."

"Do you have Derek's class tonight?"

"I do."

"Let him know what's been going on."

"For sure."

"Can I get you a coffee?"

"I'm fine."

I was reluctant to leave him alone in the showroom, but I had design work to do in my office in the back. I sat down at my desk, opened my laptop, and stared at the blank screen. I felt so bad for Jeremy. Guilty, actually. Barely twenty-one, he still seemed like a kid. I couldn't help blaming myself for asking him to pinch hit as bartender at the Pierces' house. A cloud of negativity washed over me, making me question everything I'd done in the recent past, especially my decision to move back to Willow Bluffs. Of course, I loved spending time at the cottage with Aunt Tessa. But the past two weeks had brought nothing but disaster, evoking vivid memories of my parents' accident. Would I have been better off if I'd stayed in Manhattan? I'd hoped coming back to my hometown would give me comfort and hope, and it did for a while. Yet I hadn't counted on a corpse at the bottom of a cliff and a suspicious case of fatal anaphylactic shock. I'm sure I wasn't the only one in town wondering what would be next.

I'd been curious about the intriguing text Derek had sent me last night intimating that he'd uncovered something interesting. I had no idea what he'd meant, but I assumed it was something about Gina or Glenn. I was about to call him when my phone vibrated with a new incoming text from him.

stop by my law office later
sure maybe around 1
perfect

I was dying to know what Derek had uncovered, but I didn't allow myself to think about it. Wallowing in speculation wouldn't have solved anything. Instead, I focused on designing templates for invitations to two events planned for the week before Christmas, a surprise sixtieth birthday party for the editor of the *Gazette* to be held at Grimaldi's and a lavish baby shower for a former high school classmate of mine. Relieved to distract myself from murder, Bloody Marys, anaphylactic shock, packages, and calling cards from dead guys, I delved in. By the time I finished the templates and forwarded them to the clients for approval, it was time to meet Derek.

"I have to run a quick errand," I said to Jeremy, breezing by him.

"Cool. I'll be here working on inventory. I brought lunch."

"Thanks. Shouldn't be long."

I took a deep breath as the brisk autumn air touched my face. I immediately noticed that the center of town seemed quiet for a Monday. The Bean appeared to be empty, and there were only a couple of cars on the street. I got into my VW and turned right, heading north on Willow Street for about a mile and a half to Derek's firm, Gardener and Wells, located in a charming gray and white clapboard Victorian home that had been converted to law offices. Derek had been an associate attorney there for three years, and his prominence as a young town councilman boded well for his success. When the firm purchased my father's practice after the accident, Derek became even more indispensable to them, taking the lead on many of the new matters, particularly real estate deals.

I parked in front, admiring the stately old house as I always had, although I had never been inside before. As I entered, the rich mahogany paneling, burgundy velvet sofas, and opulent

Persian rug in the reception area made a stunning first impression. The pleasant young receptionist directed me down a long, carpeted hallway to Derek's private office. He was seated at his desk with his jacket off and his sleeves rolled up, typing feverishly.

I knocked on the open door. "Hey, I made it."

"Lacey, thanks for coming by. I thought we could speak privately, and confidentially, here."

"Of course."

He got up and closed the door behind me. "Hungry? I ordered a couple of tuna wraps from Vinny's Deli."

"Great, thanks," I said, settling into a wing back chair in front of his desk. "What's going on? Your texts were kind of cryptic."

"Plenty."

"I'm listening."

"I've been going through Glenn's emails and personal files back at the town hall. He never had a chance to delete anything."

"That's a break."

"It is. I'll be turning all of this over to the police once it's organized. They haven't officially asked for anything yet, but I imagine it will help with the investigation."

"From what I've read in the *Gazette*, it doesn't sound like they've made much progress so far."

"They might not be revealing everything they have."

"I guess we should give them the benefit of the doubt for now."

"Here's the thing. It's no secret that Glenn wanted to slow down the sale of the Vander Horn acreage. He was at odds with Jim Barclay and Ron Valenti of Cliffside Builders over the use of the land. Your aunt was incredibly generous in gifting ten of her thirty acres to the community as part of the sale, but Glenn had been pressing Cliffside to donate more land. He was pushing for additional fields and park space. Even a dog park."

"Can't blame him for trying."

"Of course, that was the last thing Jim Barclay and Ron Valenti wanted to do. From the beginning, they've been planning a small strip mall on the property, in addition to the new homes and condominiums they're building."

"That's no surprise."

"The principals, Jim, Ron, and, of course, Tom Pierce, who handled the sale for your aunt, wanted to make as much money as possible. Glenn, as always, was more civic minded."

"So, Glenn had basically hit a brick wall."

"Not entirely. Here's the clincher: Glenn had been threatening to go directly to the New Jersey Department of Environmental Protection to propose that the state buy a portion of the property based on New Jersey's Green Acres Law."

"You're losing me. The Green Acres Law? I've never heard of it."

"A program created years ago that allows the state to purchase land for recreation and conservation purposes. The objective is to maximize green space. But if the state purchased part of the property, Ron and Jim's commercial plans would have been in jeopardy."

"I can't imagine Ron and Jim would have let that happen."

"You've got that right. But Glenn would have been able to put some pressure on the builders if he had the town council behind him. A big fight was brewing. If you recall, the closing on the property took place early in the morning down in South Jersey on the day of the groundbreaking ceremony. Jim Barclay,

Ron Valenti, and Tom Pierce were all there as principals. And that same morning, Glenn was supposedly heading to court to get an injunction to stop the deal from going through. Or at least delay it. I don't know what he had on Cliffside Builders, but it must have been something shady."

"And we know Glenn didn't quite make it to court."

"Exactly."

"You're assuming Glenn was killed because he was in the way."

"At this point, I don't want to assume anything, but I'd have to say that yes, that's a possibility. Glenn had a lot going on. His wife and Gina had strong motives to get rid of him. He was a low-key guy, but there were a few people who would have been happy to see him disappear."

"So much for boring old Glenn. Still waters run deep, don't they?"

"Sure do. I'm going to keep digging. I have a feeling there's a lot more to this land deal than what's on the surface."

"I don't believe my aunt was aware of any of that. And she just found out about Cliffside's tax default the other day."

"I'm sure she wasn't aware. That's all I've got so far. Oh wait, there was one more thing, and it's big. Jim sent an email to Ron—something about the books being a bit off. It sounded like he was subtly accusing Ron of skimming some money. No response from Ron. Not in writing, anyway."

"That's huge, Derek! That might explain the lack of funds to pay the municipal taxes."

"That occurred to me. If Ron was skimming money and Gina somehow found out about it . . ."

"Wow. Have you briefed Ari?"

"Absolutely. She agrees that we should bring all this to the police very soon."

He handed me a tuna wrap and a bottle of mineral water. “Let’s have lunch.”

I was happy to pivot from land disputes to tuna.

“Listen, there’s something else I wanted to mention.” I pulled Sebastian Deschamps’s calling card out of my purse and placed it in on Derek’s desk. He picked it up and turned it over, examining it closely.

“Sebastian DesChamps. Again? What is this?”

“A calling card.”

“So I see. It’s just like the one that was in the box with the cameo pin, isn’t it?”

“Exactly.”

“But this one looks brand new.”

“It is.”

“I thought these things went out decades ago.”

“You’re right. They were popular at the turn of the nineteenth century.”

“Where did you get it?”

“It was left on the front porch of the main house on the estate.”

“Someone went to a lot of trouble to have it custom made,” he observed.

“Not necessarily. Actually, any ten-year-old kid with a laptop and printer could have made it.”

“Really?”

“I’ve had custom cards printed by vendors, of course. But I’ve also done it myself plenty of times if a client is pressed for time.”

“You would know.”

“There are programs online to craft the design if you want to print cards like this yourself. All you have to do is load your printer with heavy card stock paper, press print, and there they are. Each sheet easily separates into clean edge cards. I'm sure that's what we have here."

"I had no idea. Still, it would have to be someone who knows about Sophie and Sebastian. Who would even be aware of them?"

"To begin with," I explained, "the entire cast and crew of *Edge of Darkness*, and anyone else they may have told. Julien's been terribly interested in a backstory based on Sophie and Sebastian for both the soap and a Broadway play he's working on. Apparently, the story's been a topic of discussion at production meetings."

"Could it be a prop? Maybe someone simply dropped it."

"I doubt it. I don't think they've gone that far with the idea. But, I can certainly check with Aunt Tessa. Maybe I'll pay another visit to her on the *Edge of Darkness* set."

"That might not be a bad idea."

"Another thing. A reporter from a soap opera magazine, Natalie Summers from *Soap Opera Weekly*, told me she came across Sebastian's name while researching the Vander Horns's silk manufacturing company in Paterson. She's doing a feature on Aunt Tessa. I don't know where she got her information, but she's thorough to a fault."

"So, Sebastian's name is out there."

"Evidently, it can be found. If someone is looking for it, that is."

"But the question is, why would anyone look for it?"

"That's what I don't know. Is someone out there delusional enough to think that he is Sebastian DesChamps?"

Derek picked up the calling card again, scrutinizing it.

"Do you see how the top corner is folded in?" I asked.

"Yes, I do. Odd."

"Apparently, that was deliberate. I did some reading on calling card etiquette back in the day. Turning the corner inward like that meant that the card's owner delivered it personally."

"How did you unearth that piece of trivia?"

"Online. And believe me, I wish I hadn't found it. I hate the idea that someone's been lurking around the estate, looking for someone from my family."

"Have you checked the security cameras?"

"Ugh, you know how that goes. They'd probably just show a dark, grainy image of some random guy in a hoodie. Anyway, my aunt doesn't have direct access to the footage anymore."

"We could ask Jim Barclay. Worth a shot. Thing is, I can't understand why anyone would be running around impersonating someone from your past."

"Probably the same psycho who sent the package. I don't have to tell you that this is most unnerving. I'm a wreck."

"Lacey, I think you should report this to the police."

"No way. They already think I'm crazy."

"I insist. I'd feel better if you let them know."

"I suppose I could stop there on my way back to the shop."

"Great idea. Dinner tonight after work? Grimaldi's."

"Love to. Can I meet you there about five thirty?"

"Perfect. I have a late class tonight at Oakdale. See you there. Wait, one more thing. I was talking to Tom Pierce this morning. He said he got an anonymous call from someone inquiring about challenging the Vander Horn estate. He said the caller sounded irrational."

Julien immediately came to mind. "Strange."

"Completely. The estate was settled long ago. Tom said he made his staff aware, but he let it drop."

"Nothing shocks me anymore, Derek."

"I know what you mean. See you tonight."

* * *

Driving down Main Street to the Willow Bluffs Municipal Complex, I once again had the feeling that Chief Hennessey would think I was stark raving mad. I'm not sure what I would have thought if someone had told me a wild story about a mysterious package from a dead guy who also left his calling card on the front porch of a vacant old mansion. I was afraid that when I said it out loud it would sound even crazier.

As I pulled into the parking lot behind the police station, I immediately spotted a familiar looking, fifty-ish red-haired woman. I realized she was Gina Velasco's mother. Several years before she'd worked at Amanda's, a women's boutique in town where my mother and I frequently shopped. She got into her black Ford Escape and drove off. I wondered why she'd been to the police. Perhaps Gina's autopsy results were in. Maybe the *Gazette* would have some news soon, but as I got out of my VW and walked into the station, I was more concerned about the story I was about to tell.

I inhaled slowly. Inside the small waiting area, I could see the police receptionist through a thick plexiglass window. I stepped up to the counter and spoke to her through an intercom.

"I'm Lacey Langdon. I wonder if I could have a word with Chief Hennessey."

"Do you have an appointment?

"No, I don't. I just want to follow up on a previous report, if he has a couple of minutes."

"Lacey Langdon. One moment." She scanned the list on the counter in front of her. "Funny, we were going to call you this afternoon. It seems the chief would like a word with you, too."

She picked up the phone, most likely to call Chief Hennessey. She spoke briefly, then pointed to a door adjacent to the partition and buzzed me into the station.

Chief Hennessey met me inside. "Miss Langdon, what a coincidence. I wanted to speak with you today. Come into my office."

I followed him down a dimly lit hallway to his equally dismal office furnished with a stark gray metal desk, a matching credenza, file cabinets, and imitation leather chairs.

"Have a seat," he said, ushering me inside. "I'd like to clarify a few things about your statement on the Velasco case."

"Sure. Wasn't that Mrs. Velasco I just saw outside?"

He shuffled some paper on his desk, completely ignoring my question. Mortified, I realized I shouldn't have mentioned her. "Now that a couple of days have passed since Ms. Velasco's death, perhaps you remember something more," he said. "You witnessed the entire incident, correct?"

"Unfortunately, yes."

"In your previous statement, you said that Jeremy Ellis, Ron Valenti, a few other guests, and naturally Dr. Nash were all present."

"Correct."

"Anything to add? Anyone else?"

"There were several guests around, but I honestly can't remember exactly who they were. And Derek Conover was there once the paramedics arrived."

"You also stated that you heard Ms. Velasco order the Bloody Mary herself."

"That's right. She clearly indicated that she wanted a Bloody Mary with no clam juice because she was allergic. As you know, Jeremy complied. And let me add that Jeremy Ellis is absolutely above reproach."

"Thank you," he said in a distinctly sarcastic tone that made me cringe. "Think carefully," he went on. "Did you notice anything unusual?"

Besides Gina Velasco dropping dead at an engagement party?

"Specifically," he added, "did anyone else have access to Ms. Velasco's drink?"

Jeremy said the chief had asked him the same thing. I thought for a moment. "Access? Everyone near the bar, I suppose. To be honest, I wasn't paying much attention to her or her drink."

"Did she leave the drink sitting on the bar unattended?"

"I can't say for sure, but probably. Doesn't everyone? I didn't see anyone touch it, if that's what you're getting at."

"Okay. Thanks for your time. If anything else comes to you, anything at all, please give us a call."

"Certainly. If you don't mind, there was another matter I wanted to bring up. Another strange occurrence at the estate."

He listened politely as I told the tale of the mysterious calling card. He said he'd contact Jim Barclay about accessing the security tapes and also send a patrol car a few times a day to check the estate. There was nothing much more he could do, and, quite frankly, there was nothing more I expected.

"We'll be in touch," he said as I was leaving.

I returned to Letter Perfect for what was left of the afternoon. Exhausted and distracted, I didn't accomplish as much as

I hoped I would. Between my conversation with Jeremy, seeing Mrs. Velasco, and speaking with the chief, I had a mountain of information to process.

Jeremy planned to stay in the shop and order pizza for dinner to do some reading until it was time to leave for his class with Derek at Oakdale College later in the evening. By five fifteen, I was more than ready to relax at Grimaldi's with some pasta and a glass of cabernet.

"Don't forget to talk to Derek about your interview with Chief Hennessey this morning," I reminded him on my way out.

"Don't worry. I'm on it. See you tomorrow."

Derek was already at Grimaldi's waiting by the bar when I arrived at five thirty.

"Hey, just got here," he said. "The hostess should be right out."

As we waited to be seated, Mrs. Velasco walked in alone. *Twice in one day*, I said to myself. *Unreal.*

"Isn't that . . ." Derek whispered.

"Yes," I whispered back.

She acknowledged me with a forced smile. "Hello. You own the stationery store in town, right? Letter Perfect?"

"Yes. I'm Lacey Langdon. I believe we met through my mother several years ago. Mrs. Velasco, this is Derek Conover."

"I'm so sorry about your daughter," he said. "Such a tragic accident."

"It was no accident," Mrs. Velasco asserted.

Expecting a more somber reaction, Derek and I stood before her, stunned and speechless.

"My daughter was murdered," she continued. "And I'm quite certain I know who did it." Her sharp blue eyes shot daggers across the room. "Mark my words, I won't rest until the miserable snake pays."

"Takeout for Velasco," the bartender called.

Without another word, she pivoted, picked up her order, and vanished through Grimaldi's front door.

Derek and I looked at each other in utter astonishment.

Chapter Sixteen

"It's all right, Dyl. Be right there."

Dylan's early morning barking alerted me that someone was on the estate property. From my bedroom window, I spotted Derek walking back to his Prius from the cottage. My phone buzzed with a text from him.

just left a box on your porch for ginas mom
will get it to her this morning
thanks running late for court talk later
dont worry im on it

I grabbed my purse and quickly made my way from my bedroom to the front door. I let Dylan out as I retrieved the box Derek had brought over. During dinner last night, we'd thought of the perfect ruse that would give me a plausible reason to visit the Velasco house and talk further with Gina's mother. We decided Derek would gather the personal belongings she'd left at the town hall. Since I seemed to have the closest connection to Mrs. Velasco because of her friendship with my mother, he'd then give everything to me to bring to her home. Ari, Willow

Bluffs' mayor, would call her and let her know I was coming. It sounded like a viable plan. Even if I didn't learn anything new, I felt good about going over there. It was the right thing to do.

After the bombshell Mrs. Velasco had dropped at Grimaldi's, we were certain she was chomping at the bit to speak her mind. She had been adamant that Gina's death was no accident. If everything fell into place the way we'd planned, Derek and I both suspected she would open up to me. She had a story to tell. I just needed to give things a little push.

I took a quick look inside the box—just some miscellaneous personal items. Certainly nothing that would help with the investigation. Mrs. Velasco would look at everything more carefully. I sealed the box with packing tape.

"Be a good boy, Dyllie. No worries. Arthur will come by to take you out later."

Juggling the box and my purse, I walked to my Beetle parked in the carport. Arthur had already begun his gardening chores, sweeping leaves from the front walk.

"Need help, miss?"

"Thanks, Arthur. I'm fine."

Aunt Tessa and I couldn't have managed without him. He was our gardener, handyman, carpenter, dog-walker, and watchman. He'd spoken to Chief Hennessey a couple of times about seeing someone lurking around the property in the early morning hours, but whatever he thought he had seen never came to anything. He hadn't been able to identify anyone specific, and the surveillance tapes were too dark and grainy to be of any help.

Dead end.

* * *

I made the short drive from the estate to Mrs. Velasco's home on Monroe Drive. She lived just around the corner from Glenn Hartman's Quincy Street home. Perhaps a little too close for comfort.

I picked up the box, walked up the bluestone path, and rang the doorbell. Mrs. Velasco answered the door, looking understandably tired and drawn.

"Come in, Miss Langdon."

"Lacey, please."

"Lacey. Ari told me you'd be coming by."

"I wish there was something more I could do to help."

"It's been difficult."

"I can't even imagine."

"I feel terribly isolated. I've heard from some friends, but I'm afraid some are a bit standoff-ish. The investigation, you know."

"That's unfortunate." Still holding the box, I thought I'd change the direction of the conversation. "This is everything your daughter left at the town hall."

"Oh, yes, thank you. Just put it down on the club chair next to the sofa. I'm not sure when I'll be able to deal with it."

"I know it's been terrible for you, Mrs. Velasco."

"Call me Sandra. Would you like a cup of tea?"

"Oh, please, don't go to any trouble."

"No trouble. It's nice to have some company. Please, make yourself comfortable."

I took a seat on the royal blue velvet sofa.

"Maybe you could look through Gina's things for me," she continued. "I doubt you'll find anything very interesting. Ari said it was just some personal items from her desk. I'll be right back."

I reached for the box, tearing the tape as I opened it. She was correct. Confirming my prior observations, I didn't see anything significant in the box, but that wasn't the point. I was trying to make the most of my conversation with Mrs. Velasco, and I had the perfect opportunity. Looking more closely than I had earlier, I found a cosmetic bag, a hand mirror, brush, a pair of nude pantyhose, some old birthday cards, and assorted hair ties. Nothing out of the ordinary and certainly nothing revealing. A half-full bottle of *Femme Fatale* perfume, aptly named.

Mrs. Velasco returned from the kitchen carrying a tray and placed it on the cocktail table in front of the sofa. She poured our tea from a lovely rose-patterned porcelain pot into two matching china cups. I helped myself to milk and sugar.

"My husband died three years ago, so I've been alone here the past few days. I feel like I'm frozen in time. I have to hold off on making arrangements for Gina, you know, until they're finished with the autopsy."

"That must be so difficult."

"Unbearable, actually. You know, Gina was so close to getting away from all this."

"What do you mean?"

"She was all set to move into a beautiful apartment in Fort Lee. She was going to get a new job, start a new life for herself."

I couldn't bring myself to ask about the details of Gina's new, lucrative circumstances outright. I was trying to preserve some semblance of tact. "I didn't know."

"She couldn't wait to show it to me. She was supposed to take me over there next week."

"Very sad, indeed."

"I guess I'll have to get someone to break the lease."

"She had signed a lease?"

"Yes, just a few days before she . . ." Her voice cracked in mid-sentence.

"I'm so sorry. Breaking the lease shouldn't be a problem. Do you know where in Fort Lee she was going?"

"Yes, as a matter of fact I do. Three hundred Grand Street. Wonderful views of the bridge."

"I'm sure Derek Conover from the town council could help you with that. You met him last night."

"Yes, I know who he is. Gina often mentioned him."

"He has a law practice here in town."

"That's right. I'll get in touch with him. I'm sure there will be other loose ends. Gina had moved a few years ago. She was living with a man named George. It didn't work out, and she came back home. Poor Gina always seemed to get involved with the wrong sort."

"There's just no way of knowing sometimes."

"But this time she was finally going to be completely on her own. She was coming into some money. She said she'd been doing some freelance work apart from her work with the town."

"Interesting. What kind of work?" I gently asked.

"Oh, who knows? Gina never really talked about her work very much. I think it had something to do with real estate. She didn't have a license, but she always had her eye out for a shrewd deal."

"Something local?"

"I assume so. She said she was supposed to be getting a hefty finder's fee. She had actually gotten some other fees of some type lately. Payments, I heard her say once or twice. I didn't ask questions. More tea?"

Finder's fee. What had Gina been up to? "Yes, I'd love to. Thank you." I wanted to prolong my stay.

Her hand shook as she lifted the delicate porcelain pot and refilled my cup.

"I wish I'd known your daughter better," I went on. "I only knew her by sight at Willow Bluffs High."

"She was a real go-getter. I'm devastated. I haven't slept. I haven't even been able to go into her room yet. Everything's exactly as she left it."

"Sandra, you said last night that you didn't think her death was an accident."

"Well, maybe I was overreacting a bit. I get so enraged at times. But in my heart I know I'm right. I have to put the blame on someone. It was so sudden. Unlikely. You were there."

"Everyone was in shock. We all felt so helpless."

"She's never without her epinephrine pen. It doesn't add up."

I nodded in agreement.

"As I said before, Gina always seemed to get involved with, well, I guess I'd have to say, losers. Ron Valenti was no exception. I couldn't stand that guy from day one. Made my skin crawl. He's a miserable snake, and I'd bet my right arm that he killed her."

"You've spoken with Chief Hennessey?"

"Of course. Sometimes, I think the whole thing may have had something to do with that deal she was working on. A mother's intuition. Well, that and the fact that Ron Valenti is just no good. I'm hoping the police will turn up something. But then, you know, there is that Hartman woman."

"Glenn Hartman's wife?"

"She had it in her head that Gina had an affair with her husband. Ridiculous. She was insanely jealous of Gina. Maybe she had something to do with all of this."

"If I know Chief Hennessey, he'll leave no stone unturned."

"For now, all I can do is wait for the autopsy results. I'm hoping for news later today."

"The police are super-efficient. They'll be in touch as soon as they have the report."

"They tell me the toxicology tests take some time."

"You're an incredibly strong woman, Sandra. Thank you so much for the tea." I got up.

She walked me to the front door.

"What a lovely portrait of Gina," I said, noticing the painting in the foyer.

"She was my only child, you know."

"I'm so sorry. Her beauty was truly a gift."

"Yes. Or a curse."

"If there's anything you need, don't hesitate."

"Thank you, Lacey. You've been so kind. Stop by any time."

I had an empty feeling as I pulled away from the Velasco house. Two senseless murders within two weeks. Unspeakable. Sandra Velasco had given me plenty of information to unpack. I had the feeling something sinister had been brewing. I couldn't wait to run it all by Derek.

As I made my way down Monroe Drive, a Willow Bluffs black and white squad car passed me heading in the opposite direction. I took a second look. I was sure Chief Hennessey was driving. Checking my rear-view mirror, I noticed that he turned into Mrs. Velasco's driveway. Something was up. I was sorry I'd left.

Downtown Willow Bluffs seemed busy for a Tuesday morning. As I pulled into the lot behind Letter Perfect, I noticed the Bean's lot was packed. I'd pick up coffee later after things had settled down. When I walked into my shop, Jeremy was just finishing up a call.

"Hey, Lacey. Two more party inquiries already came in. I booked the appointments for today. A wedding and a bar mitzvah."

"Great. You know, I'm shocked. That's four since the Pierce catastrophe."

"I guess it's true. There's no such thing as bad publicity."

My day was set. Besides the two appointments for major events, I planned to organize inventory for the holiday season. Before long, orders for personalized holiday cards would begin coming in, and then there would be private and business holiday parties, undoubtedly more than enough income to carry Letter Perfect through the end of the year. Talking with Derek about my visit with Sandra would have to wait until evening. He was tied up in court.

The day flew by. I finally got around to going next door for coffee for Jeremy and me around closing time. When I returned from the Bean with my latte and Jeremy's Americano, I saw that Natalie Summers was waiting for me.

"Natalie, this is a surprise," I said, placing Jeremy's coffee on the counter beside him.

"What a lovely shop. Listen, I've got a bit of a scoop."

"What's up? Something about the history of the estate? Or the DesChamps family?"

"No, no, nothing like that. I've heard from a very reliable source that Chief Hennessey will be holding a press conference a bit later about the Gina Velasco case."

"Press conference? Really? How do you know?"

Jeremy, sipping his Americano, listened intently.

"My college roommate works at the *County Record*'s city desk, and she received an alert."

"Interesting. I wonder if Gina Velasco's autopsy results are in. A press conference is rather unusual around here," I said.

"Not in a case like this one. There's been so much interest. I mean, the second death in two weeks. They apparently want to release whatever they have all at once and deal with the press head on rather than field questions for days. The reporters at the *County Record* and *Star Ledger* have been buzzing."

"Makes sense."

"My old roommate says there's even been some speculation that Velasco's and Hartman's deaths may be related."

"It does kind of make you think. What time is the press conference?" I asked.

She glanced at her watch. "In about a half an hour. Six o'clock. At police headquarters. Plenty of time for tomorrow's early editions. Want to ride over with me now?"

"I don't know. I'm not exactly a card-carrying member of the press."

"You'll be with me. You'll be fine," she insisted.

"True. Jeremy, are you interested?" I asked.

"No, thanks," he said. "It's all yours. Haven't heard from the chief all day, and that's just fine with me. You go ahead. I'll close up."

"I'll be back later to pick up my car," I said.

As we got into Natalie's white Toyota, I wondered about her unusual interest in Willow Bluffs. I understood her reasons for learning all she could about the Vander Horn estate for her article on Aunt Tessa, but I thought her focus on the Velasco case was odd.

We arrived at the town hall complex in two minutes, and we were immediately directed to the conference room at police headquarters. A long metal table had been pushed forward to accommodate rows of folding chairs and a podium. We sat down in the back of the room.

By the time Chief Hennessey and the medical examiner came in at six o'clock, about thirty reporters had appeared. The chief immediately stepped up to the podium.

"Good evening, ladies and gentlemen. I'm Police Chief Paul Hennessey of the Willow Bluffs Police Department. Joining me is the Bergen County medical examiner Dr. Allan Morgan. Given the recent homicide of Willow Bluffs Councilman Glenn Hartman, there has been considerable interest in this most unusual case, the death of Ms. Regina Velasco.

"This evening I'll make a brief statement regarding the results of Ms. Velasco's autopsy, performed by Dr. Morgan, along with the results of the Bergen County forensics lab's analysis of a drink, a Bloody Mary cocktail, consumed by Ms. Velasco minutes before she died. Copies of the respective agencies' releases will be available for you."

The chief shuffled his notes as he continued, "Dr. Allan Morgan determined that Ms. Velasco died from severe anaphylactic shock caused by ingesting an allergen known as tropomyosin commonly found in shellfish. Tropomyosin is a protein which can cause paralytic shellfish poisoning, or PSP, and ultimately, anaphylactic shock in those who are highly allergic to shellfish, as was the case with Ms. Velasco. The county's forensics lab determined that an alcoholic beverage consumed by her shortly before her death contained clam juice. Within minutes, she suffered rapid swelling of the face, neck, and throat, which caused shock and the cessation of breathing. EMTs, who arrived promptly, were unable to revive her with mouth-to-mouth respiration and repeated shocks from a defibrillator."

He looked at Dr. Morgan who nodded in approval before he went on. "I'll take a few questions," he said, assessing the pool of reporters. "Yes?" The chief pointed to a young female reporter in the first row.

"Chief Hennessey, was—"

"Please, state your name and publication," he instructed.

"Marisa Morales from the *County Record*. Was Ms. Velasco aware of her shellfish allergy?"

"Yes."

"And just to follow up, had she ever been prescribed epinephrine?"

"Yes."

"And was she carrying an epinephrine pen the night she died?"

"I can't comment on that, as it's part of our ongoing investigation."

"Let me rephrase," the reporter pressed on. "Would an epinephrine pen have prevented her death?"

Chief Hennessey leaned toward Dr. Morgan, who whispered an answer. "Yes. Most likely she would have responded to the drug," the chief replied. He then pointed to a male reporter in the back of the room.

"Joe Bergman from the *Willow Bluffs Gazette*. Did the EMTs administer epinephrine?"

Again, the chief looked to Dr. Morgan, and then stepped away from the microphone so the doctor could respond. "Yes," Dr. Morgan assessed, "but, unfortunately, at that point, it was too late. She had deteriorated rapidly."

"On the left side, by the window," the chief acknowledged.

"Allison Gregg, the *Newark Star-Ledger*. Do you suspect foul play?"

"The matter is currently under investigation."

"One more question. Chief, why would she have consumed something that contained clam juice?"

"We hope to have more information on that at a later date."

"Did she eat or drink anything else?"

"I'll defer to Dr. Morgan on that," Chief Hennessey said.

Dr. Morgan stepped in front of the microphone again. "The autopsy I performed showed that her stomach contained no other contents. The remains of the drink that were found in her stomach and the portion of the drink itself that was taken from the scene were both analyzed and found to contain clam juice and, as a result, tropomyosin. For the record, tropomyosin is found in all crustaceans and mollusks, and, therefore, any foods made with them, chowders, bisques, lobster entrees, clam dishes, etc., and all would be deadly to anyone highly allergic, such as Ms. Velasco."

I wondered how much the police were going to divulge about Gina's evening at the Pierces' party. Maybe if pressed, Hennessey would say more. I tapped Natalie on the shoulder and leaned in. "Ask him if Gina had a date for the evening."

She promptly raised her hand.

"In the back," the chief said, noticing my presence beside Natalie.

"Natalie Summers. *Soap Weekly*. Did Ms. Velasco have a date for the evening?"

"Yes."

"Sir, can you tell us his name?"

"Not at this time. In the second row."

"Jonathan Green. *Palisades Life*. May we assume Ms. Velasco's death is being treated as a homicide?"

"No, you may not assume anything. And, once again, I can't comment on the specifics of the investigation at this time."

Jonathan Green immediately followed up. "Do you have any persons of interest?"

"When will you have more information?" someone else called out.

Chief Hennessey clearly looked as though he had heard enough. "Thank you, ladies and gentlemen. You can pick up the press releases from the medical examiner and the forensics lab on the way out."

With that, the press conference abruptly came to a close.

"What they're not saying is probably a whole lot more interesting than what they are saying," I said to Natalie.

"Agreed. I thought they might say something about the town councilman's murder that occurred on the Vander Horn estate. My readers are interested in anything that has to do with Tessa Langdon Vander Horn."

"I guess we'll just have to wait for further information to be released."

"Can I drop you off at your shop?" Natalie asked.

"You know, I think I'll walk back. It's just a few blocks."

"Are you sure? It's awfully dark."

"The air will do me good."

"If you say so. Oh, I see someone I know from the *Paterson Herald*. Did you know that's one of the oldest newspapers in this part of New Jersey? Goes back to the 1820s. You should check out their archives sometime. Fascinating. There's quite a bit on your family."

"I had no idea."

"Of course, I'll be including background on your family for my feature on your aunt. I'll send you the name of my contact over there."

"I'd appreciate that. Thanks so much for letting me tag along."

As soon as I exited the town hall, I was glad I'd decided to walk back to Letter Perfect. The cool, crisp autumn air refreshed me as it touched my face. But in spite of my invigorating walk, my mind kept drifting to Dr. Morgan's graphic autopsy report and the horror of Gina's death. The image of her lying lifeless on the Pierces' great room floor, her pale skin, blue lips, and grotesquely swollen face haunted me. I couldn't get it out of my head. If only she'd brought her epinephrine pen.

I continued a few blocks down Main Street, past Grimaldi's, and through the heart of town. Normally, there wasn't much pedestrian traffic in Willow Bluffs, and tonight was no different; however, I suddenly became aware of the faint sound of footsteps on the sidewalk behind me. They grew louder and edged closer, and then whoever was behind me rapidly picked up the pace. I walked faster. I didn't dare turn around. My heart racing, I couldn't imagine why I was being followed. Practically running once I spotted my car parked next to Letter Perfect, I reached into my purse for my key fob and cell phone. Then the sound of the footsteps behind me suddenly stopped. In one quick motion, I hit the unlock button on my key fob, opened the car door, and slid into the front seat.

As I started the car, I noticed something on the windshield. It looked like a small envelope, possibly a note. Was it a trick? A ruse to get me out of the car? I knew I had to retrieve it or risk losing it. I quickly stepped out of the car, reached over the windshield, grabbed the note, and then slipped back into the front seat, immediately slamming and locking the car door. My hands trembling, I placed the envelope next to me on the passenger seat and pulled out of the lot onto Main Street. I drove straight to Willow Street and parked in the carport on the estate. I reached for the envelope first thing and opened it. My worst nightmare. A calling card. Again. With a message written in meticulous vintage script.

Sebastian DesChamps
Always beware of darkness, my dear
S.

With my hand in a chokehold around my phone, I ran into the cottage, threw my purse on the sofa, and texted Derek.

i think im being stalked

Chapter Seventeen

"Call me crazy, but I don't want to be the next one in Willow Bluffs to turn up dead," I told Derek. He'd arrived at the cottage minutes after he received my text message.

"It'll be okay," he offered, not sounding terribly convincing.

"Look, I'm still shaking," I said, holding my hands out in front of me. I fidgeted on the sofa with Dylan at my feet.

"You're aunt's not here?"

"No, she's been staying in the city. Crazy shooting schedule."

"You need to relax."

I shot him a sarcastic look. "Yeah. Thanks."

"Just trying to help. Let me get you a drink."

"Okay, if you insist. There's a bottle of chardonnay in the fridge. I think. Or maybe it's pinot grigio." I held "Sebastian's" calling card in my hand, flicking the corner with my fingernail and staring at it in disbelief.

Derek returned with two goblets and the bottle of chardy, pouring half a glass for each of us. "Take a few sips," he said. "It'll calm you down."

"I'm not crazy. Really, I'm not."

He removed his horn-rimmed glasses, rested them on the coffee table, and rubbed his eyes. "Of course you're not. But everyone's been on edge around here lately."

"Granted. However, I can assure you that those footsteps behind me and this bizarre note weren't figments of my imagination." I tossed the calling card onto the coffee table.

"So, there's no chance at all that someone was just walking through town right behind you?"

"Nope. No chance. He—or she—was following much too closely. Definitely deliberate. Not to mention intimidating."

"And you didn't get any glimpse of whoever it was at all?"

"None. The footsteps mysteriously disappeared as soon as I got to my car."

"Strange. So you think whoever left the calling card was the same person who was following you?"

"Absolutely. It was as if they wanted to make sure I got the message."

"They must have put the card on your windshield earlier."

"I'm sure. And they must have known I was at the press conference."

"Maybe Jeremy saw something."

"I doubt it. He would have let me know. This calling card stuff is beyond weird."

"Make sure you ask him, just in case."

"I will."

Derek picked up the calling card and studied it. "You've got to let the police know."

"Ugh. They were so patronizing when I called them after Sophie's brooch was delivered," I recalled.

"This is different. It's personal. Threatening."

Threatening. Intimidating. I hated those words. "Yeah. I know. Last time I called the police they said they were stepping up their patrols around the estate. I don't know what more they could possibly do."

"Tell you what. I'll call Chief Hennessey myself and tell him what's going on."

"If you insist."

"I do."

I took a couple of sips of chardonnay. "Derek, have I somehow made myself a target?"

He shrugged. "I can't imagine how—or why."

"What about the calling card stuff? Someone out there must be obsessed with Sebastian DesChamps."

"Could be. But that is as strange as it gets."

"And completely twisted. A couple of weeks ago, I never even knew that calling cards were a 'thing.' Now, I have one of Sebastian's originals that came in the package with Sophie's brooch. Then, there's the replica that was left on the porch of the main house, and the one I got tonight. Who would do this? Why me?"

"We'll get to the bottom of it," Derek promised.

"Hope so. By the way, did I tell you Mrs. Velasco brought up Glenn Hartman's wife's name when we were talking?"

"Wow! What did she say?"

"Just that Mrs. Hartman was convinced Gina was involved with Glenn, and that she was apparently insanely jealous of Gina."

"So, she kind of left the door open that someone other than Ron may have been responsible for Gina's demise."

"Exactly."

"I'm not sure Angela had opportunity, though."

"She didn't. She didn't attend the Pierces' party." I got up off the sofa to stretch my legs. "I need to change into some sweats. Be right back."

"Meanwhile, I'll call the chief."

"Thanks. When you're done, would you order a pizza from Aldo's? I don't have anything in the fridge."

"Anything on it?"

"Yeah. Half pepperoni and half mushroom."

He laughed. "You read my mind."

On the way to my bedroom, I glanced back at Derek. He had become a good friend, maybe even something more. Amazingly, he looked exactly the same as he did when we were at Willow Bluffs High School together, still boyishly charming with long blonde hair brushing over his shirt collar, an angular face, and deeply set brown eyes. It was such a comfort to have him with me after all I'd been through. I felt like he was looking out for me, and there weren't many people I could count on to do that these days.

I didn't bother to listen to Derek's end of his conversation when he called Chief Hennessey. In fact, I envisioned the chief rolling his eyes the moment Derek told him about my strange encounter. But Derek was correct. Telling the police was the right thing to do, even if I sounded like the town crank. I pulled my favorite gray sweatpants and Fordham sweatshirt out of the bottom drawer of my dresser and quickly changed. I instantly felt some of the tension release, but I knew it would take some time to recover from the uneasiness I was feeling, and I wouldn't be able to breathe until everything was resolved.

When I returned to the living room, Derek was sitting in the club chair in front of the fireplace scratching Dylan behind his ears. They looked incredibly comfortable with each other.

"How'd your call go?" I asked.

"The pizza will be here in fifteen minutes."

"Funny. You know what I meant."

"Okay. The police may want to speak with you."

"Yeah, right."

"Aw, come on, don't be cynical, Lacey. As you suspected, for now, they said they'd step up surveillance of the estate."

"I'm being completely realistic. Do they think I'm nuts?"

"I did not get that impression. Not at all."

There had been something else on my mind, something that had been worrying me ever since the package to Sophie had been sent to the cottage. "Derek, should I be worried about Aunt Tessa?"

"I don't know. I wouldn't alarm her. But you could talk to her manager. What's his name again?"

"LaFontaine."

"Maybe make him aware of everything. He's close to her, right?"

"That's an understatement. Julien makes the Secret Service look like slackers. You know, you make a good point. I think I'll go into the city tomorrow and talk to him at his office."

"Good idea to do it sooner rather than later."

I wasn't completely sure whether Julien was part of the solution or part of the problem. Derek would have been appalled if he'd known that Julien was Annabella's son and Sophie's grandson. As much as I wanted to tell him, I was sworn to secrecy.

Dylan suddenly ran to the front door, barking wildly just ahead of the doorbell.

"The pizza already? That was fast," I said.

Derek opened the door to reveal Officer Jane Kowalski, looking characteristically stoic, standing on the front porch.

"Good evening. The chief asked me to follow up on the incident you reported."

"Yes. Thanks for coming by, Officer. Lacey's right here," Derek said, ushering her inside.

I got up from the sofa to greet her. "I hope I'm not making too much of this," I said.

"We always follow up." Officer Kowalski pulled her police notebook out of her back pocket and glanced at some prior notes. "As I understand it, you were followed on Main Street and a note of some kind was left on your car."

"Correct."

"What time was this?"

"About seven this evening. They followed me for about six blocks or so. Between Monroe and Robertson. I was truly alarmed. I mean, it's not like there's a lot of foot traffic in town at that time. Everything's closed. My car was parked at my shop, and I jumped right in. I have no clue where they went after. They just seemed to disappear."

"You said they. More than one person?"

"Oh, no. 'They' meaning I don't know for sure if it was a he or a she."

"I see. And you mentioned Monroe Drive. Any other details? Think carefully," Officer Kowalski pressed.

"Nothing comes to mind. I was basically frozen."

"Any description?"

"Sorry, but once again, no. I didn't see anyone. But his—or her—presence was unmistakable." I took a few steps to the coffee table, leaned down, and picked up the calling card. "This was left on my windshield." I pointed out, handing it to her.

She examined the card closely. "'Always beware of darkness, my dear,'" she read aloud. Then she repeated it slowly and deliberately, making it sound even more menacing. "Any idea what it means?"

"No idea at all. I wish I could get into the head of whoever is doing this, but I simply cannot."

"Any disgruntled customers recently?"

"No, nothing like that." At least, I didn't think so. This seemed like something much different than that.

"Mind if I take the card with me? You know, at this point, I'm sure a photo will do." She pulled out her cell phone and snapped a picture of each side.

"Was anyone here at the cottage at the time?"

"No one, Officer. My aunt has been in the city all week."

"If you recall anything else, Miss Langdon, please contact us immediately. Even a minor detail could be important."

"Will do."

"Tonight there was an attempted break-in at a residence on Monroe Drive," she reported.

"Oh, no. That's where Gina Velasco's mother lives. I was just over there earlier today."

"Really?"

"Was it the Velasco house?" I wondered out loud.

Officer Kowalski looked puzzled at my concern. "Why do you ask?"

"I don't know. Just a funny feeling."

"We're investigating."

Derek had been listening intently to our exchange. "You said 'attempted.'"

"Yes," she explained. "The perpetrator did not gain entry."

"That's good to hear," I said.

"A window was broken and the lock on the back door was damaged. Tripped the alarm. Must have scared him away."

"Do you think the two incidents—the person following Lacey and the attempted burglary—are related?" Derek asked.

"Like I said, we're investigating," she told us, nervously tapping her pen on her notebook.

I realized Officer Kowalski clearly wasn't giving up any definitive information. "What's going on in this town?" I wondered.

"Be assured, we're increasing our patrols in the area of the estate, Ms. Langdon. And we'll be contacting Jim Barclay about monitoring the surveillance cameras around the property."

"I appreciate that."

She snapped her notebook closed and stowed it in her back pocket, indicating that she had completed her business with us. "And, if there's anything else, anything at all, do get in touch." She started out the door and then turned around. "Oh, one more thing. Looks like a couple of spotlights are out in the back. Better get those replaced."

"Absolutely. I'll get Arthur on that first thing tomorrow. Thank you, Officer," I said.

Just as Officer Kowalski was leaving, the deliveryman from Aldo's Pizza approached the front door with our order.

"On me," Derek said, reaching for his wallet.

"You're too quick." I carried the pizza, along with the brown bag sitting on top, into the living room and placed them on the coffee table. "Let's eat right here," I suggested.

"Fine with me."

"What else did you get?" I asked, opening the bag. "But be warned—if there's a card from Sebastian DesChamps in here, I'm going to scream."

"Just a Caesar salad."

"Oh, excellent! Derek, would you grab a couple of plates? In the cabinet over the dishwasher. Forks are in the drawer next to the sink."

He sat down next to me on the floor. "Pepperoni or mushroom to start?"

"Mushroom."

"Me, too," I said, serving us both a slice. "Just a hunch," I speculated, "but I don't think the burglary attempt on Monroe is related to what happened to me. Think about it. Why would some nut job running around town with Sebastian DesChamps's calling cards be interested in the Velasco house? But, for whatever reason, I do think it was the Velasco house that was targeted."

Derek shook his head. "I don't know what to think any more, but I agree that the botched break-in could have been a red herring. Maybe we'll stumble on something that will connect everything. I have a gut feeling that the real estate deal Gina's mom told you about may be a key."

"We need to find out more about that. Glenn Hartman was trying to pull in the reins on the property development. Particularly for commercial use. Gina could have killed him, you know, to put a stop to his interference once and for all."

"Yes, but Ron would have had motive as well," Derek proposed. "And Jim's suspicion that he was skimming money from the company was real. I hope he's hired a forensic accountant."

"Me, too," I said in agreement. "He's a smart guy. I'm sure he's taking every step."

"He will for his own sake, and the sake of his company," Derek said.

"Could we be overlooking Jim Barclay as a suspect? He wouldn't be the first guy to kill to protect his business," I noted.

Derek shook his head. "At this point, I don't think we should discount anyone."

"You know, we could be completely off base regarding Glenn," I admitted. "His wife knew he'd been carrying on with Gina. What's that saying? 'Hell hath no fury like a woman scorned?'"

"So true. I need to talk with Angela Hartman again." Derek laughed. "It always pays to live clean. It's boring, but definitely safer. I think I'll try the pepperoni next."

"Go for it. Don't forget, Gina was coming into money, supposedly. So, I was thinking—what if this financial arrangement had been an ongoing thing and she'd already received some cash from a real estate deal—shady or legit. More likely shady. And someone tried to break in to look for the money."

"Plausible. You have to get back into the Velasco house and take a real good look around," Derek advised.

"That will take some doing."

"I have faith in you."

We lingered, sipping wine and talking, for more than an hour in the living room. I figured whoever had followed me was long gone, especially with the police presence around the estate. I knew I'd be fine. I'd set the house alarm as a precaution and let our caretaker, Arthur, know that the police would be increasing security. After such a long, trying day, my energy had been depleted.

"Are you sure you'll be alright here alone?" Derek asked.

"Absolutely. Don't worry. Dylan's got my back."

Derek didn't look reassured.

"Tell you what," I promised. "I still have my old softball bat from high school. I'll keep it next to my bed tonight."

Fortunately, I didn't need the bat.

* * *

The next morning, I headed to Sandra Velasco's house first thing. That is, first thing after calling Arthur to ask him to replace the spotlights that were out facing the East Lawn. That had me very spooked. Thinking about the Velascos as I was on my way to Monroe Drive, I hoped I would learn more about Gina's business dealings, but I was also genuinely concerned about Sandra. When I arrived, she had just brought a box of newspapers out to the curb for recycling and was on her way back inside the house. She turned when she heard my car pull in the driveway.

"Lacey! I was going to call you. Do come in."

"I'm on my way into the city," I explained. "Is everything okay? I heard there was a break-in nearby last night."

"It was my house. What else could go wrong?"

"Oh, no. I was afraid of that. Is everything okay?"

"Barely. I've just started making the arrangements for Gina's funeral. And now this. So much to worry about."

"I'm sorry."

"I can't imagine why anyone would want to break into this house. They didn't actually get in. Just did some damage."

"Did you or Gina have anything of value? Jewelry? Cash? Or could Gina have had something you didn't know about?"

"I suppose Gina could have. I finally went into her room last night and took a look around. Come, I'll show you."

I followed her through the living room and down a hallway to Gina's bedroom. I noticed clothes tossed on the bed, shoes kicked on the floor, her makeup bag on her dresser. Everything looked as if she could walk through the door any minute.

"Look at this," Sandra said, pointing out a legal pad on Gina's desk with a list of a dozen or so dates. There were check marks next to the dates that had passed. Gina had clearly been keeping a record of something, and she was very careful not to reveal anything about it.

"Sandra, you said yesterday she was expecting some money. Maybe she had already received part of it."

"Perhaps. But it's beyond me why anyone would be interested in this."

"Do you mind if I take a quick photo of the list she made? Perhaps the dates will mean something to Derek. He worked rather closely with Gina."

"Go right ahead."

I snapped a couple of pictures with my phone. "Is there anything at all I can do for you, Sandra?"

"I'm afraid not. Thanks for coming by. Most people around here couldn't care less."

"I don't know about that. I think they just don't know what to do or say. Please, reach out if you need anything."

I got into my Beetle and headed for the George Washington Bridge. My visit with Sandra Velasco hadn't taken very long, but we now had what looked like a real clue. I was pleased to be getting an early start on the short drive into Manhattan. Luckily, traffic on the West Side Highway was light as I drove toward midtown. Still jittery, I hadn't quite put the previous day's incidents behind me. I kept looking in my rear-view mirror, nervous that I might be followed once again. I parked in my usual garage on West Forty-Fourth Street, and once I started walking through Times Square, I felt safely invisible in the crowds of tourists.

Julien's management firm, LaFontaine Creative Arts Agency, took up the entire twenty-fifth floor of Two Times Square. I wasn't completely sure why, but I felt compelled to check up on him. I hadn't called ahead to let him know I was coming. I wanted to keep it casual or perhaps I wanted to catch him off guard. I thought I'd say I was in town and thought I'd stop in. He was always in his office in the morning and then headed to the *Edge of Darkness* studio around eleven when they began taping. Kelly, his longtime receptionist, ushered me into his private office as soon as I arrived.

"Ah, Lacey," Julien greeted me, standing up as I entered his office. "To what do I owe the honor?"

"I was in Times Square to get some theater tickets, and I thought I'd stop by."

"Lovely. Do sit down. Anything I can do for you? You know I always have plenty of connections for Broadway tickets."

Impeccably dressed in a gray tweed jacket and perfectly tailored trousers, he cut a dashing figure. I'd known him most of my life, and he never seemed to age. His silver-gray hair and chiseled features gave him a look that was timeless. "Thanks, Julien, but I'm all set. I did want to mention a couple of things, however. Aunt Tessa's birthday is coming up in a couple of days, and I'm thinking of planning a small dinner party in Willow Bluffs. Just us. At the cottage." I thought I sounded convincing enough.

"Splendid, dear. You know Tessa always comes first."

"Please, keep the eleventh open. I'll be in touch."

"Absolutely. I'll get the birthday girl there. No worries." He cocked an eyebrow. "Anything else?"

I hesitated for a fraction of a second and then dove in. "There is something else . . ."

I gave Julien a detailed recap of the entire ordeal: the mysterious flowers on Sophie's grave, which he recalled; the gentleman's vintage coat; the package that was delivered to Sophie; the calling cards that were left at the manor house and on my car; how I'd been followed in town.

Julien shifted nervously in his chair but looked genuinely concerned. "I had no idea. Sophie and Sebastian must be more well known than we realize. What an ordeal for you, Lacey. I knew, of course, of the two deaths in Willow Bluffs. A murder and a suspected murder, correct?"

"Yes. That's right."

"That woman who they think may have been murdered—what was her name?"

"Gina. Gina Velasco."

"I remember her from Glenn Hartman's funeral and, of course, from the Pierces' party," Julien said. "A bit of a tart, I dare say, was she not?"

"Yes, you could say that. Somehow, I think she may hold the key to everything that's been going on around town."

"Interesting," Julien said.

"I wanted to bring you up to date, but I didn't want to alarm Aunt Tessa. She's not aware of everything, you know."

"I understand. Most unusual."

"And disturbing."

"Mum's the word," Julien promised. "And don't worry about your aunt. She comes from good stock. She's as tough as she is beautiful. I'll keep an eye on things from here. I run interference for her all the time."

"I know you do, Julien."

"If I think it's necessary, I won't hesitate to hire security."

"Thank you. I hoped you'd say that."

"Would you like to walk over to the studio with me?"

"Actually, I don't want Aunt Tessa to know I was here. Besides, I really do have to get back to the shop."

Julien's secretary buzzed him. "Yes?"

"Miss Vander Horn is here," she announced.

"Oh, no," I blurted out. "Now what?"

"I'll handle it," Julien assured me. "Follow my lead."

Aunt Tessa breezed into Julien's office, clearly surprised to see me. "Lacey, I didn't know you were coming in."

"Just a last-minute thing, Tessa," Julien explained. "She had to sign some beneficiary forms for the royalties on the new syndication agreement. Time is of the essence."

"I see."

I wasn't sure she was buying it.

"Today's taping is delayed till one, Julien," she announced. "I thought we'd have lunch at Sardi's."

"An offer I couldn't possibly refuse, Sophie."

Sophie, I thought.

Aunt Tessa shook her head. "You've been working too hard again, Julien."

"Everything's for you, Tessa. You know that."

Turning to me, she said, "Lacey, dear, you must join us."

"Thanks, Aunt T. That's very tempting, but I'm afraid I have to get back to the shop."

"Ah. Pity." I noticed something skeptical in her tone.

"Another time for sure, Aunt T." I kissed her cheek.

"Sorry to summon you here on such short notice, Lacey. But I'm relieved we could take care of that little contract detail right away."

"Never a problem, Julien," I said.

I exhaled as I exited his office and walked to the elevator bank. As I left the building, I felt I had succeeded in alerting Julien to the possible threat of danger; unfortunately, I might have inadvertently aroused some suspicion in Aunt Tessa.

Once outside, I found Times Square was even more jammed than it had been earlier. That was nothing new. I didn't mind. I felt happily anonymous, lost in the crowd. Clutching my purse under my arm as I snaked my way through the swarm of people, I felt my phone vibrate. I slowed my pace as I took a look. A text had come in from Derek.

still in the city?
just leaving walking to my car
good you need to get back asap
whats up
ron valenti was arrested and charged with the murder of gina velasco

Chapter Eighteen

I made it to Letter Perfect by ten thirty. Jeremy, seated behind the counter, looked up from his laptop as soon as I walked in.

"I thought you'd never get here. Have you heard?"

"I did. Derek texted."

"Best news ever. I finally feel like I'm off the hook."

"I don't think you were ever actually a suspect, Jeremy. They knew you were just the bartender mixing drink after drink."

"Still," he remarked.

"Yeah, I get it. I suppose I'd feel the same way."

I noticed Jeremy refreshed his laptop screen a couple of times, looking intently at what came up. "Here it is," he announced. "Finally. The press release is up on the WBPD website. Listen to this—'The Willow Bluffs Police Department reports that detectives obtained a warrant and subsequently arrested Ronald D. Valenti of Willow Bluffs, New Jersey, for the murder of Regina Velasco. Valenti is currently in the custody of the Bergen County Sheriff's Office. Charges for first-degree murder and attempted burglary are pending.'"

"Wow. It's official."

"Wait," he remarked, frowning. "Attempted burglary? Is that a joke?"

"No, not at all. They must think he's the one who tried to break into the Velasco home last night. This will be all over town in no time."

"Are you kidding? It already is."

I noticed an incoming message on my phone. Derek.

town council emergency meeting

ok heading over to the paterson herald soon looking for info on the vander horns especially sophie

cool talk later

"I'll bet there'll be other charges coming. Probably something relating to the development of Aunt Tessa's property," I stated. "Just a hunch."

"Wild. Well, he's totally done."

Jess suddenly burst in like a tidal wave. "I need to take refuge. The Bean is a circus. The entire town has gone mad. I brought a latte for you, Lacey, and Jeremy's Americano. On me."

"Thanks. I can use this," I said, taking a couple of gulps. "You have no idea."

"Awesome," Jeremy agreed.

"Just when you think things can't get any worse in this town! Do they think Valenti killed Glenn Hartman, too?" Jess wanted to know.

"Doesn't sound like it," I said.

"So, two different murderers? Who would have thought? Right here in Willow Bluffs. Unbelievable," Jess said, shaking her head.

"Yeah, and that means Glenn's killer is still out there. Scary stuff," Jeremy observed.

So many unanswered questions and strange occurrences, I thought. I didn't know why it suddenly seemed so compelling, but Natalie had told me to check out the archives at the *Paterson Herald*, and I figured there was no time like the present. If history truly repeated itself, maybe I'd come across some clues about the Vander Horns's illustrious past—maybe even something about the elusive Annabella. No one could account for her after she had given birth to Julien. "Listen guys, I don't mean to be rude, but I have to run out again."

"But you just got here," Jeremy protested.

"I know. I have to drive into Paterson, and traffic should be light right now." I chugged what was left of my latte, grabbed my purse, and headed for the door. "I'll be back in no time."

Jess and Jeremy shot each other a sideways glance. "Want company?" Jess offered.

"I'll be okay," I assured her, heading out to my VW.

She shrugged, looking disappointed.

Not surprisingly, all day I had been oddly distracted by what had happened in town the night before. Maybe that had been the point. Someone could have been trying to scare me, throw me off the scent, and keep me from getting any cozier with Sandra Velasco and what she might tell me. Something was inexplicably out of kilter, and I felt uneasy as I sailed down Route 80 into Market Street in Paterson. I parked in a lot that served the *Paterson Herald*'s offices. Maybe I was destined to find some clues inside.

I took the elevator down to the *Herald*'s newspaper morgue in the basement. *Morgue*, I thought to myself. So fitting. I couldn't seem to get away from death. I walked into the depressing, cavernous area, which was actually nothing more than a huge storage room with gray metal shelving and fluorescent overhead lighting that cast eerie shadows on the grimy, dull beige walls. A gray-haired sixty-ish lady sat at the reception desk in front of the stacks.

"May I help you?"

"I'm not sure. I'm Lacey Langdon. I'm interested in researching my aunt's family, in-laws actually, the Vander Horns. Their roots go back several centuries here in Paterson, I understand."

"I'm Patricia Moorehead, director of information services here in the morgue." She paused and smiled. "My goodness. Would your aunt be Tessa Langdon Vander Horn?"

"Yes. One and the same."

"Imagine. I've been a fan for years. In fact, I DVR *Edge of Darkness* every day and watch it when I get home."

"Aunt Tessa would be delighted to hear that!" And that was one hundred percent true. "I'll be sure to tell her."

Now beaming, Ms. Moorehead asked, "Are you looking for anything specific?"

"I'm not exactly sure. I was wondering if you might have any old articles on the family. I've heard so many names. Particularly, the brothers who founded the E. and F. Vander Horn Silk Company, Eduard and Frits. And Frits's daughter Sophie, Aunt Tessa's cousin by marriage, and Sophie's suitor, Sebastian. I'm also interested in Sophie's daughter, Annabella Van Dyk."

"Yes, some of these names are vaguely familiar. The family is part of Paterson's history. I'm certain we have archived clippings. Let me take a look on the computer." She typed quickly, running a search of her database. She then printed the list of hits that came up and handed it to me. "You know, you're the third person in the past couple of weeks to ask for information on the Vander Horns."

"Really? The third?"

"Yes, there was a young woman from *Soap Opera Weekly* who's writing a piece on your aunt."

"Oh, yes, that must have been Natalie Summers. She's the one who suggested I come here."

"Lovely woman. And then, we had an inquiry from a gentleman."

"A gentleman? Do you recall his name?"

"I'm afraid I don't. Not off hand. But I can pull it up," she said, looking down at her screen as she searched. "Ah, here's his email. Stephan Champion. He was looking for information on Sophie Vander Horn as well. Popular lady."

"Indeed." I made a mental note of the name. Stephan Champion. Sebastian DesChamps. Somehow, the similarity couldn't have been a coincidence. My thoughts drifted to Julien. Had the news of his adoption finally put him over the edge? I tried to convince myself it was impossible, yet the shadow of a doubt remained.

"I sent the gentleman some links from our online archives. Society pages with births, weddings, social events. And, of course, the obits. Goldmines! I told him how to conduct his own search. We digitized several years ago. Everything we could, that is. We are required to keep hard copies of some of our records. But digitizing was a real game changer, you know. So easy for our reporters to find backstories. Here you go," she said, sliding another printout across the desk. "The email from Stephan Champion and my reply. I assume you'll be interested in the same information, so this should save you some time."

"I appreciate it. By the way, did he ever come in?"

"No, he did not. I was surprised."

"Oh, too bad. Sounds like an interesting guy. I'll try emailing him."

"He said he lived quite a distance away. It's a pity because, as I said, in addition to the digitized information, we also have hard copy files that contain so many essential supplemental items. Reporters' notes, photographs, interviews, personal papers. Anyone researching the Vander Horns would find the material fascinating. Note that any of the hardcopy articles you find in the file can also be accessed online."

"Amazing. I had no idea so much backup material was kept."

"We have a substantial hard file on the Vander Horns. I'll pull it for you."

Ms. Moorehead disappeared into the stacks and immediately returned with a bulky, brown expanding file with worn edges. She dropped it on the counter in front of me.

"I'm afraid it can't leave the morgue, though. You'll have to look through everything here. Whatever gets filed in the morgue, stays in the morgue," she said with a smile. "That's our motto."

Librarian humor. I smiled back. "Of course."

"You can use one of the carrels behind my desk."

I carefully removed everything from inside the file onto the carrel's desktop. It was truly a treasure trove: old photographs, original clippings, and a reporter's notepad, which was most intriguing. I scanned one of the clippings dated April 30th, 1920, with the headline *Sebastian DesChamps Tragically Falls to Death on Vander Horn Estate.* Someone, most likely a reporter, had inked notes in the margins that were faded but still legible: *where was Lucas Van Dyk? police investigation? murder charges pending? Eduard and Frits Vander Horn?*

When Aunt Tessa had originally told me the story of Sophie and Sebastian, she had hinted at that.

Lucas Van Dyk might have been responsible for Sebastian's demise, but if there had been suspicions at the time, it seemed that they were swept under the rug, undoubtedly at the insistence of the Vander Horn brothers. Too late now. I knew there was no statute of limitation on murder, but how would I search for information for a crime that was committed over a century ago? Moreover, police records would be impossible to access if they ever existed at all.

Most of the items in the morgue file came from society events. Of course, one of Sebastian DesChamps's original calling cards jumped out at me, stapled to a guest list from Sophie's eighteenth birthday party, which had been elaborately celebrated in the Vander Horn Estate's ballroom. I found several clippings on Sophie's wedding. "Miss Sophie Vander Horn Weds Mr. Lucas Van Dyk." "Willow Bluffs Wedding of the Century," complete with an engraved wedding invitation addressed to the *Herald*'s society reporter, Abigail Andersen, and vintage photographs that must have been featured in the newspaper's rotogravure.

Sophie, although beautiful in her ivory taffeta gown, appeared distant and forlorn, exactly as she looked in the portrait I loved so much that hung over the fireplace in the cottage. Such a sad life. I found a clipping announcing her daughter's birth, but nothing at all about Annabella's later years. Aunt Tessa must see all of this, I thought. Family history from a bygone era made everything real. I snapped some photos with my phone, which would have to do for now, and packed everything up.

"Thank you, Ms. Moorehead," I said, handing the file back to her. "Fascinating stuff."

"Come back any time. Regards to your wonderful aunt!"

Left with so much to digest, my mind wandered as I drove back to Willow Bluffs. Stephan Champion/Sebastian

DesChamps. Was that the key? Was Sebastian murdered? And, what about Sophie's daughter Annabella? Did she eventually marry and have more children? There would have to be records, I assumed. I wondered what Natalie Summers had concluded. She hadn't revealed much when we spoke.

Intrigued, although thoroughly shaken, after looking through the records on the Vander Horns, I decided to make a quick stop at the estate on my way back to the shop. I wasn't taking any chances. I wanted to make sure Arthur had replaced the burnt-out spotlights on the East Lawn behind the main house. And with Ron's arrest, I felt like things were finally coming to a head. I was anxious to speak with Derek. I wanted to hear all about his emergency town council meeting, hopefully before the end of the day. I wondered if the police were investigating Ron's partner at Cliffside Custom Builders, Jim Barclay. Jim had always seemed as straight as an arrow to me, but on the other hand, he had as much to gain as Ron with Glenn Hartman out of the picture. I didn't know what to think.

As I pulled into the estate's carport, I noticed Arthur watering the mums on the South Lawn.

"Arthur, I'm so glad I caught you. I just wanted to make sure you took care of the spotlights."

"Yes, miss. First thing. All four were out. Mr. Barclay was surprised. He said they put new ones in before the closing."

"Mr. Barclay's here?"

"Yes. With an architect, I think. Some business about the sunroom."

"Oh, I think I'll go inside and say hello."

"One more thing, miss. After I finish up this afternoon, I'd like to go to my son's place out in Chatham for a couple of days, if it's okay with you. Everything's ship shape around here. Nothing to be concerned about."

"No problem, Arthur. Have a great time."

I immediately ran up the front steps and entered the main house through the double front doors. I followed the voices I heard to the back of the house where I spotted Jim Barclay and another man discussing winterizing the solarium.

Jim greeted me as soon as he saw me. "Lacey, good to see you. Something I can do for you?"

"Just stopping in for a minute. Thought I'd say hello. How are you?"

"Absolutely stunned by Ron's arrest."

"I think everyone in town's been traumatized by what's been going on," I said. "So hard to believe. I guess the murder charge is just an allegation at this point, but nonetheless. And, the investigation is ongoing, but it's really all too much." I wanted to get his reaction, so I threw out one more comment. "I hate to think the worst, but I wonder if Ron will be charged with Glenn Hartman's murder as well."

"No way," Jim said adamantly. "Ron was with me early that morning at the estate closing."

"Oh, that's right." I'd completely forgotten about the closing.

"In fact," Jim went on, "because of another deal, the closing had to be held in our lawyers' South Jersey office after a couple of postponements. We had actually gone down the night before to look at some beachfront property in Ocean Grove. We got back to Willow Bluffs just in time for the groundbreaking."

"So you were miles away."

"At least one hundred miles away, and nowhere near the estate. I have to tell you Ron and I were absolutely shocked when we heard about Glenn's death at your reception."

Jim seemed awfully eager to explain. My mind raced. Who else could have struck Glenn and sent him off the cliff? Tom Pierce had attended the closing as well. Did Glenn's wife Angela have opportunity? No, it just didn't sound like her style. Perhaps someone else he worked with? A disgruntled subcontractor? The list of suspects was narrowing. "It sounds like we may be on our way to closure," I said to him, trying to determine if he knew more.

Jim frowned. "Hope so. Lovely to see you, as always, Lacey."

I knew an abrupt dismissal when I heard one. Walking back to my car, I noticed Arthur carrying the garden hose back to the shed, probably tidying up before leaving for his visit with his son's family. I was happy for him; he deserved a few days off. Jim Barclay seemed like he was moving on with business as usual, in spite of his partner's arrest. Somehow, I didn't think he was as shocked as he had said.

Driving down Willow Street on my way back to the shop, I thought about what a crazy day it had been. Sandra Velasco's house to Manhattan to the shop to the newspaper morgue, to the estate and now back to the shop. It must have been nervous energy. And I was dying to talk with Derek. As I pulled into my spot at Letter Perfect, I noticed Bean Around's parking lot was full. Gossip central, for sure.

Jeremy greeted me as I breezed in. "That was fast."

"I was on a mission."

"Cool. Hope you found what you wanted."

"You know, I'm not sure. What did I miss?"

"Nothing much. Mrs. Bartlett is coming in on Monday about her daughter's wedding."

"Fine."

"Jonathan McCracken wants to make a change in the menu for the library gala. You need to give him a call."

"Will do."

"And someone named Denise Chapin called. She said she's from your high school's alumni association."

"Ugh. Probably a fundraising drive. Thanks. I'll be in my office."

Focusing was difficult. I had a nagging feeling that I had missed something terribly important when I went through the morgue file on the Vander Horns. I hoped whatever it was would hit me like a ton of bricks at any moment, but I was drawing a blank. Fortunately, there was nothing urgent pending. I decided to concentrate on planning an intimate dinner party in the cottage for Aunt Tessa's birthday; it would be me, Aunt T, Julien, and Derek. I was certain I could handle that.

I called the caterer and ordered assorted canapés; tricolor salad; filet mignon with mushroom sauce, haricot verts, and whipped potatoes; and a beautiful coconut birthday cake. Bluff Liquors would deliver a couple of bottles of her favorite champagne, Veuve Cliquot Brut. And I asked Willow Bluffs Petals to design a gorgeous centerpiece with mums, gerbera daisies, and lemon leaves. I'd set a beautiful table, and we'd be ready for a perfect evening. Julien had said he'd easily take care of bringing her over on the pretense that we'd all go out to dinner, and I had no doubt he'd come through. She'd be thrilled to spend her birthday quietly at home. Our plans were set. At least I'd accomplished something on this impossible day. I'd finished following up on the most important things on my agenda when a text finally came through from Derek.

meet me at Oakdale tonight before my class lots to tell
ok
campus café in the student union first floor 5:30ish
got it see you there

That left me with one more stop. Oakdale College in Westerville, about six miles north of Willow Bluffs.

"I may see you later tonight," I called to Jeremy on my way out.

"Seriously?" he replied.

"I'm meeting Derek on campus. I may sit in on his lecture."

"Derek, huh. Totally cool. I'll walk you out. I'm going to the library before class."

* * *

Oakdale, a small college perched high on the Palisades, attracted a large number of commuters, many of them working people, like Jeremy, attending part time. The main administration building, Wright Hall, a sprawling stone structure dating back to the mid-eighteenth century, anchored the campus. Most of the classroom buildings and dormitories were built in the 1950s when the school began to flourish.

I parked, found the Student Union easily, and grabbed a booth in the Campus Café. Within a few moments, Derek rushed in, looking characteristically disheveled and harried. He took a seat across from me and said, "Let's order. We only have about a half an hour."

I glanced at the menu posted over the grill. "What do you recommend?"

"Keep it pretty basic."

"Would a cheeseburger and coffee be basic enough?"

He caught the eye of the young student-waitress. "Two coffees and two cheeseburgers." He turned to me and went on. "Here's the lowdown. Fortunately, the mayor's been kept in the loop. Ari was briefed by both Chief Hennessey and an assistant district attorney, and then she brought the town council up to speed. Sounds like they have an airtight case against Ron Valenti."

"Details?"

"Do you remember when Gina collapsed at the party, and no one could find her purse?"

"Of course. I'll never forget it."

"If you recall, Jim Barclay never found it."

"Awful."

"Chief Hennessey immediately confiscated her purse, and when they searched it, the epinephrine pen wasn't there."

"How odd."

"Exactly," Derek agreed. "Sandra Velasco swore to the police that Gina never went anywhere without it."

"She said the same thing to me. A couple of times. So, what happened?"

"This is where things get dicey. The police found the pen stashed in Ron's trunk, and his fingerprints were all over it. In other words, he must have deliberately removed and hidden it."

"Wow! Totally premeditated."

Derek continued as the waitress served our coffee and burgers, "It was just dumb luck for Ron that Gina had forgotten to bring the purse into the party. It made her death look like a total accident. At least for a while."

"Oh, I see," I said. "Ron had hoped she would have brought the purse inside, but the pen wouldn't have been there. It would have looked like she had forgotten to put the epinephrine pen in the purse. Wow!"

"Bingo. But it never came to that."

"Nope. There was no purse at all until Barclay went to look for it."

"The investigation goes even further," Derek went on. "They really dug deep the past couple of days. Ari found evidence in the building department that Ron was taking kickbacks from suppliers on the community park construction project and making payments for phantom materials that were never to be delivered. Phony invoices. The guy was brazen. He had stolen a couple hundred thousand."

"Unreal. Right under Jim Barclay's nose. And let me guess, Gina found out about it and was blackmailing him."

"Yup."

"That list of dates I found was really a list of payments due. Blackmail style payments."

"You've got it," Derek said. "Ron decided to end it with one easy shot. Get rid of her and make it look like an allergic reaction. This is just the tip of the iceberg. They've confiscated Ron's personal and office computers to confirm the financial irregularities, shall we say. They're trying to determine how he got ahold of the poison—the tropomyosin—that he must have slipped into her drink. That will be the slam dunk."

"Ron probably added clam juice. The medical examiner said it naturally contains a little tropomyosin. He must have added the juice to Gina's Bloody Mary somehow, along with an extra dose of tropomyosin, to make sure he got the job done."

"Sounds like that was the plan."

"But, you know, the bottom line is we still don't know who killed Glenn Hartman."

"Maybe we never will," Derek admitted.

"If Dylan hadn't found that bloody rock, we'd still be thinking he committed suicide. Turns out Ron has an airtight alibi for the morning Glenn was killed. So does Jim Barclay. They were both at the closing."

After we finished what passed for dinner, we crossed the campus quad to Dayton Hall, where Derek's class was meeting. Law and Justice in America couldn't have been timelier considering our local crime wave. Derek came alive in front of the class, and his students, especially the young women, seemed to love him. Just out of an abundance of caution, he assured me, he followed me home in his car after class and walked me to the door.

"Oh, no. What's this?" I asked in disbelief.

Someone had left a small box on the front porch right in front of the door. Derek leaned down to pick it up. "There's a note. 'Found this in the shed behind the cottage. Movers must have misplaced it. I'm heading to my son's house in Chatham. Arthur.'"

"That's a relief. It's probably just a few more of Aunt Tessa's things. As long as it's not something bizarre from Sebastian DesChamps." *Or Stephan Champion.* Or whoever.

"Don't even go there," he advised.

"You're right. But still keeping my old softball bat nearby just in case."

Chapter Nineteen

It was about time. We deserved a party. My entire day had been full of anticipation for the evening's dinner celebration for Aunt T's birthday. When I finally got home after a hectic schedule at the shop, I shifted into high gear to get everything ready. I set a spectacular table with a crisp, white linen cloth, matching monogrammed napkins, Aunt Tessa's prized Aynsley Pembroke china, Waterford Lismore crystal, and, a true heirloom, Uncle Jonathan's mother's sterling silver flatware. Aunt Tessa would love it.

My favorite florist, Willow Bluffs Petals, delivered a stunning centerpiece of oversized yellow and white mums accented with magenta gerbera daisies and lemon leaves, artfully arranged in a rectangular white vase. For once, I had taken plenty of time for myself as well. With my hair swept up in a chic chignon, I'd dressed to the hilt in a slightly retro, long, black taffeta skirt with a white silk ruffled blouse to fit my role as hostess, not something I did every day.

Aunt Tessa would surely appreciate celebrating at home rather than in a restaurant. Classic Caterers had delivered the filet mignon dinner earlier; all I had to do was reheat it, which even I'd be able to handle. I looked up at Sophie's portrait, confident that she would have approved, and exhaled. We'd enjoy a quiet, intimate evening, free of distractions or intrusions from any of Aunt T's many admirers.

Dylan, barking loudly, ran toward the front door just as I heard a soft knock.

"Oh, good, you're home," Aunt Tessa said as I opened the door. "Forgot my keys. Again."

"Happy birthday, Aunt T. Shall I even bother to ask how many candles we'll need?"

"You know better than to ask a question like that, my dear. In fact, I've completely lost count." She looked around, noticing the table. "Oh my, are we dining in?"

"I thought it would be cozy."

"Perfect. Absolutely love it. I see you've unearthed all of my favorite things! Thank you, my dear. This is wonderful." She paused as she took everything in. "Four place settings?"

"Derek is joining us."

Aunt Tessa smiled. "Ah, I see."

"I thought Julien would be with you," I said.

"He'll be along very shortly. I had my driver bring me out. Julien's meeting with the Broadway people and then coming directly here. He may be a bit early."

"That's fine. What can I get you to start off the celebration?"

"Oh, I wouldn't mind a touch of cabernet."

"You've got it."

"By the way, you look stunning tonight, Lacey."

"Thank you, and likewise." Aunt Tessa glowed in a rich, cerise double-breasted suit paired with elegant black pumps. As always, with her perfectly coiffed blonde bob, she was the picture of elegance.

"How's that Broadway project going?" I called from the kitchen.

"Now that he's part of the family, as it were, he's more passionate than ever about the production, if that's even possible. It's all he talks about. He tells me it's all coming together. Slowly, however. We have a script that's in great shape and a theater. The Lamont. Only problem is that investors are just trickling in, not exactly gushing."

"I have no doubt that Julien will come up with backers when push comes to shove."

"Actually, there are a couple of people right here in Willow Bluffs he'd like to approach. Tom Pierce, for one. And Jim Barclay, once he gets on his feet again."

"I know that Jim will come back swinging now that Ron's out of the picture. Derek said he should be able to recoup some of his losses."

"I agree."

"I'm sure the financing situation will change once a buzz gets going. Break a leg and all that. I can't wait to see *Edge* on stage!"

I brought two glasses of cabernet and an assortment of canapés into the living room on a tray and set them down on the coffee table.

"Ah, there's our lovely Sophie," Aunt Tessa said, looking up at her portrait.

"You know," I said, admiring the exquisite cameo that had caused so much trouble, "today is a very special occasion. You should wear the brooch. And the earrings as well."

"Why, yes, that would be appropriate, wouldn't it? After all, the brooch was sent here, even though under the most suspicious of circumstances," Aunt Tessa recalled. "And the earrings were a delightful and most generous gift from Genavieve Leigh. The brooch is actually in my bedroom. Lacey, would you be a dear and get it for me? Top right drawer of my dresser. Black velvet box."

"Sure, be right back." I hurried upstairs to Aunt Tessa's bedroom and checked the top right dresser drawer, but it was clearly missing. I rummaged through her lingerie, but there was no sign of it. "Oh, no," I called to Aunt T. "It's not here."

"What? Impossible."

"When did you last see it?" I called.

"I'm not sure. Perhaps I left it at my place in the city," Aunt T considered. "But I don't think so."

I came downstairs to join her in the living room.

"The earrings are locked in a safe in the studio," Aunt Tessa continued. "Julien insists that I wear them when we start taping the Sophie and Sebastian story line. I don't think the brooch is there, too, but I suppose it's possible. There's nothing we can do about it now. I'll check thoroughly when I'm back at the apartment. It couldn't have disappeared into thin air."

I heard my phone chime. I had left it on the mantle. A text from Derek.

clients were late be there in half an hour so sorry

I couldn't hide my disappointment.

"Problem?" Aunt T asked.

"Looks like Derek's going to be late, too."

"Ah, the young man who isn't your young man."

I let that slide. "We may as well enjoy the canapés. We have salmon with Dijon sauce, country paté, and gruyère with prosciutto."

"Marvelous."

The doorbell rang, setting off Dylan again.

Startled, I jumped up to answer. "Julien! So glad you made it."

"Hello, Lacey. Thank you so for the invitation. And, happy birthday, my dear Tessa," he said, handing her a bouquet of lovely, long-stemmed yellow roses. "I hope I'm not too late. Fortunately, traffic was light for once."

"Thank you, Julien. They're lovely. You look exhausted. A little pale, I dare say. Feeling all right?" Aunt Tessa asked.

His gaze was fixed straight ahead. "Fine."

Practically trance-like, he didn't look fine to me.

"Just an excruciating day," he went on. "You must understand my commitment to our family history. It's the money that's so challenging. I need a windfall. An angel investor. I couldn't possibly have negotiated another thing. Broadway is a tough sell, you know."

"A tough sell, indeed," Aunt Tessa agreed. "But the story is fascinating." She paused for a moment, grinning knowingly. "Especially the bootlegging."

I tried to change the subject. "Have some hors d'oeuvres," I offered. "I'll get you a glass of cab. That should refresh you." When I brought the roses back into the kitchen to place them in a vase, I couldn't help thinking of the similar yellow roses that had been left on Sophie's grave.

Interesting coincidence, I thought, or possibly something more.

As we sat sipping our wine, Julien went on about his tireless plans to memorialize the Vander Horns. Clearly agitated, he began to sound almost maniacal. My concern intensified. I hoped Derek would be along soon. Meanwhile, my filet mignon and accompaniments warmed in the oven. I couldn't hold dinner forever.

Julien suddenly stood up and motioned to us to follow him to the door. "I have a surprise for you both. Come."

"Where to?" I asked. "The oven's on. I don't want dinner to burn. My beautiful filets will be hockey pucks."

"Just outside. You'll see. It'll be fine."

"Oh, Julien, *reaaallly*," Aunt Tessa scolded, as she reluctantly got up from the sofa.

A troubling alarm went off in my head. Something didn't feel quite right. I left the oven on, and the front door unlocked, hoping that we would, in fact, be back shortly. Julien led the way across the East Lawn to the shed behind the cottage.

"Beautiful night. Perfect for young lovers," Julien said.

"Young lovers? Julien, have you lost your mind?" Aunt Tessa asked.

I couldn't imagine why Julien had taken us to the old, dilapidated tool shed. No one ever ventured inside, except Arthur.

"Enter, ladies. It will all make sense. I know you'll be pleased. I've been planning this for months."

We entered the shed, albeit uneasily. Aunt Tessa and I exchanged an anxious glance as we fixed our eyes on what was before us. Blown up photographs of Aunt Tessa and Sophie adorned the walls. We saw a small card table in the middle of the shed, covered with an old canvas cloth and set with place settings for the three of us. The floral-patterned dinner plates and champagne coupes had obviously been pilfered from the estate, along with the large, sterling silver candelabra holding eight glowing candles, which Julien must have lit beforehand. I was baffled and disturbed. The scene was totally bizarre.

"Do take your seats, ladies. But first, something for you, Sophie."

I grimaced. *Sophie?*

He reached behind him, bolted the door, and then grabbed something from one of the wooden shelves. With a sweeping gesture, he unfolded what looked like a long velvet cape with a white lace collar and fastened it around Aunt Tessa's shoulders. "There. Beautiful," he remarked. "And totally worthy of you, I might add."

"Thank you," was all Aunt Tessa could say, shooting a perplexed look my way.

He then replaced his tweed sport jacket with a knee-length, navy blue wool cutaway coat, cinched at the waist, double-breasted with brass buttons and velvet trim on the collar and pockets. Nineteen-twenties style. I felt sick. I recognized it immediately. It was most definitely the coat that had been placed on Sophie's grave.

As we sat down, Aunt Tessa and I both noticed elaborate, handwritten invitations that had been placed upon our dinner plates. As I tried to make sense of it all, I could see that Aunt Tessa was just as baffled.

You are cordially invited
to a dinner party at the Vander Horn residence
celebrating the engagement
of Miss Sophie Vander Horn
to Mr. Sebastian DesChamps
the twelfth of November
nineteen hundred and twenty
at half after six o'clock in the evening

Aunt Tessa and I looked at each other in disbelief, both of us realizing that Julien had gone stark raving mad. He seemed to believe that he had assumed the identity of Sebastian Des-Champs and Aunt Tessa had become Sophie Vander Horn. And there was something about the penmanship that was vaguely familiar. Was this some kind of a joke? Was he rehearsing a scene for *Edge of Darkness*? Where was Derek? We needed help. Desperately.

"Of course, I have engagement presents for you, lovely Sophie," he said, placing two black velvet jewelry boxes in front of her. "I do hope you'll be pleased."

Aunt Tessa pretended to be surprised when she opened each box to reveal the unmistakable blue and ivory cameo that Sophie had worn in her portrait, and the earrings that Genavieve had given us.

"Put them on!" he insisted, his tone forceful.

My anxiety heightened.

Aunt Tessa was smart enough to comply. She fastened the brooch to her collar and removed her large pearl earrings, replacing them with the matching cameos. I didn't know exactly why, but as she placed the earrings she'd been wearing on the table I surreptitiously covered them with my hand and hid them in my skirt pocket. I had to keep my wits about me.

"You look divine, Sophie. Angelic. We are finally together. This is how it was always meant to be. I let you slip away once, but I've come back to fight for you till the end. Lucas Van Dyk will rue the day he tried to steal you away from me."

"Yes, Sebastian. You know you are my one true love."

He reached behind him to retrieve what looked like three *Edge of Darkness* scripts. "This is the true story of us, Sophie and Sebastian. A veritable masterpiece. This is how we will be remembered. I've made everything right. Rewritten history. No one will ever hurt us again."

Aunt Tessa opened the script and pretended to read. "Brilliant work, Sebastian. Just brilliant," she said, managing to assuage him without sounding patronizing. "You've told our story the way it always should have been."

I glanced at the script as well. Did he actually want us to act out the scenes he had written? This charade had progressed from bizarre to downright insane. And Julien of all people. He had always been such a rock. The voice of reason. How far would he take this elaborate delusion?

Once more, the tragic tale of Sophie and Sebastian had come back to haunt us. Lucas Van Dyk, the suitor Sophie's father had preferred, had almost certainly killed Sebastian Des-Champs so he could marry Sophie himself. There it was right before us, with Julien now avenging Sebastian's fate in a deranged fantasy. There was no better actress to play along with the charade than Aunt Tessa. "You're so right, Sebastian," she said. "I belong with you, to you. I've waited so long for this moment."

"Champagne is in order," Julien/Sebastian announced grandly. "Then, we must go to the house to play our scene for Eduard. He's in the library. He'll be so happy about our engagement, Sophie. Everything's changed now. Don't you see?" His eyes wild, he popped a bottle of Veuve Clicquot and filled our coupes, then raised his glass. "To us, Sophie."

As I lifted my glass to toast, I considered throwing the champagne in his face. I thought better of it, concerned I might miss and we might not be able to get away. I'd have to think of something else, and I knew I'd better do it quickly. He was drifting further and further off the rails.

Julien turned to me. "And young Annabella, I see you've joined us from the future. An omen. Now, you'll be the child of Sophie and me. Not Lucas's daughter," he proclaimed, his eyes glazed and distant. "This is the way it was meant to be."

His mind had short-circuited.

"Sebastian, we mustn't be hasty. Are you sure my Uncle Eduard will be ready to accept us? Perhaps we should wait a few days to tell him."

"How could he not be pleased for us, my dearest?"

I was in awe of how the usually steady, even-tempered Julien had become so irrational and disjointed. How long had he been conjuring up this twisted fantasy? I felt helpless, terrified. My mother's mantra echoed in my head. *Give it all you've got, no matter what.* Of course, that was my only option.

Aunt T blotted her forehead with her napkin. "I'm feeling a little lightheaded, Sebastian. I need a bit of air. Too much excitement. Would you open the window?"

As he turned around to do so, Aunt T looked at me and nodded in the direction of the candelabra. I acknowledged her desperation with my eyes. Before "Sebastian" rejoined us at the table, I reached for my champagne glass and in one motion deliberately knocked over the flaming candelabra.

"Oh, no," I shrieked. "What have I done?"

"Annabella, you stupid, clumsy child," Sebastian chided. "I knew we shouldn't have invited you. It was against my better judgment. You know, you should never have been born at all."

A half-dozen candles tumbled from the table, falling against the shelving and onto the floor, causing the old, dry wood to ignite in a flash of red and yellow flames. Aunt T and I immediately jumped up and bolted to the door, holding our napkins over our faces to protect ourselves from the building smoke.

"Just one moment," Julien, as Sebastian, demanded. "A little fire won't spoil our celebration." He pulled what looked like a white mother of pearl antique pistol out of his coat, pointing it directly at Aunt Tessa and me.

"Sebastian, you do not want to do this," Aunt Tessa pleaded. "What about us?"

"I know exactly what I'm doing. We're all leaving together."

My heart palpitated.

"Sophie, take that candle," he demanded. "We're going to the house to confront Eduard," he said, pointing his gun's long barrel to the single candle that remained in the candelabra.

Removing the candle, Aunt Tessa said, "Yes, Sebastian, dear, we must leave at once," she said, choking on the smoke. "And, whatever you do, you must not let Lucas interfere. He'll spoil everything."

The flames spread rapidly to the walls of the shed as he followed us out the door, his pistol at our backs.

We proceeded across the lawn, toward the main house. There was no escape.

"If Lucas is on the property, I must stop him," he proclaimed once again. "He'll be the one to die this time."

Holding the gun in his left hand and pointing it toward us, he reached inside his coat pocket for the house key, no doubt stolen from Aunt Tessa and duplicated. He opened the front door, prodding us with the gun to enter ahead of him. Aunt Tessa and I proceeded reluctantly into the hallway with him following close behind until we reached the library.

"I don't understand," Sebastian said. "Eduard's not here. We had an appointment. Unless . . ."

He pulled the lever under the bookcase that opened the hidden passageway to the secret room.

How had he discovered it? I could feel my blood pressure rising.

"And you, Annabella, you wretch. You started the fire intentionally, did you not?"

"No, no, no," I protested. "It was an accident."

"I think the best thing would be to leave you locked in Eduard's hidden private room where no one will find you for a long, long time. You're nothing but a nuisance. A heinous offspring of that godforsaken Lucas."

"No, Sebastian. I need her with me," Aunt Tessa implored.

"She'll be nothing but trouble."

"People will look for her," Aunt Tessa reminded him.

"They'll never find her here."

"Her father will find her. He often comes here with Eduard. You know that."

"Then maybe I should just get rid of her once and for all," he declared, pointing the gun directly at me.

Julien had turned Sebastian into a monster. My pulse raced, and I could barely breathe. In his delusional state, he was capable of anything.

"No, Sebastian," Aunt Tessa pleaded. "They'll know it was you. Don't spoil everything now."

"I know all about Eduard's secrets," he said. "He didn't think I knew about his bootlegging business, but I did. That's the beauty of all of this. He knew better than to cross me. I told him if I couldn't have Sophie, I would expose him. Scoundrel. Two could play his game."

"Sebastian," Aunt Tessa implored, "I just realized . . . Eduard must be outside on the cliff with Lucas. They're probably waiting for you. If you want to rewrite history, this is your chance."

"Yes, Sophie, you may be right. Okay, let's go," he said. "Both of you. We'll go out to the cliff."

Come on, Derek, I prayed. Where are you?

The spotlights were on, thankfully, and the moonlight illuminated the South Lawn just enough so that smoke could be seen billowing from the shed. It wouldn't be long before it was completely engulfed in flames. Surely, someone would notice. Where were the security patrols Chief Hennessey had promised?

We exited the house from the back door and walked across the lawn toward the cliff, Julien following closely behind Aunt Tessa and me. About halfway across the lawn, I purposely let my napkin fall to the ground, then slipped my hand inside my skirt pocket and stealthily dropped Aunt Tessa's pearl earrings. I also slid the gold bangles off my wrists and let them fall onto the grass, with the prayer that someone, hopefully Derek, would get here and follow the trail.

We approached the gate to the cliff. As if being kidnapped by a madman wasn't enough, my fear of heights had now kicked in. My chest tightened. I pushed the gate wide open. Derek, or someone, would surely see it, hopefully in time. Julien led us out to the rocky cliff. Still at gunpoint, Aunt Tessa and I faced the South Lawn and the main house, while "Sebastian" looked toward the river, searching for his nemesis, Lucas.

"You were right, Sophie. Lucas will be here. Mark my words. I've challenged the coward. No one will hurt you again, Sophie."

"I need you, Sebastian. You must protect me," Aunt Tessa adlibbed.

"I always do. I'll put an end to Lucas Van Dyk exactly as I disposed of Glenn Hartman, another lout who wanted to hurt you, Sophie. He tried to interfere with the sale of your estate.

Destroy your deal, your profits. You'll never have to worry again, my dear."

"You killed Glenn?" Aunt Tessa pressed. "For me?"

"Of course. Anything for you."

I could barely breathe. Julien had just confessed to murdering Glenn Hartman.

Through the trees and shrubbery, I could make out a pair of headlights as a car pulled into the carport. It had to be Derek. Surely, he'd see the flames burning through the walls of the shed. He'd call 911. Almost certainly, he'd go inside the house to look for us and then come outside to the lawn and find the clues I'd left.

Julien had become practically incoherent. "History *must* be rewritten," he exclaimed. "We'll be reading Lucas Van Dyk's obituary in the *Herald*, not mine. No one will come between us ever again, Sophie. No one."

I was certain I heard the faint sound of sirens in the distance. Derek must have called the fire department. Aunt Tessa's sidelong glance told me she heard them, too. I hoped Julien wouldn't panic.

"Listen," he said. "They're coming for him. Yes, they're finally coming for Lucas. We'll be free of him, Sophie."

With that, I saw a shadowy figure in the moonlight moving slowly toward the cliff's gate. Derek had found us. With what looked like my old softball bat in his right hand, he inched stealthily toward us on the cliff, raised the bat, and struck Julien in the back of the head. Julien fell, unconscious, onto the rocks. I exhaled. Aunt Tessa looked ashen.

"Derek, thank God. Grab the gun," I managed. Dizzy, my legs were about to give out.

Within seconds, fire engines and patrol cars rushed onto the estate. A patrol car bolted toward us, racing over the lawn and stopping by the gate. Chief Hennessey jumped out. Upon seeing Julien lying motionless on the rocks, he drew his gun and took the pistol from Derek. Officer Kowalski immediately backed him up.

"Is everyone all right? Miss Vander Horn? Lacey?" Chief Hennessey asked.

"Barely," I managed.

"I'm numb," Aunt Tessa said. "I could use a stiff drink. Or something."

"Kowalski, call an ambulance. We have a 10–96. Some oxygen, too, Kowalski. And blankets. Pronto. Get the EMTs over here. What happened, Miss Vander Horn?"

"My agent, Julien LaFontaine. He's had some sort of breakdown," Aunt Tessa managed, trembling. "Unfathomable. Beyond anything I could ever have imagined."

Aunt Tessa, Derek, and I sat on the lawn in a state of shock. Before long, the estate was crawling with county investigators, police, EMTs, and firemen. Julien was rushed to the Palisades Medical Center's trauma center by ambulance, under police escort.

"I'll need statements from all of you," the chief said.

"Perhaps everyone would be more comfortable in the cottage," Derek suggested.

With the fire in the shed under control and Julien on his way to the hospital, we all relocated to the cottage, including Chief Hennessey, but I'm not sure we were more comfortable. I turned off the oven as soon as we walked in. My filet had turned into a dry, shriveled mess. I was still shaking. I looked up as we sat in the living room, and to my chagrin, there was Cousin Sophie, Sebastian DesChamps's *objet d'amour* and the cause of all the trouble, presiding over us.

"The mind certainly works in strange ways," Derek said.

"How did we not see any signs?" I asked.

"Because there weren't any," Aunt Tessa said.

"I've never seen anything like it," I added. "A total psychotic break."

"Will he get the help he needs, Chief?" Aunt Tessa asked.

"Yes, I'm certain of it," he assured us.

"Medical and legal, I trust," she added. "I'd like to see him transferred to a private hospital as soon as possible."

"His family will have to make the necessary arrangements," the chief explained.

Aunt Tessa frowned. "Julien's family is complicated."

"We'll work it out, Aunt Tessa," I said.

"Meanwhile," Chief Hennessey reminded us, "I will need your statements."

We were in for a long, long night.

Chapter Twenty

Aunt Tessa and I spent two endless days in seclusion at the cottage, utterly consumed by the horror of Julien's breakdown. We were both catatonic, not even focused enough to watch television or read a book. Any hint of Julien's obsession with Aunt Tessa, Sophie, or Annabella had completely escaped us over the past few months. But as I thought about it—and I had nothing else to do but think about it the last two days—there had been some clues, although elusive. He had always shown up at the cottage at precisely the right—or wrong—time. He was preoccupied with Sophie and Sebastian's tale of woe, and he had become unusually fixated on the Vander Horn heirloom jewelry that had been found. And, of course, the revelation that he was Sophie's grandson must have shocked him. He had always been totally devoted to Aunt Tessa. But I never put it all together. Nobody did.

Jeremy stepped up to take the helm at Letter Perfect, and Aunt Tessa arranged for a brief hiatus from *Edge of Darkness*. The writers got around her absence by sending Caroline Manchester to visit her sick sister in Albuquerque for as long as it would take Aunt Tessa to recover, but if I knew my aunt, that would be soon. Derek had called several times urging us to get out of the house, but, paralyzed by the reality of what had happened, we simply couldn't manage it. I knew he wouldn't give up. I was outside on the South Lawn with Dylan Saturday morning when I saw him pull into the carport.

"Come on," he insisted. "We're going out."

"Oh, Derek, I don't think I'm ready."

"You have to *decide* you're ready. Now is as good a time as any. We're just talking about coffee, no big deal."

"I don't know," I said, with a bit less hesitance. "This is way more than coffee."

"Just coffee. I'm not taking no for an answer. Get your aunt. If you can't do it for yourself, do it for her. Please."

I sighed. "Okay. I'll see what I can do."

I'll have to venture out sooner or later. Maybe we are ready.

I somehow managed to convince Aunt Tessa. She threw on a pair of beige wool trousers and a matching silk blouse and grabbed a pair of sunglasses. I looked fine, for coffee anyway, in jeans and a sweatshirt. Derek, pleased that he'd successfully argued his case, drove us over to Bean Around.

The three of us slipped into a quiet table in the corner, and none of the early morning customers seemed to notice us. Or perhaps they were kind enough not to acknowledge us.

Jess, looking surprised to see us, came right over. She struggled to find the right words. Smiling faintly, she gently placed her hand on my shoulder.

Derek broke the ice. "Lattes and croissants all around?"

I nodded in approval.

"I'd love a brioche," Aunt Tessa decided.

Aunt Tessa and I settled in and relaxed at the table, relieved to be off the estate. Derek appeared ready to fend off any curiosity seekers.

"Join us," I said to Jess when she returned with our order.

"Love to. This is on the house, by the way. I can't tell you how wonderful it is to see you both. And looking so well at that. I wish there was something I could do. I mean, what an unbelievable ordeal you've all been through."

"It's been devastating, to say the least," I told Jess.

"To think that someone could have been so completely obsessed," she said. "And go off the deep end with no warning."

"So unfortunate that we didn't see the signs," Aunt Tessa lamented.

"Lacey, from what I've heard, you and your aunt could have been killed," Jess blurted out.

I shot her a look that said, "you shouldn't have mentioned that."

"To tell the truth, I have never been so absolutely terrified in my life," Aunt Tessa admitted.

"You handled it with complete grace, Aunt T."

"Julien will get help," Derek said. "But it is truly a tragedy that we didn't realize the extent of his illness sooner."

Thankfully, no one except Aunt Tessa, Derek, the police, and me knew the full details about Julien's episode. The police reported it to the press as a mental health crisis and left it at that. Right after the incident we told Derek that Julien was Annabella's illegitimate son, but we vowed to keep it strictly between us. No one needed to know the Vander Horns's secrets.

"He's been transferred to the Ridgewood Sanitarium. The best facility in the area, from what I understand," Aunt Tessa said.

Jess looked around. The café was filling up. "I hate to leave you, but I need to get behind the counter."

I smiled appreciatively. "Thanks for this, Jess."

"There will be charges against him, of course," Derek explained. "The murder of Glenn Hartman, attempted murder of Lacey and Tessa, kidnapping, theft, to name a few. He'll need a top-notch criminal defense attorney."

"Do you know anyone, Derek?" I asked.

"I could make some discreet inquiries. He confessed to Glenn's murder. It will be a challenge."

"We witnessed it," Aunt Tessa affirmed.

"I spoke to the chief earlier today. He said it's as if Julien drifts in and out of his psychosis," Derek said. "The uncanny thing is that every time we've seen him the past few months, he's seemed normal. Razor sharp."

Aunt Tessa grimaced. "I blame myself."

"No, no," I countered. "Julien has an illness that he cannot control. He needs psychiatric intervention. It clearly wasn't your fault, Aunt Tessa. It wasn't anyone's fault."

"But it was all because of me," Aunt Tessa went on. "Months ago, I made the fatal error of letting Julien know that Glenn was the only councilman who opposed the sale of the estate. He was incensed, certain I'd be hurt financially. Glenn was threatening to go to the Department of Environmental Protection to press for more of my property to be donated to the community."

"Yes. The Green Acres Law. That could have hurt Tessa's profits considerably," Derek explained.

"He knew I needed the sale to go through as planned. Of course, I wanted to make as much as possible on the deal. Julien was counting on me to invest a portion of the profits in the Broadway production of *Edge*."

"In Julien's twisted mind, Glenn had to be stopped at all costs." Derek pointed out.

"And then he went off the deep end when he learned about Sophie and Sebastian, irrationally transferring all of those feelings to me."

"Finding out about his birth mother after years of searching was the last straw. Unbelievable that it turned out to be Annabella."

"Of course there will be an insanity plea," Derek said. "He clearly lost touch with reality. But that presents its own unique challenges. It's a very low percentage defense."

"You know, I think we could all do with a bit of therapy after what's happened," Aunt Tessa admitted.

"I won't argue with you there," I said. "Don't forget, Aunt T, that Natalie Summers's feature article about you in *Soap Opera Weekly* will be out soon. And she's pushing for that biopic for the network. You'll need to be prepared for some attention."

"True," Aunt T sighed, "And I suppose they'll want me back on set soon. I do miss it."

"I'm ready for things to return to normal here in Willow Bluffs, whatever that is," I mused. "I don't think there's anywhere in the real world that fits the stereotype of the suburban fairy tale."

"Remember when parades, picnics, football games, fireworks were about all we had for excitement around here?" Derek recalled.

"Um, after the past couple of weeks, no, not really," I admitted.

"At least Jim Barclay will be able to get Cliffside Custom Builders back on track now that Ron's out of the picture. I don't think it will take him long to recoup his losses, considering his reputation," Derek pointed out.

"Yes. Jim had quite a setback, thanks to Ron and Gina. But I believe you are one hundred percent correct," Aunt Tessa said.

"He'll bounce back. I hope I can help in some small way. Jim has always done right by me."

"The forensic accountant uncovered phony invoices that enabled Ron to embezzle a small fortune. Then, when Gina began blackmailing Ron, things got desperate," Derek disclosed. "You know, I think if he hadn't killed her, she would have killed him."

"I'm glad we're talking," Aunt Tessa said. "I think it's been therapeutic."

"You're absolutely right, Aunt Tessa, but enough about our local drama." Turning to Derek, I said, "How's this for some old-fashioned hometown excitement?" I offered. "We have our Willow Bluffs High School ten-year reunion coming up in June."

"Oh, no. Don't remind me. I wouldn't be caught dead there."

"Don't tempt fate," I warned.

"High school was bad enough the first time around. Practically killed me back then. I was a social zero," he lamented.

"Oh, come on. You were not. You have to go. You were president of the student body," I pressed.

"True, but still, hell would have to freeze over."

"I've been recruited for the reunion committee, you know," I told him.

"Does that mean I have no choice?"

"Yes, that's exactly what it means."

Aunt Tessa beamed with delight.

"You'll find that life is all about creating memories, my dears." She paused a moment. "Good and bad. And speaking of memories. Lacey, have you considered relocating Cousin Sophie's portrait? Perhaps to the attic?"

"An inspired idea, Aunt T."

Acknowledgments

I would like to thank the many people who encouraged and supported me during my journey as *Invitation to Murder* came to life:

My husband Frank, who listened patiently to my ideas and read each draft tirelessly; my daughter Marisa Floriani and son-in-law Michael Macrides, who were constant cheerleaders; my wonderful agent Cindy Bullard of Birch Literary; my talented and perceptive editor Tara Gavin; my dear friend and reader Patricia Hartig; and, of course, the dedicated Crooked Lane dream team who made the magic happen, Thaisheemarie Fantauzzi Pérez, Rebecca Nelson, Julia Abbott, and book cover illustrator Lulu Dubreuil.